W9-BVO-520

Murder in the Palais Royal

ALSO BY THE AUTHOR

Murder in the Marais
Murder in Belleville
Murder in the Sentier
Murder in the Bastille
Murder in Clichy
Murder in Montmartre
Murder on the Ile Saint-Louis
Murder in the Rue de Paradis
Murder in the Latin Quarter

MURDER in the
PALAIS ROYAL

Cara Black

Published by
Soho Press, Inc.
853 Broadway
New York, NY 10003

Library of Congress Cataloging-in-Publication Data
Murder in the Palais Royal / Cara Black.
p. cm.
ISBN 978-1-56947-620-8 (hardcover)
1. Leduc, Aimee (Fictitious character)—Fiction. 2. Women private investigators—France—Paris—Fiction. 3. Palais-Royal (Paris, France)—Fiction. 4. Murder—Investigation—Fiction. 5. Paris (France)—Fiction.
I. Title.
PS3552.L297M83 2010
813'.54—dc22
2009041046
10 9 8 7 6 5 4 3 2 1

Vengeance? Kill the one they love.

—A GYPSY SAYING

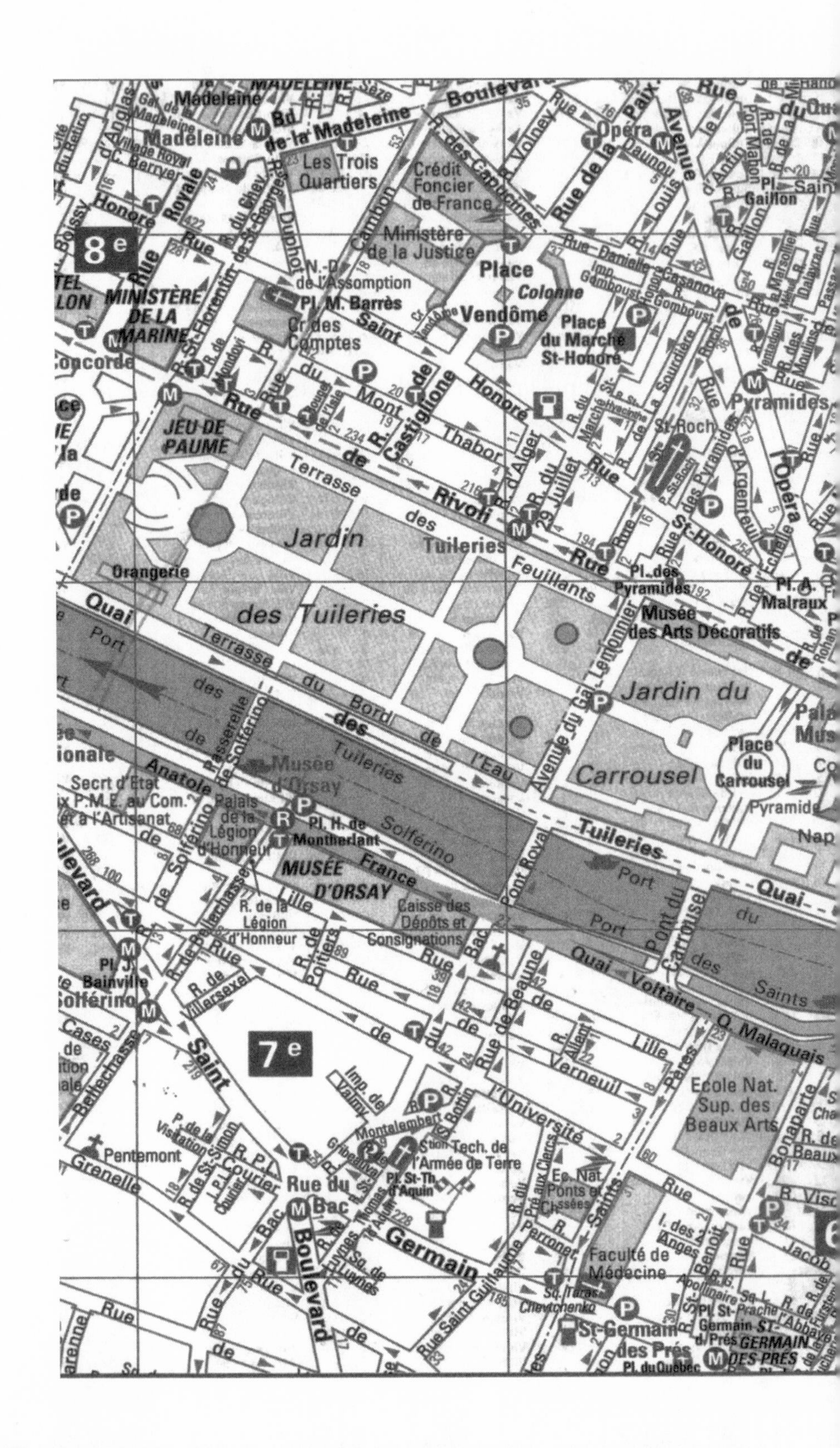

8e
7e
Madeleine
Bd de la Madeleine
Boulevard
Les Trois Quartiers
Crédit Foncier de France
Ministère de la Justice
R. des Capucines
Opéra
Rue de la Paix
Avenue
Place Vendôme
Colonne
Place du Marché St-Honoré
N.-D. de l'Assomption
Pl. M. Barrès
Cr des Comptes
MINISTÈRE DE LA MARINE
Concorde
Rue Royale
Honoré
Rue du Mont Thabor
R. de Castiglione
Rue de Rivoli
JEU DE PAUME
Orangerie
Terrasse des Feuillants
Jardin des Tuileries
Terrasse du Bord de l'Eau
Pyramides
St-Roch
Rue St-Honoré
Pl. des Pyramides
Pl. A. Malraux
Musée des Arts Décoratifs
Jardin du Carrousel
Place du Carrousel
Pyramide
Avenue du Gal Lemonnier
Quai des Tuileries
Quai Anatole France
Passerelle de Solférino
Port de Solférino
Musée d'Orsay
Pl. H. de Montherlant
Palais de la Légion d'Honneur
MUSÉE D'ORSAY
Secrt d'Etat aux P.M.E. au Com. et à l'Artisanat
Caisse des Dépôts et Consignations
Pont Royal
Port des Tuileries
Pont du Carrousel
Port des Saints Pères
Quai Voltaire
Q. Malaquais
Rue de Lille
Rue de Bellechasse
R. de la Légion d'Honneur
R. de Poitiers
Rue du Bac
Rue de Beaune
Rue de Verneuil
Rue de l'Université
Ecole Nat. Sup. des Beaux Arts
Rue Bonaparte
Boulevard Saint-Germain
Pl. J. Bainville
Solférino
Imp. de Valmy
Montalembert
Stion Tech. de l'Armée de Terre
Pl. St-Th. d'Aquin
Ec. Nat. Ponts et Chssées
Pentemont
Grenelle
Rue du Bac
Faculté de Médecine
Sq. Taras Chevtchenko
St-Germain des Prés
Pl. du Québec
ST-GERMAIN DES PRÉS
Rue Jacob
Rue Saint Guillaume
Boulevard Raspail

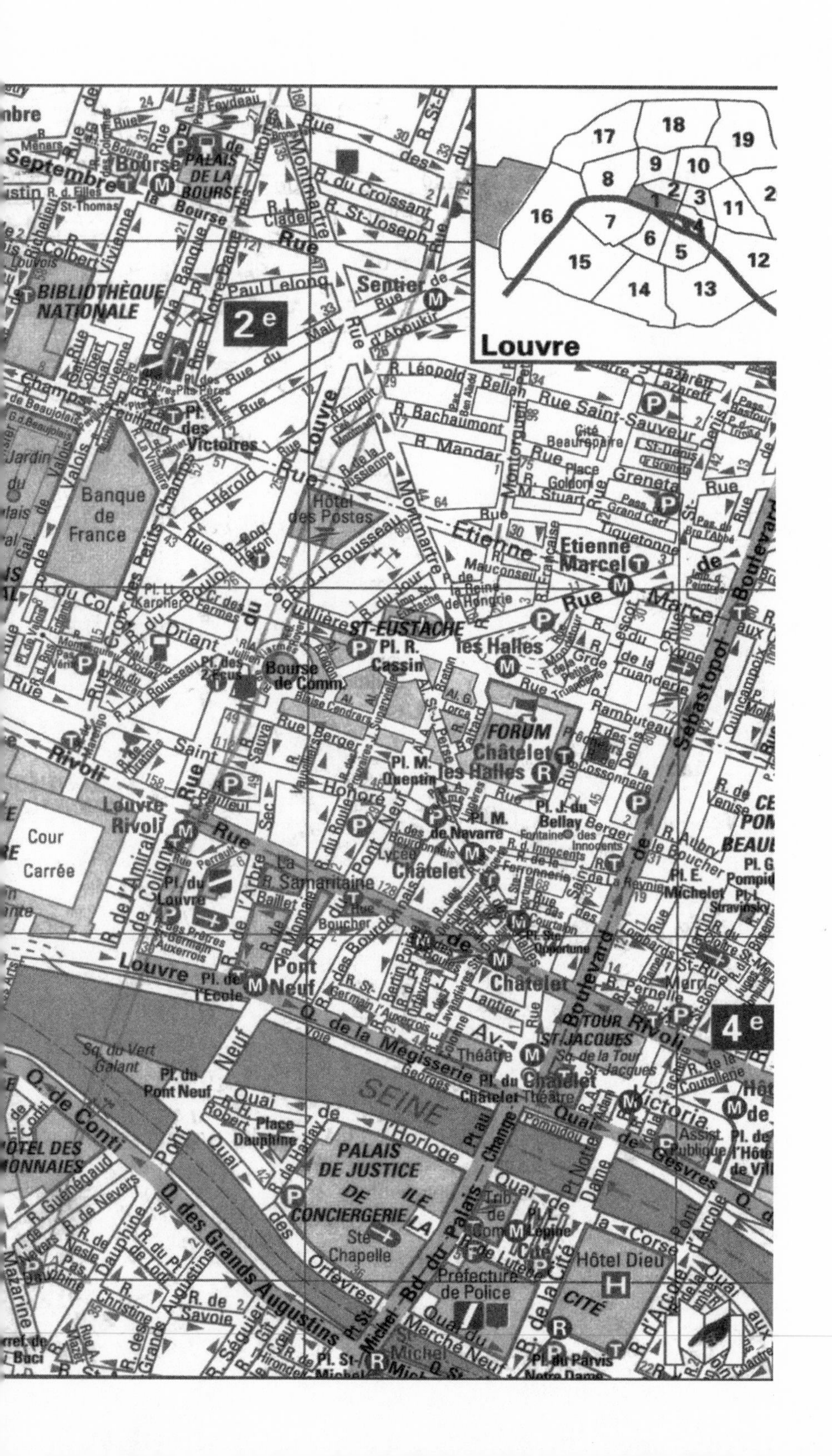

Louvre
17
18
19
9
10
8
1
2
3
11
16
7
6
4
5
15
14
13
12
2e
4e
BIBLIOTHÈQUE NATIONALE
PALAIS DE LA BOURSE
Bourse
Septembre
R. du Croissant
R. St-Joseph
Sentier
Rue d'Aboukir
Rue Montmartre
Rue du Louvre
Paul Lelong
Rue du Mail
Pl. des Victoires
R. Léopold Bellan
R. Bachaumont
R. Mandar
Rue Saint-Sauveur
Rue Greneta
Rue Montorgueil
Rue Etienne Marcel
Etienne Marcel
Hôtel des Postes
Banque de France
Jardin du Palais Royal
R. J.J. Rousseau
R. Hérold
Rue Coquillière
ST-EUSTACHE
Pl. R. Cassin
les Halles
Bourse de Comm.
FORUM Châtelet les Halles
Rue Rambuteau
Boulevard de Sebastopol
Rue Berger
Pl. M. Quentin
Rue Saint Honoré
Rivoli
Louvre Rivoli
Cour Carrée
Pl. du Louvre
La Samaritaine
Rue de l'Arbre Sec
Rue du Pont Neuf
Lycée Châtelet
Pl. J. du Bellay
Fontaine des Innocents
Pl. E. Michelet
Pl. G. Pompidou
Pl. I. Stravinsky
Rue des Lombards
Rue de Rivoli
Av. Victoria
Châtelet
Pl. de l'Ecole
Pont Neuf
Q. de la Mégisserie
TOUR ST JACQUES
Sq. de la Tour St-Jacques
Théâtre
Pl. du Châtelet
Châtelet Théâtre
SEINE
Sq. du Vert Galant
Pl. du Pont Neuf
Place Dauphine
Quai de l'Horloge
PALAIS DE JUSTICE
CONCIERGERIE
ILE DE LA CITÉ
Ste Chapelle
Bd du Palais
Préfecture de Police
Hôtel Dieu
Quai de Gesvres
Quai de Corse
Pont d'Arcole
Pl. de l'Hôtel de Ville
Assist. Publique
Pl. du Parvis Notre Dame
Q. de Conti
HÔTEL DES MONNAIES
Q. des Grands Augustins
Quai des Orfèvres
Pl. St-Michel
Marché Neuf
R. Guénégaud
R. de Nevers
R. Dauphine
R. Christine
R. de Savoie
R. Séguier
Mazarine

For the ghosts

MURDER in the PALAIS ROYAL

Paris

October 1997

Monday

Aimée Leduc smoothed her vintage Lanvin blue silk blouse, a flea market find. She was determined, for once, to play by the rules. The rules in this case were set forth in an *Elle* article: "Now that you've met him, don't blow it. • RULE 1: Bad boy or not, *he* likes good food." She hoped this was true of Mathieu, media liaison for a fashion house.

Opening the balcony doors of her apartment to the twilight, Aimée inhaled the crisp autumn air. Below, streetlights lining the Ile Saint-Louis cast yellow slants of light over the Seine.

Fallen rose petals on the walnut dining table emitted a faint scent. The slow melodic twang of Django Reinhardt's guitar sounded in her dining room. She lit the beeswax tapers on the candelabra, blew out the match, watched the slow gray spiral of smoke rise, and crossed her fingers.

Chloë's voice came from the kitchen. "But how well do you know him, Aimée?" Tall, with blunt-cut reddish-brown hair and black-framed round owl-like glasses, Chloë had recently sublet the upstairs apartment.

"Who really knows anyone, Chloë?" Aimée asked.

Chloë shot her a warning look. "Take it slow. Why rush?"

But when had she taken anything slowly? Mathieu ignited a spark in her that she hadn't felt in a long time.

Miles Davis, Aimée's bichon frisé, pawed at his leash. "You're sweet to take him tonight, Chloë."

"Don't do anything I wouldn't." Chloë grinned before the door closed behind her.

Aimée heard her footsteps down the hall. The doorbell rang.

* * *

MATHIEU'S DEEP-SET EYES gleamed at her over the black trumpette mushroom fricassee drizzled with white peppercorns. He tore out the nub of the *ficelle*, a thin baguette. "*Eh bien*, you should have told me that you cook."

She didn't; she hoped to God she'd weighted down the take-out cartons from Fauchon deep enough in the garbage.

"You're quite the gourmet, Aimée. Impressive," he said. Mathieu was lean and muscular under his V-neck sweater. A silver stud earring showed under his black curling hair as he ran the back of his warm hand along her cheekbone. "What else haven't you told me?"

Told him? That tomorrow she was flying to New York to find her brother, a younger brother she hadn't known existed until two weeks ago when she'd discovered ten-year-old letters with a Manhattan return address. At least that gave her a place to start.

It was a shame she'd connected with Mathieu on the eve of her departure. But she'd figure that out later, if later happened.

Her phone rang. She ignored it until the voice of René, her partner, boomed on the answering machine. "Aimée, care to explain the hundred thousand francs making us richer this evening? A payoff from an Eastern European arms dealer? Or did you furnish the Colombian cartel with a safe bank account?"

Mathieu's eyebrows rose. She grabbed the phone, explaining, "My partner! A joker. Excuse me."

She ran to the kitchen, checking the oven she never used to see if the roasted rosemary chicken had warmed up. "Damn embarrassing, René. Some joke? I'm not laughing."

"Me, neither," René said. "Not that we couldn't use the money. Is there something you're not telling me?"

"I won the lottery?" Had she even remembered to buy a ticket this week?

"Lottery winnings arrive in nice big checks, Aimée."

He sounded serious.

"I don't understand, René."

"No client owes us even half that much," René said.

"You checked our overdue accounts?"

A snort came over the line. "Double-checked."

Mathieu . . . and the rosemary chicken was burning. "There's got to be a bank error. A mistake."

"Get over here, Aimée, and deal with this. I'm up to my neck organizing the Nadillac investigation." René exhaled. "Their fee is legitimate money, remember?"

She racked her brain. No explanation for such a sizable unexpected deposit came to mind.

"*Bien sûr,*" she said, reaching into the oven and burning her hand. "*Merde*! I'll get back to you soon."

Another snort. "Hot date, eh?"

"In more ways than one, René." But he'd hung up.

Monday Night

IN LEDUC DETECTIVE'S office, René Friant stood and stretched, all four feet of him. Stress, he knew, aggravated the pain of dysplasia common in dwarves his size. Sometimes stretching would alleviate it.

The beveled mirror over the office's marble fireplace

reflected his computer's flashing green cursor. A brass arm lamp hanging over his desk provided the only other light. Above him, the chandelier and the woodwork of the carved nineteenth-century ceiling disappeared in shadow.

This addition of a hundred thousand francs to the business's currently strapped bank account raised alarms in his head. Hadn't Aimée championed their latest economy move, insisting that he order printer toner in bulk? And now, no doubt, she was writhing in the arms of another bad boy, too distracted to deal with the bank problem. He tried to push her out of his mind, to repress his feelings for her. As he always did.

Mentally, he replayed the ongoing computer security projects from which they earned their bread and butter. He knew every client, every firm. There was no explanation for the payment of such a sum. He re-checked the bank's e-mail notification of the wire transfer. Perhaps the bookkeeping department had made a numerical error.

Or was Aimée in trouble? Hiding something? Something involving this wild-goose chase across the Atlantic to look for a "brother" who might not even exist. But he and Aimée were best friends, she always said. How could he suspect her?

Shouts and yells came through the office wall. He sighed. Those crazy Italians in the new travel office next door were watching a soccer championship match, like everyone else on their floor this evening. He switched on *Radio Classique*. Strains of a Haydn sonata filled the room. Before he dealt with the computer surveillance dossier for Nadillac's impending trial, he needed a break. The compromising findings in Nadillac's data files had to be plainly presented. He needed to clear his mind.

René assumed a yoga position on the hardwood floor, closed his green eyes, inhaled a cleansing asana breath, then exhaled.

After a half hour of stretching and yoga poses, he sat up, his limbs and spine more limber, ready to deal with Nadillac.

He heard the faint tumble of the lock; then the frosted glass door of Leduc Detective opened. Yells came from the soccer fans down the hall.

"About time, Aimée," he said.

He heard only footsteps, then the groan of her desk drawer opening. He turned down the radio and looked up. But the office was dark and the partition blocked his view.

"Giving me the silent treatment?" he asked.

René got to his knees, taking his time. There was no reason to throw his back out of alignment before she revealed what she'd withheld over the phone.

He heard her rooting around in her desk drawer.

"So you're angry about our phone conversation."

She didn't answer. He saw a blur in the darkness heading to the coat rack.

"*Zut alors!*" René said. "If you're in trouble, tell me, Aimée." In the coved doorway he saw light hit the visor of the motorcycle helmet she wore. He hadn't heard her scooter pull up in the street but then why would he, up here on the third floor?

Still, why hadn't she hung up her helmet?

Yells erupted from the open door of the travel agency. "Another goal!"

Then he saw the glint of the gun barrel. Her Beretta.

"Aimée?"

The muzzle flash illuminated the room for an instant. Amazed, he heard the crack of a gunshot and felt a dull thud in the back brace he wore underneath his handmade Charvet shirt. The impact knocked him sideways.

Aimée shooting at him?

He shoved his orthopedic chair, propelling it across the

polished wood floor, his five years of judo and black belt training paying off. The chair wobbled as it struck his desk, deflecting the second shot. Then a force like hitting concrete slammed against his chest. The acrid reek of cordite filled the air.

Pain ripped through him, each breath like a knife twisting inside his chest. Shouts came from the hallway.

Warm blood spattered his desk, his face. A haze filmed his open eyes. The next shot he didn't feel.

Monday Night

AIMÉE'S CELL PHONE rang from somewhere on the floor. Her legs were entangled with Mathieu's on the recamier, his breath hot in her ear, his musky scent enveloping her. The phone rang again. And again, insistent. Coming up for air, she scrabbled around and felt for it, locating it lodged under her leopard-skin high heel.

"Leduc Detective," she said. "I mean, Aimée Leduc."

"Mademoiselle Leduc," a businesslike female voice said. "Emergency ward, Hôtel Dieu."

Hôtel Dieu, the public hospital, calling? She tried to sit up, but most of her was under Mathieu's bare chest.

"You're the contact listed for Monsieur Friant in his medical information?"

"*Oui*, but what's happened?"

Loud pinging noises and the squawk of a loudspeaker broke up the words on the phone at Aimée's ear. Then she was told, "Monsieur Friant's in surgery right now."

René in surgery. She sat up, pushing Mathieu aside, shaking with fear. René drove like a speed demon behind the wheel. A car accident?

Her fingers trembled as she zipped up her skirt.

She'd grabbed her bag and her jacket before she remembered Mathieu, who gazed at her, wide-eyed. He'd shifted his position and stood zipping his jeans.

She put her hand over the phone. "Sorry, an emergency, Mathieu. Got to go."

He'd put his jacket on, a nervous look in his deep-set eyes. "Me too."

The hospital lay a few minutes away on the next island, opposite Notre Dame. "Please, what's happened?" she said into the phone.

"Ask the police."

* * *

THE FLUORESCENT LIGHTING in Hôtel Dieu's green hospital corridor flickered, hurting Aimée's eyes. She'd waited more than two hours with no report on René's condition, no details except that he'd suffered gunshot wounds. She was not permitted to wait in the relatives' area. And there had been no sign of the *flics*, who'd left to respond to another call.

Horrified, she paced back and forth, breathing in the cloying pine disinfectant. Although it was sparkling clean and antiseptic, she hated hospitals. Most of all, she hated having no information as to René's condition.

She'd known René since they'd been at the Sorbonne. After her father's death on the job in an explosion—a bombing—in the Place Vendôme, she'd veered away from criminal investigation to refocus Leduc Detective on computer security.

She'd talked René into bringing his computer skills into the business, and he'd become her partner.

"Excuse me, *s'il vous plaît.*" She leaned on the counter. The reception nurse was on the phone, her back to Aimée. "Any word on Monsieur Friant?"

The nurse shook her head, not even turning around. The Emergency door pinged open. Aimée heard the thump and squeak of a gurney's wheels rolling over the linoleum. Then footsteps, more footsteps, running. The flash of green scrubs. What Aimée had taken for a gurney was a mobile wheeled unit, the cardiac shock paddles velcro'd to it.

"OR Room 3, the gunshot patient. Code Blue!"

Aimée's heart dropped. René!

Frantic, she tore past the surgery doors.

"This area's restricted," a nurse shouted. "You can't come in here."

She met angry looks from the green-gowned and masked surgical team. Beside her an aluminum cart held surgical instruments; plastic bags of blood hung hooked to a trolley. "What's happening? How's René?"

"Subdue this woman. Get an orderly to assist!"

Strong arms grabbed at her. "Can't I donate blood?" Tears welled in her eyes. "We're both O-positive."

"Control yourself, Mademoiselle, or leave the hospital."

She found herself on a plastic chair in an inner waiting room opposite a picture of a stone farmhouse in rolling green fields, reminiscent of her grandmother's Auvergne farm. Salty tears were stinging her cheeks.

Across from her stood a statue of the Virgin Mary cloaked in blue. Near the statue, a woman fingered a rosary and rocked on her chair, her eyes pools of pain.

"My baby." A sob escaped the woman.

"I'm sorry."

"Sorry?" The woman blinked. "You don't know how it feels."

Aimée didn't know what else to say. Silently, she watched the woman rock, wondering how a woman could stand knowing her child was suffering. Wondering if her own mother would have been as bereft, had she been hospitalized. Would that have kept her at home instead of leaving when Aimée was eight years old?

But self-pity would get her nowhere. Or René.

"*Désolée*, you're right," she said. "It's just that my best friend René's life's at stake." Her throat caught.

The woman set the black-beaded rosary in Aimée's hands. "Pray with me."

So she did. Prayed for this woman's baby, prayed for René, prayed she could take back every mean thing she'd ever said to him, every idea of his she'd ignored, the way she'd dismissed him on the phone. She didn't know if prayers would help him or the baby.

Tuesday Morning

AIMÉE RUBBED HER eyes; the clock showed 5 A.M. High heels in her bag, she crept from the waiting room, down the hospital corridor. The cold smooth linoleum chilled the soles of her feet.

In the next corridor, a glassed-in ICU held ten patient beds, each surrounded by machines. Staff, in green scrubs and white lab coats, consulted computers. Behind the reception area, an erasable board listed patients and bed numbers. Beside #6 she saw the name Friant, R.

She stepped into her heels, combed her fingers through her hair, and opened the glass door to the ICU. Her eyes adjusted to the bright lights. A steady thrum of beeping noises came from machines, and the smell of alcohol pervaded the room.

"*Excusez-moi*, may I see Monsieur Friant?"

"You're a relative?" the nurse asked, looking up from a chart.

"I'm listed on his medical card. The hospital called me."

The nurse pointed to a curtain on the left.

"What's his condition?"

She heard short beeping sounds, then an alarm rang. "Cardiac arrest in 10," shouted someone.

"The doctor will explain," the nurse said, rushing off on crêpe-soled shoes.

Aimée took a breath and parted the white curtains of #6.

René lay there clad in a child's hospital gown printed with red fire trucks, his head bandaged, eyes closed, a ventilation tube filling his mouth, a large dressing taped to tubes snaking from his chest.

She gasped. Helplessly, she watched the rise and fall of the ventilator machine breathing for him. The blip, blip, blip of a cardiac monitor beat in a steady rhythm. She bent down and kissed him, her lips lingering on his fevered cheek.

She uttered a mantra, "Save him, save him," to the steady rhythm of the blip, blip, blip. She pulled up a stool near his bed, sat, and took his hand.

"Don't die on me, René," she said. Her lip quivered. "Don't you dare."

She stroked his limp hand. IV drips were connected to tubes taped to his wrist and his dressing. Dawn's rose-orange glow peeked in a pattern through the hospital window lace curtain. She focused on the band of light streaking across the metal headboard, praying René would wake up. Praying he'd live.

She heard the patter of footsteps, the clinking of the curtain rings being pulled aside.

A surgeon in green scrubs, glasses atop his thinning brown hair, consulted René's chart, then scanned a monitor labeled OXYGEN SATURATION.

"Is he in a coma, Doctor?"

"He's under deep sedation, Mademoiselle. Standard practice during surgery and the intubation procedure."

She nodded. The terms, lodged in the recess of her mind from her stint at pre-med, sounded familiar.

"His numbers look good, Mademoiselle."

That standard phrase, used by physicians, guarded and neutral. Her hand flew to her mouth. The École des Médecins professors had advised using that term for anything from routine to terminal.

"And if his numbers drop?"

The surgeon pulled his chin, his eyes tired.

"Please, Doctor. I'm on his medical card, but no one's told me anything."

"I apologize. We have a full ward, as you can see."

She steeled herself to listen. "Tell me."

"The bullet entered the chest cavity by the nipple and bounced off a rib, puncturing the right lung," he said. "A through-and-through, resulting in a 'dropped lung.' But a good clean exit wound."

From bad to worse.

"Will he live?"

She grew aware of the aroma of coffee, as the curtains

parted further. She looked up to see a man, tall, mid-thirties, wearing a brown jacket with a lived-in look from which a loose button hung. The odor of cigarette smoke clung to his clothes. He was hollow-eyed, with an up-all-night drag to his gait. He verged on attractive, she thought, given sleep and a shower. He stared at her.

The doctor beckoned to Aimée. "Mademoiselle, please step outside."

"Not just yet, Doctor." The man flashed his badge. "Melac, with Brigade Criminelle. I need to question your patient."

"He's recently come out of surgery and is still sedated."

"It's imperative. I only need to ask him one question."

The surgeon studied the monitors. "Can't this wait?"

"Give me just a minute."

"The breathing tube stays in until he's stable. He won't be able to speak."

"But he can signal, can't he?" Melac said.

"I could lighten the sedation," the surgeon conceded. "But I warn you, patients often panic when they find themselves in pain and with a tube down their throat. His lung collapsed, but we've sealed the puncture. So far, he shows no artery or nerve damage. But we don't know."

Aimée stared at Melac.

The surgeon gestured to a nurse, who checked the IV. "Lower the drip a milliliter per second." He turned to Melac and Aimée. "We had difficulty locating the pediatric instruments required by his small chest size. I warn you, the moment he exhibits stress, I'll re-up the medication."

Aimée stood. "I'm Aimée Leduc, René's partner. Concerning the shooting, Detective. . . ."

"Inspector Melac," he said. "You're a hard woman to find."

"Did you check the waiting room?" she asked. "I've been

there since the hospital called me. Do you think René knows who shot him?"

Melac's face was impassive. "Last night at ten o'clock—"

"He was shot at ten?" she interrupted. "Where was he?"

"I'll ask the questions."

The sheets stirred. "He's coming around, Inspector. A minute only," the doctor said. "Monsieur Friant, you're in the hospital. The detective wants to ask you one question. But you cannot speak: you have a breathing tube in your throat. Try to raise your left hand, if you can, to respond. Can you hear me, Monsieur?"

René's eyelids quivered.

"René, you had me worried, partner," Aimée said, forcing a smile and squeezing his hand.

One green eye opened, then the other. His dilated pupils were as big as centime pieces.

Melac leaned in from the other side of the bed.

"Monsieur Friant, I need your help. Witnesses allege your partner shot you. But we need your positive identification," he said.

Open-mouthed, Aimée stared at the detective.

"Monsieur Friant, did this woman, Aimée Leduc, make an attempt on your life?"

She didn't want to believe what she was hearing.

"Did she shoot you, Monsieur Friant?" he asked.

Aimée's heart jumped.

A look of bewilderment and pain contorted René's features. His left arm shot out toward Aimée.

Melac's gaze darted from René's face to Aimée's with a probing look that raked her skin.

Did René actually think she'd shot him?

René scratched at the tube, trying to pull it out. Panic

showed on his face. A sputter of a cough, a choking sound came from the tube.

"That's enough." The surgeon nodded to the nurse, who was re-adjusting the drip. "Monsieur Friant, you're going back to sleep."

Aimée got to her feet, grabbing her bag from the floor. "What witnesses?" Her throat caught. "Who says I shot my best friend? That's crazy."

"You were seen by Italian soccer fans partying in the office next door," Melac said. "They interrupted the shooting and saw you flee the scene."

She stiffened. "If I shoot, I don't miss. All you know is that a woman who looked like me broke into our office. Maybe she shot René. I didn't." She'd found her tongue.

René's eyes had closed. The ventilator whooshed, breathing for him.

"We discovered a Beretta and a cartridge casing in your desk drawer."

"She used a Beretta?"

"And left it for us to find. Do you have a license for the Beretta?" Melac checked for dirt under his fingernails.

"For *my* Beretta, of course." Somewhere. Where had she put it?

"Otherwise, that's two counts against you."

"Last time I checked, seventy-eight Berettas were registered in Paris. Who says it's mine? And why would I come here if I had shot René?"

"We see it from time to time. Maybe remorse." He shrugged. "Or a way to cover up."

"Impossible. Last night I had someone over for dinner. Ask him. We were together until the hospital called."

"But your partner pointed at you when I asked if you had shot him," Melac said.

The surgeon gestured toward the hallway. "Outside. You're disturbing the conscious patients."

She looked at René, his bandages, the lines hooked from his wrist to the IV drip. A deep pain welled inside her.

"Patients panic coming out of deep sedation; they feel suffocated and exhibit a gag reflex," the surgeon said. "They often try to pull the tube out, as Monsieur Friant attempted. I warned you. His gesture is inconclusive. We keep patients under and immobile to monitor closely for possible complications. And considering the low bone density and narrow chest cavity common in dwarves his size, we have to be cautious. Now, if you'll excuse me?"

The glass door shut behind him.

A pair of handcuffs appeared in Melac's hand. He gestured to the EXIT sign.

This wasn't happening. "You're arresting me?"

"Consider this a request to assist in our inquiries." Melac consulted an old pocket watch on a chain. "If you'll accompany me, Mademoiselle Leduc?"

How could she leave, with René in ICU?

"I'm on my second shift, and my patience is wearing thin," Melac said.

She hesitated. "You'll keep a guard here?"

"Hospital security's been alerted, Mademoiselle," Melac said. "My car's downstairs. By the way, officers found packed suitcases in your apartment hallway and your dog with your nice concierge." Melac motioned to the Air France folder sticking out of her bag. "Looks like you're planning on going somewhere, *non?*"

"New York. No law against that."

Her flight left in two hours. A local detective was meeting her at JFK with a car. He'd said he had a lead to her brother.

Impossible to go now. "It looks like I'm canceling my trip."

"I'd say so." Melac unlocked the handcuffs and took a step toward her.

She swallowed. "That's unnecessary."

"Procedure, Mademoiselle."

Tuesday Morning

AIMÉE'S HEELS TAPPED on the worn wood floor as she sat behind bars in the Brigade Criminelle's unheated holding area. Melac had yet to question her or take her statement. Her mind burned with questions about René's prognosis, who might have shot him, and why Melac thought she had done it. René had been confused and disoriented by medication, hooked to a machine with a painful tube breathing for him. When he reached out, had he been trying to pull her closer, to tell her something?

The handcuffs chafed her wrists. She tried rubbing her hands, sticky from the gunshot-residue tests, then grimaced at the spots made by the double-sided carbon adhesive on her silk blouse; no amount of dry cleaning would remove them. And the procedure had taken up valuable time that she would have spent finding the shooter.

Further down the wooden bench in the holding area, a man in handcuffs, wearing tight jeans, ran his tongue over his lips as he'd done for the last ten minutes. His eyes rested on her cleavage.

She stood to catch the duty officer's attention. Young, smelling of pine cologne, his was not a face she recognized. "Can I give my statement to Melac now?"

He scanned the roster. "Melac's off duty."

He hadn't told her. "*Et alors*, what's going on? Who's responsible for the investigation now?"

"Would you know if I told you?" he said.

This could take all morning. Her father, a former *flic*, had always moaned that transferring case files to the new shift took forever. Often investigators were called out on a new case and the backlog waited. But time was what she didn't have.

"I want to see Commissaire Morbier," she said.

"So do a lot of people."

His pine cologne got to her. No doubt it had been on special at the local Monoprix.

"I've known him all my life."

The *flic* eyed her silk blouse, pencil skirt and leopard print heels, and the mascara smudged around her eyes.

"And you'd like a café crème and *Le Figaro* to read while you wait." There was a grin on his face. "A brioche to go with that, perhaps?"

"Please, let him know his goddaughter's here," she said, ignoring his sarcasm. She hoped to God that Morbier was working today. "Try Commissaire Morbier's cell phone for me, please: 06 88 32 49."

"You're making that up," he said.

"Only one way to find out. I'd do it, but. . . ." She jangled her handcuffs. "You took my purse."

"And if I do?"

She could see the wheels turning in his head.

"My eternal thanks and I'll put in a good word for you," she said, summoning a smile, "mentioning your efficiency."

He dialed the number on the black rotary phone. She was unable to overhear the conversation. Then he looked at her, surprised. "Wonders never cease," he said. "Follow that officer."

* * *

DETERMINED TO IGNORE the fatigue weighing down her shoulders, Aimée accompanied a female officer, who knocked on the third floor *Groupe R* office.

"*Entrez*."

Morbier stood hanging a white silk scarf on the coat rack. Instead of his usual worn corduroy jacket and mismatched socks, he wore a tuxedo, formal evening shirt, dangling bow tie, and cufflinks. And spit-shined black-tasseled loafers.

Aimée's jaw dropped.

But Morbier's drooping basset-hound eyes, dark hair—now more salt than pepper—the cigarette hanging from the corner of his mouth, were the same.

He caught her expression. "Just call me a dancing fool."

"Who is she, Morbier?"

"I was at a colleague's retirement party, Leduc." Morbier tapped ash from his cigarette in the full ashtray on his desk.

"Tough night, Leduc?"

"You could say that. Tougher for René. He was shot."

Morbier's hand paused in midair. Dust motes floated in the desk lamp's rays trained on his glasses and folders.

"Ask the officer to remove the cuffs and I'll tell you about it."

Morbier sat, sighing, and nodded to the officer. Then he pulled off his black-tasseled loafers, wincing.

The officer unlocked the cuffs. Aimée rubbed her sore wrists. Little red indentations marred her skin.

"Two espress, officer, *s'il vous plaît*," said Morbier.

Since when did Morbier say "please"?

"What happened this time, Leduc?"

He unbuttoned the shirt collar, stretched his neck. Then held up his hand. "*Non*, don't tell me. That's the Brigade's turf, not mine. Not for a long time now. You know that, Leduc. I hoped this was a social call."

"Melac suspects me of the shooting." She paused and took a breath.

"*Did* you shoot René?"

She shook her head.

"Start at the beginning, Leduc," he said, his face expressionless.

So she did.

"So René was shot at your office with your gun?" Morbier flicked a kitchen match against the edge of his desk; the match flared, and he lit an unfiltered Gauloise. His eyes narrowed. "And you want my help?"

Where was that coffee? Her heavy eyelids drooped.

"You gave me that Beretta, Morbier. Remember?"

He shifted in his chair. "And I hope you licensed it."

"But it could belong to anyone. None of this makes sense." She rubbed her eyes. "Would I shoot René with my Beretta, then walk in here and tell you about it?"

"Stranger things happen."

"Who the hell shot René, and why does everyone think it's me?" She tried to slow down, control the rising panic in her voice. "I want to give my statement and move on to more important things. Like finding who did this."

"As I said, I can't help you."

"Then who can?"

The aroma of freshly brewed espress filled Morbier's office. The female officer set a tray down on his desk.

"*Merci.*"

Aimée looked around her. Hanging on his coat rack, the

white scarf was out of place beside his mouse-brown raincoat and worn blue wool duffel coat. A few framed photos hung on Morbier's walls; his desk was littered with files and stray papers. There was not much here, but it all spoke of Morbier.

She dropped two brown sugar cubes in the demitasse and stirred.

"How is René?" Morbier took a sip and set his demitasse down.

"His right lung was punctured. I still can't believe anyone would shoot him."

She noticed the black-framed photo on the wall: Morbier at the Elysée Palace with the president. "Since when do you hob-nob with Chirac?"

"It's me and twenty others in the photo, Leduc. Another retirement reception. That's all I go to these days. Retirement functions. Mine too, soon."

He'd said that for years. But he kept his mouth closed about his work on the Brigade Criminelle's third floor in *Groupe R*, which had been upped to a few days a week. She observed the age spots on his hands, the wrinkled neck below his jowls, the weariness in his expression. Yet he'd come to work still wearing his tuxedo. His loyalty to the job came first, she'd give him that.

And she'd use it.

The steaming espress, bitter and strong, sent a jolt to her head.

"You haven't answered me, Morbier. I want you to get Melac off my back and steer this investigation the right way."

"You know it's not in my hands."

"A word in the right ear, Morbier, that's all I ask." She gave him the biggest smile she could muster. "Melac's off duty. They bagged my hands for GSR, but it's been two hours and no one's taken my statement. They haven't processed any admits all morning." She leaned forward. "Who'd want to hurt René? Can't you request that this investigation be placed in the right hands? Who's the golden boy detective right now?"

"You really want to know, Leduc?"

"I want the pro. The best. René deserves it."

"And you don't, of course," Morbier said.

"Why are they wasting time, Morbier? I've got an alibi."

"No doubt you rubbed someone the wrong way, Leduc. And if you don't behave, they'll keep you longer."

"Like twenty-four hours in *garde à vue?* You're my godfather, Morbier. Would you let them?"

"Melac's the best, Leduc."

"What?" A sinking feeling came over her.

"Forget Melac's attitude," Morbier said. "He's the one I'd want if I were a suspect."

"A suspect? But I had a man over for dinner last night. He can confirm it. I couldn't have shot René."

"You cooked?"

"In a manner of speaking."

"Until the GSR reports come back negative and your alibi's confirmed, you're Melac's point of attack."

"Meanwhile, evidence will be lost or contaminated," she said. "Melac's not like you. And you call him the best?"

The air in the office was thick with cigarette smoke. Only the distant ringing of telephones in the outer offices broke the silence.

"We're all different, Leduc. Look below the surface," Morbier finally said. "Besides, it's a new world now. Computers, forensics, this DNA. And the young ones who know how to use these things. They call me a dinosaur."

She did too, but not to his face. Yet no computer could

replace Morbier's brain as it catalogued names and facts and put them together. And he never forgot a thing.

"What's this job gotten me, Leduc, but a life sentence?"

He had no family except for a grandson in Morocco who he'd lost custody of. His job was his life. His only life.

The red lights of Morbier's phone console lit up like cherries, all in a row. He lifted the receiver. "*Oui?* They've been asking about her? *Bon*, she's ready."

Morbier hung up. "They're ready to take your statement." He sighed. "I've bailed you out one too many times. It's not my job any more; I've ruffled too many feathers."

"Has that ever stopped you?"

With Morbier, it always came down to a deal. What could she offer?

"You want me to cooperate, Morbier?" she said. "I will."

"That's a first." He lit another Gauloise. The smoke spiraled in a gray trail to the ceiling. His eyes narrowed. "You promise?"

Like hell she would. "Count on it, Morbier."

"It's Melac's call, Leduc. But behave and I'll see what I can do."

Morbier reached in his drawer and put a fifty-franc note in her hand. "Buy René some flowers."

René needed a lot more than flowers.

She joined the police escort at his door. Paused. "*Merci.*"

All the way down the wide stone staircase, past the black-suited magistrates huddled in conversation, a thought nagged at her. Morbier had referred her to the New York detective, yet he had neglected to mention it now. So unlike him. He never forgot a favor owed.

* * *

IN THE FIRST-FLOOR cubicle, Aimée stared at Vichon, the duty detective. Late thirties, shaven head, and barrel-like chest, he dwarfed the small metal desk. He inserted a sheet, aligned the paper, and pecked at the ancient typewriter keyboard with two fingers.

"WHERE'S YOUR COMPUTER?" Aimée asked. "It's 1997."

"Blame it on your tax francs *not* at work," Vichon said. "They hook the new system up next week. Or so they say."

He had that right, she thought. Half of the Commissariat's computer systems were incompatible with the others. Red-faced, the Brigade Criminelle had tried to hide the fact that its budget didn't provide for enough computers to handle Britain's MI5's communications, an embarrassment in the more than a month since Princess Diana's car crash in the Pont de l'Alma tunnel. Referred to as '*La Crim*,' the Brigade Criminelle's investigation into the phantom Fiat Uno seen speeding away still had turned up nothing.

"You've got security on my partner's hospital room, *non?*"

"Now you're telling me how to do my job, Mademoiselle?"

Somebody needed to, but she swallowed her words.

The Brigade Criminelle was allowed to hold her in *garde à vue* for up to twenty-four hours. Better to shut up, not push Vichon. She couldn't find the person who'd shot René from a jail cell.

A knock sounded on his cubicle window.

"*Oui?*" Vichon heaved himself up and conducted a conversation in the hallway with a blue-uniformed *flic*. The only word she caught was *indicateur*, an informer.

Aimée saw a blonde in zebra-striped hot pants, lace-up stiletto boots, and matching black leather bustier. Her hands were cuffed behind her. Attractive, apart from the black eye and the dried blood on her cheek.

Was this what they did to informers? Aimée's shoulders tensed. Vichon stepped back into the cubicle.

Aimée passed him a slip of paper with Mathieu's phone number on it. "Call him. He'll confirm that we had dinner last night at my apartment. He stayed there until the call came from the hospital."

Vichon shrugged. "All in good time."

Twenty minutes later, she'd signed her two-page typewritten statement and pushed it over his desk.

And then it hit her. He'd typed out her statement, but not on the standard Procès-verbal form. And she knew why. Filing the Procès-verbal kicked the administrative wheels into action: duration of custody, her right to an attorney, and assignment of a procurator and *Juge d'Instruction*. A loss of power for the police. The elitists at *La Crim* hated being on the *juge d'instruction's* leash. Termed "hunters," they preferred to investigate in their own way, to remain "unofficial" until they were certain before documenting their investigation "officially."

A bad sign. Since Napoleon's time—and before—the police had spied on French citizens. That hadn't changed. They could tap her phone, follow her, give her rope with which to hang herself.

Vichon thumbed the pages in the report, scratching his chin, ignoring her statement.

Aimée drummed her chipped Byte-me Blue lacquered nails on the desk. "*Alors*, I've got an alibi. Besides, I have no reason to shoot my partner. He's my best friend."

"Witnesses at the scene identified you."

Surprised, she leaned forward. "But I left my office at five

P.M. to pick up the rosemary chicken. Ask the Fauchon clerk at Place de la Madeleine."

"One witness was very clear in his statement," Vichon said, ignoring her words. "The one who saw you running away down the stairs."

"Saw me? You mean the drunken Italians down the hall? What was I wearing?"

"Forget the fashion questions, Mademoiselle."

The stale air in Vichon's cubicle was getting to her. She stood, smoothing down her skirt. What else had the Italians said? What had Vichon left out? "The Italians weren't the only tenants on our floor partying when I left. Ask the ad agency."

"Until we get a confirmation of your alibi," Vichon said in a measured tone, "you're the suspect we're working with, Mademoiselle. Why are you in such a hurry?"

She dropped back into the chair, staring at him. "I know procedure and, of course, I want to assist in any way I can." She didn't mention that she was tired, hungry, in need of more espress, and wanted to brush her teeth. "I can help you, Vichon. I do computer security, but my background's criminal investigation; I'm a licensed PI. Whatever I find out will go right to you. Procedure followed and adhered to." She watched him. "And you'll get the credit."

"But you're not my type."

She wanted to hit the sexist *salaud*. Instead she bit her lip. "How does that enter into an investigation?"

"This is *La Crim's* case." He leaned back in his chair. "No amateur help needed, especially an amateur with a plane ticket out of the country and her bags packed."

"But Commissaire Morbier will vouch for me," she said. "Not half an hour ago in his office upstairs he commended Inspector Melac. He told me Melac was the best."

Vichon sat up. "He said that?"

"And you'd like him to speak of you that way, wouldn't you, Vichon? Not express concern over pointlessly detaining me, his goddaughter, in the *garde à vue*."

Vichon's fists clenched.

"Now, do we need to call my godfather," she said, "or may I have my bag?"

* * *

OUTSIDE LEDUC DETECTIVE, Aimée stood on the scuffed wood floor of the landing. Yellow crime-scene tape criss-crossed her frosted glass office door, which was ajar. She pushed it open.

Inside, she saw a figure with an orange POLICE armband opening his metal fingerprint kit. Through the window came the whine of a siren, the hum of midday traffic, and cooing from a pigeon perched on the black iron grillework.

As usual.

But it wasn't.

Graphite powder dusted the woodwork and file cabinets. The contents of her desk drawer—a tube of mascara, software encryption manuals, keys, and stop-smoking patches—littered the floor.

"Didn't you notice the tape? No entry," said the fingerprint technician.

She pursed her lips.

"It's my office, Monsieur."

"And it's *my* crime scene."

She needed to get inside. "Then you can take my prints now. It will save you an extra step later."

La Crim had taken her prints already, but she doubted the technician knew that.

"If I need your assistance, Mademoiselle," he said, "the investigator will inform me."

This technician went by the book.

"Then don't let me disturb you," she said, tiptoeing a few steps farther inside. "You can watch me, make sure I don't touch anything."

"Afraid not, Mademoiselle," he said, blocking her path.

"How long does this take?"

His mouth pursed.

And then she saw the dark red brown patch of René's bloodstains on the parquet floor. Her stomach lurched and she grabbed the door ledge.

"That's my partner's blood. Could you hurry, Monsieur?"

"I've got a job to finish," he said. But a flicker of sympathy crossed his face. "I must follow procedure."

At least he might let her look around.

"And that means?"

"Finish fingerprinting the crime scene, call in the results, and then, after approval, I can release the crime scene."

She opened her mouth to speak, but before she'd said a word he continued, "So if you'll leave and let me get to work, Mademoiselle?"

She backed out. She'd use the time to question Luigi at the travel office next door. He'd moved in a few weeks ago and the smell of fresh paint still hovered in the hallway. She'd find out what he'd really seen.

First, she had to inform the New York detective that she'd missed her flight. Yet each time she attempted to leave a message, his voice mailbox was full. She'd have to try again later.

Aimée knocked on the door of Viaggi Travel.

No answer. "Luigi?"

Still no answer. She was about to knock again when the door opened.

"What now?" said Luigi, a young man in his twenties, dark-haired, with charcoal stubble shading his chin. His wrinkled shirt looked like he'd slept in it. After a moment, his face darkened as he recognized her.

"*Madonna mia* . . . you!" His bloodshot eyes widened. He tried to shut the door. "Get away."

She'd stuck her boot inside. "Been to the eye doctor's lately, Luigi?"

She pushed the door open. "*Non?* Time to get your eyes checked." The odor of stale smoke and spilled beer met her. The little travel agency needed airing out. Peroni beer bottles filled the garbage bins, and ashtrays overflowed. A large-screen *télé* filled one wall; posters of Roma and Isle of Capri along with red and gold soccer pennants adorned another.

"*Assassina!*" Panic showed in his eyes. "You tried to kill Monsieur René. I call the *flics*." He began to run and tripped, sending beer bottles scattering over the floor.

"Why are you accusing me? It doesn't make sense," she said. "Remember, yesterday you recommended a shop to me for antipasto and truffles? Why would I—"

"Drugs. You take drugs. Act crazy." He pulled himself up and reached for the phone, then clutched his stomach as a wave of nausea passed through him. "You go to jail."

"Look at this place." She tapped the bin of beer bottles with her pointed toe. "How much beer did you drink? All that partying, watching the game, the noise, the dark hallway. What did you really see?"

He clutched his stomach again.

"René's my partner, my best friend, Luigi," she said. "I want to find the person who *did* shoot him."

He backed away, eyeing the phone. "Maybe you have gun, want to shut me up too?"

"You need Schoum," she said.

"*Como?*"

"A time-honored antidote to hangovers." The yellowish herbal mixture came in a blue-and-white label *Traitement d'appoint de douleurs fonctionelles d'origine digestive*, and worked wonders.

She blocked his way to the phone.

"Monsieur René . . . the blood . . . how could you shoot this little man?" Luigi said, white-faced.

Perspiration beaded her brow; the atmosphere in this office was stifling. But she had to get him to talk, to get information.

"Weren't you watching the championship match?"

"Torino versus Palermo. . . ." His voice trailed off.

She cleared a space on a cracked leather chair. "Sit down. Let's discuss what you remember, what you actually saw."

"I saw *you*." He pointed his finger accusingly.

"Me? Did you see my face?"

"I saw your raincoat. The one you wear yesterday. I hear shots . . . terrible. Like when robbers held up my uncle's store in Torino. I never forget the sound." He glared at her. "Next door, Monsieur René's shouting 'Aimée.' Then you run down the stairs."

"Maybe you only saw a woman my height?"

"I give Monsieur René CPR, try to pressure the wound." Luigi's voice quavered. "But so much blood."

"You saved René's life, Luigi." She rocked on her heels. "Thank you."

For a moment, doubt appeared on Luigi's face, a fleeting look of concern. "I don't like to believe my eyes."

And then the look vanished. "I tell Arnaldo, call *polizia, ambulanzia*. You run away."

"And the *flics*—"

"I give statement," he interrupted. "The police find your gun."

He clutched his mouth as nausea overtook him.

"I know why you come back. Now you kill me."

She stared.

"*Non*—" then Luigi stopped himself. Fear shone in his dark eyes.

"What did you actually see, Luigi?"

"Your helmet. Fancy helmet you wear," he said.

"My helmet? But it's here in the office."

Blue Fever helmets like hers carried a price tag of over eight hundred francs; they were made in a limited edition.

"Why would I keep my helmet on, Luigi?"

"You crazy . . . I don't know."

"Can't you see, Luigi, the shooter wore the helmet to hide her face? And frame me."

"I tell *polizia*." He leaned forward, breathing hard. "Please, they investigate."

Given Vichon's attitude and the snail's pace of the investigation, she wouldn't count on it. Valuable time was slipping away as they spoke.

"Luigi, I'd never hurt René. Believe me."

As long as she was the main suspect, and until Mathieu was reached by the police and asked to confirm her alibi, the real shooter would have ample time to disappear. Or worse, she might make another attempt on René.

She ran out into the dimly lit hall. The crime-scene tape still hung over Leduc Detective's closed door. A knot of worry filled her chest.

She had to get in. She turned the doorknob with a measured

twist, tiptoed inside, and heard the technician, somewhere in back, whistling. Her helmet hung from the coat rack. She grabbed it.

"Who's there?"

Aimée shut the door, ignored the wire cage elevator, and ran down the steps two at a time. Out of breath, she hailed a taxi on rue du Louvre.

"Where to, Mademoiselle?"

The shooter thought she'd gotten away with it, Aimée thought. Not while there was breath in her body. She'd find the guilty woman, and protect René.

A police car with flashing red-orange lights pulled up across rue du Louvre. Had the fingerprint technician alerted a patrol car? Or had Luigi reached the *flics* in record time? She didn't care to find out.

"Place du Marché Saint Honoré," she said, breathless, to the taxi driver.

An easy place to lose a tail.

"But it's not far." Not worth the fare, he meant.

She slipped him fifty francs. "And I'm sure you know a short cut."

* * *

BY MID-AFTERNOON, SHE'D visited six motorcycle accessory stores. ToutMoto, the last carrying the Blue Fever line on her list, occupied a former bakery. Faded gold lettering and mill scenes on painted glass panels were still in evidence. ToutMoto nestled among upscale boutiques near the Madeleine and Hotel Ritz: an exclusive chunk of real estate.

Aimée entered ToutMoto to a thumping heavy metal beat and whining strains of a guitar pouring from overhead speakers. "*Bonjour,*" she called.

"*Un moment,*" came a woman's voice from the rear.

Aimée scanned the racks of pink lambskin leather jackets, Kevlar jeans and the displays of tiger-striped handlebars, and the helmets lining the walls. The Blue Fever helmet was featured, the type she wore.

A woman in a figure-hugging red leather jacket and matching leathers emerged and set a coffee cup down on the counter.

Aimée smiled. "My friend bought me this helmet here."

"*Mais oui*. A chic line. We sell two or three a year. You want to return it? Only store exchange is permitted."

"*Non*, but it's a bit tight. Here," Aimée pointed to the chin strap. "She said you'd know how to adjust it. I think it was you," Aimée said. "Maybe you remember her?"

"My clients range from 'golden girl' bankers to Sorbonne students. We're the *exclusif* female motorcycle and scooter accessory store." The woman sipped her coffee and checked the strap. "But this helmet's worn," she said. "There's a scratch here."

A tiny scratch, almost unnoticeable, on the visor. *Merde*. She couldn't pass it off as new.

The woman took another sip, her gaze hooded now. "We carry the newest Blue Fever model. This is last year's."

"*Vraiment?* But I thought. . . ." Aimée paused, trying to think of another angle. "That's confusing. She gave it to me for my birthday."

The woman shrugged.

"It's scratched already, and she's trying to pass it off as new?"

"She's your friend."

Two woman entered the store laughing and zeroed in on the sale rack.

"Why does it matter, Mademoiselle?"

Aimée blew air out of her mouth. "Like I'm going to buy her an expensive wedding gift if she bought my birthday present at the flea market? Bet she got herself the newer model, one of those." She pointed to the Blue Fever helmet decorated with lightning bolts in the window.

A delivery man entered, wheeling a dolly stacked with boxes.

"Take the strap to a leather shop," the woman said, wanting to get rid of her. "They'll stretch it for you."

"*Merci*. But I can't believe it! She told me she bought it yesterday. Or was it the day before? I'd like to understand."

"I've helped you all I can, Mademoiselle."

"But you remember her, *non*?"

Anxious for Aimée to leave, the woman scanned a sales transaction log. "Yesterday I show a cash transaction for a Blue Fever. It was a busy time. That's all I can tell you."

Aimée's shoulders slumped.

The woman took a clipboard from the delivery man and signed. Desperate, Aimée tried again. "You've been so helpful. I know this sounds petty, but—"

"*Ça suffit*, Mademoiselle! I don't know what kind of scam you're trying to pull." Anger vibrated in the woman's voice as she stared at the sales transaction log again, then glanced at Aimée, a knowing look in her eyes. "It was *you* I sold the Blue Fever to, *n'est-ce pas?*"

"What do you mean?"

"Oh, the dark glasses, the scarf don't fool me. You're an amateur. Now if you don't leave, and quietly, I'll ask the delivery man to escort you out."

* * *

ACROSS NARROW RUE des Capuchines, Aimée took a window table in the *café-tabac*: blond wood, Formica counter and a worn sixties interior, family-run by the look of children's pictures on the mirror. A line formed before the cashier, who sold cigarettes, LOTO tickets, and Métro passes. Locals perched at the counter. She paused to think.

A woman impersonating her had bought a helmet that looked almost like hers, entered Leduc Detective, and shot René with a Beretta.

Forget convincing Melac that she was being framed. He'd question the woman at ToutMoto and her case would look worse.

For a moment, her mind went back to Mathieu's warm breath on her neck. What reaction would he have to being questioned by *La Crim*?

Had the shooting made the press? The shooter could be lurking anywhere, might even be stalking René while Vichon sat on his fat behind catching up on old cases.

Crowds thronged the pavement: delivery men, shopgirls, and couture-clad women with little dogs peeking out from their oversize Dior bags. Cars, motorcycles, trucks, bicycles ringing their bells wove through the narrow street of this commercial quartier, thrumming with activity, around the corner from Place Vendôme.

The shooter had made one small mistake: she'd bought the newer helmet.

The waiter, gray-haired and past retirement age, set a double espress and brioche before her. He might remember something.

"Did you work lunch yesterday, Monsieur?"

"Mondays, we're closed."

"*Merci*."

She reached Hôtel Dieu on her cell phone and asked for the intensive-care nursing station. Busy. On her second try, a nurse answered.

"Monsieur Friant's condition remains stable," the nurse responded to her query.

Thank God!

She had so many questions. "Can you tell me if he's able to speak on the phone?"

"Not now, Mademoiselle," the nurse interrupted. "Talk to the doctor. We're run off our feet."

"And his name?"

"Dr. Soualt," the nurse said. "Give me your number and I'll attach it to Monsieur Friant's chart."

She did and hung up, none the wiser. She dunked her brioche into her coffee. Crusty buttery flakes fell onto the worn marble tabletop.

A blue and yellow postal van had double-parked, creating a jam in the street. Horns blared. A taxi driver got out of his car, shaking his fist.

And then she noticed the video surveillance camera mounted above the *parfumerie* shop next door to ToutMoto. A *parfumerie* also selling gloves, evidenced by the sign *Maitre Parfumeur et Gantier*.

She finished the flaky brioche, downed her espress, and slapped ten francs onto the table.

* * *

THE *parfumerie* EXHIBITED crystal flacons topped by gold stoppers, exuding a heady mix of scents: cypress, vetiver, musk, a touch of fig. Glass display cases contained opera-length gloves made of lambskin, deerskin, peccary, and silk, according to the hand-lettered signs. At hefty prices, she thought.

"Don't tell me." An older man in a black suit waved his hand back and forth in the air. Sniffed. "You go for the classic, Mademoiselle."

"Pardon, Monsieur, but your video camera—"

"You're wearing Chanel No. 5."

"How did you know?"

"I have the nose, Mademoiselle." He beamed. His prominent nose, red-veined cheeks, and wavy white hair gave him a distinguished look. "May I interest you in a mix, classical but light, earth tones layered by a hint of mulberry?"

Sounded good enough to eat.

"Another time, Monsieur," she said. "I'm interested in your video camera's capability."

"State-of-the-art model, yes," he said. He tented his fingers, rocking forward on his heels, a look of concentration on his face. "I'm the first merchant on the street to employ the device. It's foolish not to use modern technology these days. I've aired my views at our merchants association. One is already in place over at the Ritz. You've seen Princess Diana getting into that Mercedes via the camera at the rear. Such a sad testimony to her last minutes of life."

He liked to talk. And she lusted for the ostrich leather wrist-length gloves displayed on the counter. But not right now.

"Beautiful, *non?*" He'd noticed her gazing at the pale citron-scented gloves. "Just a tinge of green apple mingling with the color of Normandy butter, and as soft."

Exquisite.

"Quite a history to them. Henri IV's mother was poisoned with a similar pair. But Catherine de Médicis didn't just poison rivals, she turned perfuming gloves into a high art."

Aimée had had no idea. "Fascinating, monsieur, but—"

"We work in close collaboration with the most famous glovemaking houses. Our perfume mixes with the natural scent of leather, producing a new olfactory combination as it mingles with the scent of one's own skin."

To forestall a further sales pitch, she showed him her PI license with its unflattering photo, her mouth pursed as if tasting a lemon. "May I review your video surveillance footage from yesterday noon?"

She took out her checkbook. "Of course, I'm prepared to pay."

"It's important, Mademoiselle?"

"Four hundred francs," she said without skipping a beat.

A minor dent in the price of the gloves she admired. "That would, of course, include the tape itself, Monsieur."

* * *

HILAIRE, THE NOSE, led her beyond packing cases to a dark back room. Corked glass bottles containing floral essences, a glass beaker, and crushed gardenia petals in a mortar and pestle stood on a work table.

"Of course our scents come from Grasse, but I like to experiment," Hilaire said.

Mounted in a niche in the wall were two screens. One viewed the shop interior, the other rue Capuchines. The latter had a clear shot of ToutMoto's entrance.

"You're looking for something or someone, Mademoiselle?"

Wasn't she always looking? She suppressed a sigh. The elusive bad boy, always out of reach.

"Aah . . . I see." He gave a knowing smile and adjusted his cravat. "Aren't we all?"

"A woman, my height, dark glasses, scarf," she said. "Let's try from 11:30 A.M. onward."

He hit a button. She heard a click and the whirr of rewind. The crushed gardenia petal scent hung in the small room. Hilaire stopped the tape, then hit PLAY. The time counter in the right corner read 11:00. Passersby moved in slow motion.

"Fascinating, *non?*" Then he sped it up.

Aimée concentrated on each woman entering ToutMoto. None wore dark glasses. The time counter showed noon, then

12:10, 12:20; still no one. Had the woman at ToutMoto lied to get rid of her?

"I'll need to change the tape at 12:30," Hilaire said. "That one?" he asked. Hilaire was pointing to a figure. "Her?"

He hit PAUSE. On the screen she saw a figure in a raincoat like the one she'd worn yesterday. Tall, thin, with a scarf over her head, wearing large sunglasses.

"She looks like you," he said.

From a distance, she did. Maybe she was a tad shorter. Aimée's hands trembled.

"Can you fast-forward?"

A whirr. Now the door opened and the woman emerged from the shop, her back to the camera, clutching a large shopping bag. The helmet, Aimée figured. The woman stepped off the pavement into a taxi. A matter of seconds, and she was gone.

"Monsieur, can you replay that in slow motion?"

Aimée studied the woman and the taxi. After the seventh replay, she'd made out the taxi company logo and the taxi number, 1712 or 1713. With this information, she had a lead.

* * *

OUT ON RUE Capuchines, heading to the Métro, she called the taxi dispatch office. "I'm enquiring about the destination of the passenger picked up at 5 rue des Capuchines at 12:20 yesterday, by either taxi number 1712 or 1713."

"We don't give out that information to the public."

"*Bien sûr.*" She reached in her bag for her worn Vuitton wallet and read off her father's police badge number. "But I'm a *policier* involved in an investigation. Could you hurry, please?"

"We comply of course, but regulations require that this request be made in person."

Some new regulation? Or a ploy by the taxi service to discourage any follow-up?

"I'm on surveillance," she said. "Can't you help me out this once?"

She heard an expulsion of breath over the line.

"*En fait*, we don't like it either, but the dispatch log is kept in my supervisor's office."

"Your address?" she asked.

Waves of passersby darted around her as she scribbled the address inside the cover of her checkbook.

She shouldn't impersonate a *flic*, or do the Brigade Criminelle's work, she told herself. But she hated to deal with Vichon. She chewed her lip. On the other hand, she would relish seeing the look on Vichon's face when the woman was traced and her identity established. Not only would they get the shooter and her motive, but Aimée would be off the hook.

But would René? Running down the Métro steps, she pulled out her cell phone, punched in the Brigade's number, and reached for her lipstick.

* * *

SHE FOUND THE taxi dispatch office in the crumbling, stone-blackened Passage de la Reine de Hongrie—Passage of the Queen of Hungary—near the sixteenth-century Saint-Eustache, in the midst of Les Halles on the fringes of the professional kitchenware district. But she wasn't here for sauce pans or Le Creuset enamelware; she was here to find out where the taxi had dropped the woman who'd shot René.

"*Alors*, not a place one finds in the guidebooks. But atmospheric," a voice said. "The old Paris, eh?"

She knew that voice.

Melac.

Wasn't he off duty?

"But I'm not here for a tour." Melac stepped around garbage and discarded newspapers blowing over the stones. A more rested freshly shaved Melac in a black turtleneck sweater and tapered black jeans. He cleaned up well. At least she'd applied fresh lipstick in the Métro.

"I need to talk with you, Mademoiselle."

"After you view this evidence," she said. "I hope they passed on my message. Did you bring the camera?"

He pulled a compact video camcorder from his pocket. "Going to give me an explanation?"

"Better that you see this first." She inserted the tape that she'd bought from Hilaire at the *parfumerie* and played it.

"That's you," Melac said. "So?"

"It's someone *disguised* as me, buying a helmet."

"It looks like you."

"From a distance maybe, Melac. Wrong shoes."

"Wrong?"

A gust of wind wrapped a newspaper around her leg. She kicked it off.

"You wouldn't catch me dead in beige crocodile loafers," she said. "And I already own a helmet. This one." She showed him the helmet she was carrying in her bag. "Why would I buy another one? Luigi saw a woman wearing a helmet very like mine. Of the seven stores in Paris selling this Blue Fever model, only ToutMoto sold one in the last eight months. Yesterday. To her. We have to hurry."

Melac took out a small notepad. "Who videotaped this?"

"Monsieur Hilaire, who owns a *parfumerie* next to Tout-Moto. He has a video surveillance camera outside his shop."

Impatient, she strode toward the ground-floor taxi office fronting the passage. "The dispatcher will give you the address the taxi took this woman to. You'll need backup, a stakeout team . . . who knows how many—"

"Telling me my job?" But he reached for his phone.

In the taxi dispatch office, a man sat at a phone console, chewing a pencil.

"*Mais*, Madame. I don't speak Hungarian," the man said into the phone. "Understand? It's just our dispatch office address. Where do you want to go?"

He rolled his eyes, gestured for them to wait. A two-year-old *Marie Claire* magazine and a thick, much-thumbed Le Redoute mail order catalogue from last Christmas took up the only seat. She preferred to stand. Melac edged into the corner, deep in conversation on his cell phone.

"No Hungarians here," the dispatcher said. "But my drivers will take you anywhere. *Quoi? Non*, that's just the name, Madame!"

Like every schoolchild, Aimée knew the ironic history behind the passage's name. Julie Bécheur, a vegetable seller who had lived in this passage, petitioned Marie Antoinette to better market women's conditions. Taken with Julie's likeness to her own mother, Marie-Thérèse, Queen of Hungary, Marie awarded Julie's audacity by naming her passage for the Queen of Hungary. Conditions improved for a while. During the Terror, Julie's royalist sentiments brought her to the guillotine.

Melac flashed his badge. "Show me the taxi dispatch log, Monsieur."

By the time the dispatcher returned from a back office with the taxi log, Aimée was almost jumping out of her skin.

Melac crowded the counter, blocking her view. After a moment, he flipped the pages of his notepad.

"But *you* live on Ile Saint-Louis at Quai d'Anjou."

"And the Métro runs till midnight. So?"

She elbowed Melac aside and read the log entry: At 12:21 P.M., 5, rue des Capuchines, Pickup.

She stared at the taxi destination listed, and her mouth went dry: 17, quai d'Anjou.

Her address.

Tuesday

BLACKMAIL NEEDN'T GET fancy, Clémence Touvier thought, as she cut words from the newspaper with her manicure scissors. She'd seen this done in an old black-and-white film and figured the technique would still work. Besides, given the stakes, she felt certain that no detective or crime lab would ever examine her cut-and-paste job.

Clémence hunched over the upturned cask in the arched stone wine cellar below the Palais Royal bistro. Dust-covered wine bottles lined the racks in the naturally cool cavern with a temperature of a perfect 18 degrees Celsius. Only two more words to cut out.

"Clémence?" Someone pounded on the locked wine-cellar door. "You there?"

Merde! Carco, the chef and her sometime boyfriend, had arrived in the adjoining kitchen to prepare the evening sauces early. How had he known to look here? There were only ten minutes left before her wait shift, and she had to finish this.

Despite her queasiness from the sharp tannin smell of red wine, she made herself keep absolutely still. She heard voices, then shuffling footsteps, from the tunnel. He'd given up. She clipped her blond hair back, tiptoed to reach the glue she'd hidden behind a bottle of Saint Emilion, and got back to work.

The last word applied, the glue drying, she stared at her work. Simple and to the point. Fifty thousand francs would buy her silence.

She'd never be caught. She wore plastic dishwashing gloves from Monoprix. No fingerprints.

Nicolas, her ex, had never talked about his money source. But his payments had ceased and she was broke. Last night, desperate, she rummaged through Nicolas's belongings stored in her basement. She discovered a newspaper article and realized it held a link to Nicolas's aristo friend.

What the connection was, she didn't know yet, but the article gave her enough to allow her to bluff and suggest she did. She figured the threat of leaking a scandal to the press would suffice. That money would buy her ticket out of Paris.

Aimée Leduc had put Nicolas behind bars. She would worm the information out of him. Clémence had taken care of that too.

A slap on the stone, a muffled grunt, and then voices came from the tunnel outside the wine-cellar door. Again she heard Carco's voice. "That's the last delivery. Anyone seen Clémence?"

She held her breath. Pots clanged in the kitchen. She had to hurry.

Tried and true worked best, *non?* As her uncle, the *salaud*, would say. Her uncle had raped her in the woods the summer she was ten. It all came back to her: the dense heat of those afternoons; pine needles scratching her back; the resin scent mingling with his wine breath. How he'd put his tobacco-stained fingers over her mouth.

The fear that everyone would know.

Much later, her uncle had been imprisoned for killing a bank guard. At sixteen, she'd left Toulouse but found Paris, like other provincials before her, as gray at heart as its gray-cobbled streets. No sunflowers nodding in the fields, only rare splashes of color, no life embracing Provençal humor, only Parisian irony: that half-smile, the brittle shrug.

Now at twenty, Clémence refused to struggle with dead-end jobs. Her attitude had ended work cleaning offices and flats in the prestigious 16th arrondissement where even the maids wore pearls. But a job in the high-end Palais Royal bistro run by a fellow Toulousian where she could joke with clients made life bearable.

Clémence unlocked the cellar door, closed it without a sound, and padded through the tunnel. She'd reached the staircase to the bistro when she felt a hand on her shoulder.

A shiver went through her. Then she recognized Carco's stocky frame and flushed face, topped by his chef's hat. Along with crated zucchini and net bags of onions, he blocked her way in the tunnel.

"What's with the gloves?" he asked.

Her shoulders tensed. She had to find a way past Carco and deliver the letter before her shift began. "Last pair, too!" she said. "I need to polish the copper pots."

"I waited for you last night, Clémence."

He could wait forever, as far as she was concerned.

"I'm sorry. You know how tired I get after my shift, Carco."

"Why don't I come to your place tonight after work, Clémence?"

The last thing she wanted, in her condition. Not only that: her roommate despised him. And his temper.

But his cousin was a *flic*. She'd better watch her step and keep Carco happy, for now.

"My place?" She grinned, leaning against his white, side-buttoned chef's jacket. "Why?"

"We'll watch that video you have, you know. . . ."

"How about *your* place?"

He lived in a closet of a room near the Gare du Nord; the smell of grease from the Turkish kebab place below, and recorded prayers on the radio from the adjoining apartment, would wake her up at dawn.

"Promise?"

She'd promise anything to get away; her gloved fingers clutched the envelope in her pocket. She winked. "Of course."

Tuesday Afternoon

Gabrielle de la Pecheray shut the Ministry of Culture Press Conference Room door with a sigh of relief. Under her private office's high, gilded ceiling, she toyed with the idea of a massage. Her feet ached. Keeping the wolves at bay took its toll. She'd spent an hour fielding journalists' questions over the proposal to unseal National Archives Occupation-era documents. Now she collapsed in the Louis XV chair and kicked off her heels. This week she'd noticed a fine line cornering her lip.

Her eye fell on the envelope marked "Personal, Gabrielle

de la Pecheray" lying among the correspondence on her desk. What now? She shook her head in a quick motion, her thick blond hair held back by a black bow in a coiffed ponytail.

Gabrielle slit the envelope open to find cut-out words from a newspaper pasted on a sheet of cheap paper.

> Olivier was involved. I have proof. Leave fifty thousand francs CASH in an envelope at the antiquarian bookshop in Galerie de Valois, Palais Royal by 4 P.M. today.

Proof . . . proof of what? What did this crude blackmail attempt mean?

She shook the envelope, and a creased newspaper article dated January 1994 fell out, along with a grainy photo of flames and a gutted building. A sinking feeling overtook her.

> Suspect convicted of arson in Marais synagogue fire. The 18-year-old member of a neo-Nazi group, *Les Blancs Nationaux*, has been sentenced at the Tribunal for the November 1993 burning of the Marais synagogue. Trial evidence centered on the defendant's boast on video of setting fire to the synagogue, as part of group initiation into the notorious skinhead group, and testimony from the Leduc Detective agency who obtained this video. The accused—and now convicted—Nicolas Evry, his name revealed by the authorities, remains at La Santé. Due to his age, he received the minimum sentence of four years.

But hadn't they taken care of this, paid Nicolas off? She'd shielded Olivier, her son, who'd flirted with Le Pen's youth party and mixed with neo-Nazi skinheads, *Les Blancs Nationaux*, but that was over.

And why now, why threaten her four years later? Olivier's latest occupation, apart from "student," was party boy, according to the tabloid columns of *Voici*.

Her manicured hands trembled. The black marble clock on her desk showed 3:45. She reached for her cell phone. Time to make a call, squeeze her contact. Get this handled.

But the recorded voicemail message said: "Out of the country. No messages taken."

Whatever this "proof" consisted of, she couldn't risk having it made public. Not now. Gabrielle stared from window overlooking the flowering Palais Royal garden, the fountain, the alley of trees and shops under the colonnade. Peaceful, almost bucolic. But her insides churned. It smelled like the threat of an amateur. Then again, this could mask more sophisticated forces at work.

She took our her wallet, found five thousand francs. In her desk drawer was another five thousand. She took a sheet of paper and started to write. Her hands shook so much that the ink blotted. She tore it up, tried again, and wrote "The rest when I have the proof."

Her cell phone rang. The minister's number appeared. Of all times, she thought.

"*Oui*, Minister Ney."

The minister cleared his throat. An ominous sign.

"Gabrielle," he began, "I'm concerned that your staff cocked it up over the junior deputy's little indiscretion."

Cocked it up? "I think your junior deputy already did that, Monsieur le Ministre," she said. "The *flics* caught him with a fifteen-year-old hooker."

She couldn't deal with this now. She had to hurry to the antiquarian bookseller, to question him herself.

A small expulsion of air came over the line. "But how can

one tell these days?" said the minister. "I mean, they don't provide birth certificates, do they?"

Gabrielle wondered if Minister Ney spoke from personal experience. But that wasn't anything she wanted to know.

Gabrielle stuffed the money into the envelope and shut her drawer.

"Fix this the usual way, Gabrielle."

Did the whole bureau depend on her for damage control? For once, couldn't the minister invoke national security and cover up the old-fashioned way?

"But Monsieur le Ministre, he not only ran a red light but resisted arrest with an underage illegal Romanian hooker in the car."

"Gabrielle," Minister Ney said, "it's important that he interviews well on *Opinions* tomorrow. We must bolster public support against the delegation's proposal. It's in no one's interest to unseal those documents in the National Archives."

No need to remind her. More than a few government officials feared that their past would appear in the media if certain documents were made available. Especially now, given the upcoming wartime collaboration trial in Bordeaux of the former Vichy official Papon.

She reached for her bag. "I can't make this go away, Monsieur le Ministre."

Opinions was the highest-rated political-commentary show on the *télé*. And she'd scheduled the junior deputy's interview more than a month ago. Unfortunate, since—despite the junior deputy's underage proclivities—he influenced a significant delegation in the Ministry.

She glanced at the time. 3:55 P.M.

"I don't care what you do, Gabrielle," he said. "Or how you do it. Make the moderator sympathetic."

"But Cédric's a well-respected political analyst."

"And he's got a little file he'd like kept quiet, as I recall."

Cédric led a discreet life, apart from his fondness for cocaine. An old charge of possession had been swept under the carpet, standard procedure for influential celebrities, but ready for activation as needed. Cédric was her old classmate from ENA, witty and intelligent. The thought of smearing him sickened her.

"Minister, he's been in rehab. That chapter's closed. I can't do that to my friend," she said. "Couldn't we find some other way?"

But for all her damage-control expertise, what it might be escaped her.

"Can't, or won't, Gabrielle?"

His words dangled over the line.

"Your husband Roland's up for a ministry position, isn't he? I wouldn't want your lack of cooperation to affect that. This is not the time for you to grow a conscience."

What else could she do but agree?

"*D'accord*, Minister. I'll take care of it tonight."

She'd never figured her years spent at ENA and *Hautes Etudes Politiques* would lead her to a career of bleaching the dirty linen of Ministry officials.

"I'll expect a list of questions prepared for the moderator in an hour."

More than the usual *crise de jour* for a Tuesday.

"But first come to my office. I'll expect you momentarily." And with that the minister hung up.

Cornered, she heard the clock chime four o'clock.

Tuesday

AIMÉE LEANED ON the taxi dispatch counter. "Impossible," she said in disbelief. She checked the dispatch log again. "Yesterday, René and I shared sushi at lunch, going over my upcoming testimony for the Nadillac trial next week."

Melac watched her, expressionless.

She remembered René in his orthopedic chair coaching her on points and answering techniques for the trial. René was worried that she'd forget to charge her cell phone. As usual. Funny, the little details she remembered. She'd give anything to go back to yesterday.

She grew aware of Melac's scrutiny. He was speaking.

"Often, in cases of mental illness, it's hereditary. The hidden disease was the old term for schizophrenia."

That snapped her to attention.

"Some pyschobabble from a Brigade Criminelle training session, Melac?"

"Patients often want to be caught," Melac continued, "to be stopped. They feel helpless to stop themselves."

"I've been framed." She re-checked the log for the third time. "Monsieur, was this a check or charge transaction?"

"Cash."

"Did the driver report a tip?"

"Not according to this. But then they don't always, eh?"

"See, Melac? Cash, no trace." She summoned what little bravado she could muster. "I tip big. It earns me good taxi karma on rainy nights. Drivers remember me."

"You're digging a hole for yourself, Mademoiselle."

"*Non*, though it looks that way," she said, exasperated. "I don't know who disguised themself as me. Or took a taxi to my place. Why would I go to all this trouble, get this tape and show you, if that woman was me?"

"We'll continue this at the Brigade." Melac flipped his notepad closed. "I'd suggest you revise your statement, Mademoiselle."

"What are you talking about?" Fear coursed through her veins. "René? Has his condition worsened? Is he . . . he's—"

"Stable."

In the few blocks to the Brigade Criminelle, Melac was busy on his cell phone. Frustrated, her fingers worked at the worn car upholstery. "What's this about, Melac?" she asked as he pulled past the gates.

"You'll find out."

On the third floor, occupied by the Brigade Criminelle, he showed her to a dark space like an old film projection booth. Through a rectangular slit of a window, she saw a man seated at a wooden table with only his shoulders and the back of his head visible.

"He can't see or hear you," Melac said.

Not a standard lineup. Odd, she thought. "If you want me to identify him, he'll need to turn around."

Melac gave her a look she couldn't fathom.

"Your job's to listen."

Melac closed the door. A key scraped in the lock. And she felt like a baited rat without any cheese. Stupid. She'd walked right into it, shown Melac the evidence, played by the "rules." And look where it got her. No one to blame but herself. No René to count on. No one to extricate her from her predicament. She twisted the copper puzzle ring Yves had given her more than a year earlier, the night before he was murdered, then pushed aside her thoughts of him. This was no time to wallow in reflections on what might have been.

Whoever shot René had planned it to a T. Knew where she lived, her schedule, movements, even her clothing. The thought made her shiver.

The shooter had counted on the *flics* tracing the helmet. Instead, she'd beat the *flics* to it, and dug herself deeper into the pit. Now he thought she was schizophrenic.

She took out her cell phone and punched in Morbier's number. No answer.

Melac entered the room below and sat. The sound system crackled and voices became audible.

"Thanks for making the time to give your statement," he said. "I understand you have a busy schedule, Monsieur."

"Busy? It's the fall collection! Our preview and runway show is this week."

She knew that voice. Those shoulders, that earring. Mathieu.

Finally! At last, with her alibi corroborated, Melac would concentrate on finding the woman who had impersonated her.

"Please read your statement aloud."

"Again?" Mathieu shrugged. "Monday night, my wife and I attended our daughter's preschool play at the crêche near Place Vendôme. The performance lasted an hour. At 8 P.M. we ate dinner at Léon de Bruxelles on the Boulevard Beaumarchais, then returned home by 11 P.M., where I spent the rest of the night."

Aimée's mouth dropped open. Mathieu was married? And had a child? And she prided herself on spotting a married man a kilometer away: the walk, the furtive look. But this time her radar had failed her. Even after consulting Chloë's *Elle* article, she'd scored zero. So much for this "bad boy." The liar.

"Your wife will corroborate this?"

"*Bien sûr,*" he said. "But she's in Milan now. Talk to her when she returns."

Aimée pounded on the door. She had to confront the liar.

Playing by the rules always backfired. Big time. She'd think twice before doing her civic duty, if she ever got another chance.

Today she should be sitting in a coffee shop with her brother on Manhattan's Upper West Side. A brother who'd be a young man now. She'd hoped to get to know him.

And then she noticed the message light flashing on her cell phone. The number of Hôtel Dieu. René? But the extension looked like his doctor's. She hit the callback number and got the nurse.

"Dr. Soualt, *s'il vous plaît*," Aimée said.

"He's in surgery."

Great. She'd missed the doctor's call. She forked her fingers through her zig-zag-cut streaked blond hair.

This time she wouldn't let a nurse fob her off.

"Monsieur Friant, a patient, please connect me to his room."

"Friant? Monsieur René Friant's been moved from intensive care."

Good news.

"Wonderful, please connect me to his new room."

"I am sorry, Mademoiselle. He's been discharged."

"I don't understand," she said. "He had surgery only late last night. Where is he?"

"The consulting doctor referred him to a private facility."

That quick? He'd had a collapsed lung.

"Were there complications? Where is he now?"

"The confidentiality rules apply, Mademoiselle. I can't divulge that information."

Had they placed him in protective custody, in a private clinic?

She took deep breaths and had calmed down by the time a blue-uniformed *flic* unlocked the door and escorted her to Melac's office.

"Where's René?" she asked him.

"Safe." His eyes were on her knuckles, reddened from pounding on the door.

"You mean René's in protective custody and you're not going to tell me where? I demand to know."

"Sit down," he said. "Regulations forbid my giving a suspect information as to the victim's location. In all cases we must protect the victim."

She wanted to kick the base out from under his swivel chair. "Look, Melac. . . ." She made herself take a breath, trying to control the anger welling up in her. "I don't believe this. Rene's my partner!"

"But that's not why you're here," Melac interrupted. "Mathieu Albret stated he was with his family Monday night. You heard. You have no alibi, Mademoiselle."

She sat before she said something she'd regret in a big way, took another deep breath, and observed the ring on Melac's fourth finger.

"Forget that you think I'm schizophrenic," she said, after a moment. "Won't wives lie for their husbands?"

Melac shrugged. "Mine didn't."

And she understood. Seen it before with so many *flics*. "And you're divorced, paying child support, and still carrying the torch, right?"

Melac blinked.

"Seeing your children every other weekend," she said. "Shared holiday time in August, *non*?"

A sad ghost of a smile flitted across his features. "Actually, the last part of July."

"I bumped heads with Mathieu in the fast lane at the pool two days ago. It led to coffee, he invited me for dinner. Instead I offered to cook *chez moi*."

Melac leaned forward. Listening. Like a good *flic*. Like her father. For a moment he seemed almost human. She'd give anything to know what he was thinking.

"Of course, you were attracted to his mind, not his Speedos," Melac said.

"So he fools around on his wife," she said, "he lied. She's 'conveniently' in Milan. Maybe she was on Monday, too. Why don't you check the airlines? My only proof lies in my garbage bins."

"How's that?"

"Eight Fauchon takeout cartons. I can't cook."

"Fauchon's for gourmets," he said. "I buy frozen meals at Lidl."

The low-price supermarket. Aimée pictured his single room in police housing, crayon drawings from his children on the walls, the suitcase he lived out of. Waiting for the weekend to visit his children.

"Single men usually do."

Melac blinked again. He pulled his notepad from his pocket and flipped it open, now in professional mode.

"Let's get back to the point, Mademoiselle Leduc," he said. "Mathieu Albret furnished his statement. You have no alibi."

"Time for marriage counseling, I'd say."

Her mind turned over the little Melac had: Luigi's drunken description, René's ambiguous gesture.

"Of course, you realize Luigi had been drinking all afternoon and evening, Melac?"

"We're checking on that."

She continued, "In robbery and cases of assault with a deadly weapon, you need more than circumstantial evidence, which you don't even have. There was no gunshot residue on my hands, for one thing. No motive, for another."

"We find that motive boils down to revenge, love, or, the

most common, money." His mouth narrowed. "Call it my gut feeling. Your partner's afraid of you."

Her mouth went dry.

"Maybe you threatened him in the ICU."

"You call that trusting your instinct?" she said. She crossed her legs so she wouldn't kick him. "I think you just don't like me."

His ears reddened.

"I do my job," he said. "And I'm aware of your father's history. But here at *La Crim*, you get no special treatment."

She grabbed her bag and stood. "Are you going to arrest me?"

"That's up to *La Proc*," he said. "She's looking at the assembled evidence."

"Part of which I furnished, proving that someone set me up. Given Mathieu's statement, as yet uncorroborated by his wife, you've got nothing, Melac." She leaned forward, her palms on his desk. "*La Proc* can't take this to the *juge d'instruction*. As she's explained to me on previous occasions, her job consists of assembling admissible evidence. You know that."

"And you have no alibi, Mademoiselle," he repeated.

"Say that after you've checked the Monday Milan flight manifests for Madame Albret, Inspector."

"Dealing with you, as Commissaire Morbier told me, makes herding feral cats look easy," Melac said.

Great help, Morbier! But she bit her tongue. Things were stacked against her.

"Going to nail my shoes to the floor, Melac?" she asked. "Or may I go?"

Melac tented his fingers. His expression was shuttered. Then he gestured to the office door. "For now."

She stuck her hands in her pockets, so Melac wouldn't see them shaking, and strode out of his office.

Tuesday Afternoon

RENÉ HAD NO enemies. Who would shoot him? Or implicate her?

She had to start at the office. Go through their clients' files, their work calendar, René's daily agenda, his address book.

This woman dressed like her, knew where she lived, as well as the address of her office. She'd shot René and framed her. Calculated, and chilling.

Leaves crackled under her feet as she headed toward Pont Neuf. Sirens whined. The smell of oil from a barge, chugging below on the Seine, floated on the wind.

She squared her shoulders and noticed the kiosk headlines: TRANSPORT UNION NEGOTIATIONS REACH IMPASSE. STRIKE THREATENED.

Another strike, a typical autumn.

But not for her.

She'd pick up her scooter from the garage repairing it. No use battling for taxis this week, with an impending Métro strike.

An hour later, she parked her faded pink Vespa in an alley off rue du Louvre. Diffuse, vanilla light filtered down from the mansard rooftops, but it did not dispel the chill emanating from the worn limestone. She snapped her denim jacket closed, knotting her scarf, wishing she'd worn her high boots instead of the pointed mid-calf vintage Valentinos.

Time to face the office, an office without René, and a daunting search through their files. Then she had to figure a way to force Mathieu to rescind his statement.

She headed to her building, an eighteenth-century soot-stained edifice with scrolled wrought-iron balconies and the thirties' neon sign: Leduc Detective.

Maurice, the one-armed Algerian war veteran who manned the newspaper kiosk, handed her the evening's *Le Soir*.

"Controversy over inquest—was Princess Diana pregnant?" Maurice read. Shook his head. "The stuff that sells papers!"

More than a month had passed since Diana's crash in the Pont de l'Alma tunnel, but the press hadn't quit.

"They put this on the back page!" Maurice pointed to a six-line article reporting grave desecration in the Jewish section of Père Lachaise cemetery. "Skinheads defaced the star on my mother's grave. Again."

"*Désolée*, Maurice." She'd had no idea.

"There've been vicious attacks in the Métro, outside the Orthodox school in Belleville," he said. "These crimes go unpunished. You'd think, after Bergen-Belsen, they'd done enough. But it never stops."

She set a franc on the counter.

"Weren't you going to New York?" Maurice asked.

Would she ever get there? "My plans changed."

A line formed behind her. She walked the few steps to her building.

Viaggi Travel's door was dark. The crime-scene tape had been removed from Leduc Detective's door. Inside, the rooms lay deserted and silent, without René. And to carve out time for her trip, she'd finished her work, for once.

Past the office partition, she viewed René's desk. His laptop, files, his empty workspace. The stain left on the floor by his blood.

She felt adrift on a rough sea of lies. But she had to concentrate. The answer must lie here. Somewhere.

René's laptop held sensitive data, clients' files, operating systems, the works. Had a competitor broken in and shot

René? Or was it an attempt to taint their firm and the computer security of the companies they monitored?

At her desk, she booted up her computer and checked network sharing and hardware, and looked for a break in the firewall. Nothing. Relieved, she accessed René's e-mail for threats or ambiguous messages. Apart from a confirmation of the upcoming Nadillac hearing, there was nothing.

Nadillac, a short, overweight, twenty-something whiz nerd, had turned to his hobby—black-hat hacking—for revenue. He did what a growing number of hackers did: he'd employed "0days" or "zero days," information and code enabling the penetration of the software run by governments, private citizens, and, in his case, the corporation Nadillac worked for. He'd deployed 0days, resulting in minor disruption of his company's Web site, and then he'd paralyzed it. But she and René caught him before he'd taken total control of the company's network. They'd submitted the incriminating findings of their investigation to his firm. Next week, she was slated to testify against him in court.

René's four color-coded files were on his desk: IN PROGRESS, FUTURE PROJECTS, PROPOSALS SUBMITTED, and PROPOSALS ACCEPTED. For twenty minutes she checked each file but found nothing missing. The phone rang, startling her.

"Good afternoon, Mademoiselle Leduc." A honeyed voice, indicative of a sales pitch or request for donation. "Paribas bank here. I'm inquiring about the recent deposits to your business account."

She sat up, alert, remembering René's accusation from the previous night.

"Can you tell me which deposits you're referring to?"

"This is a courtesy call, Mademoiselle," the honeyed voice continued. "For such large sums, we suggest a higher interest yield account."

"*Excusez-moi*, but which deposits?"

With all that had happened, she hadn't checked their account for the sums René had mentioned.

"I'm in the sales branch. Sorry, I don't have that information."

"Why not?"

"Your business's banker keeps that. Think about moving funds to a higher yield account and increasing your portfolio's value, Mademoiselle. We offer competitive rates." The honeyed voice turned to vinegar. "I'll call you later this week for your reply." The phone went dead.

She should have checked this sooner! She accessed it online and scrolled through the bank statements, and gasped. A one-hundred-thousand-franc deposit, just as René had said.

No one owed them so much money.

No doubt there had been an electronic error, perhaps an account number mistyped by data entry. All too easy a mistake for a late-night data entry shift. But surely it would be simple to take care of; her bank would find the error and correct it.

After punching in their banker's extension, she was put on hold.

With the phone crooked between her neck and shoulder, she went through René's top drawer. It took five minutes to sort through the account files.

"Monsieur Guérin, at your service," the banker's recorded voice answered. "I'm in meetings today but will check my messages and get back to you before the close of business hours. Please leave your number."

She left a message. She found nothing else new in René's file drawers. But in his bottom desk drawer, she found his brown moleskin office diary.

No appointments yesterday. On Monday, she saw a conference call with Cybermatrice penciled in for the morning.

There were notes to himself in the margins: train at Dojo; call Félice, EXPLAIN!; order chocolate *Maman's* birthday; and a red line through the following week, Aimée NY.

Think. She had to think. Who might have had it in for René?

He'd broken up with Félice, a fellow student at the Dojo. Didn't she have a new boyfriend? She remembered René saying he was a biker, a jealous type who'd done time in prison, not someone René thought worthy of Félice. And he had a motorcycle. For a moment she wondered if it came down to a jealous boyfriend. A stretch, but worth checking out.

But she recalled René's grumblings last week over the tactics of Cybermatrice, their rival, his complaints over their underhanded tactics. She called Cybermatrice, but only got a recording. Frustrated, she left a message.

She thumbed through René's diary and found Félice's number. And she had the perfect excuse to call: René was in the hospital.

"*Allô?*"

"It's Aimée," she said. "Remember me, René's partner?"

"Where's René? Our Dojo practice just finished. He never misses a class."

Aimée heard a gong reverberating in the background.

"Félice, he's in the hospital," she said.

"*Mon Dieu!* What happened? Is René all right?"

"He's stable," Aimée said. "Someone shot him." She didn't know how to put her question. "René said your boyfriend's the jealous type."

"Manu? But we broke up. *Alors*, you can't think he'd shoot René."

"I need to eliminate him as a suspect. Where is he?"

"Good luck," Félice said. "The *salop* took my keys and locked me out of my apartment yesterday. It took hours until the concierge came."

Aimée heard an expulsion of breath over the phone.

"Manu's got problems, but he wouldn't hurt René, my friend, my Dojo partner. Even after. . . ."

Pause. The gong sounded again.

"After what, Felice?"

"It's a long story," she said.

"I need to hear it."

"But I'm late for work."

"René's hooked up to machines, Félice. The *flics* suspect me because the shooter used the gun in my desk."

Félice gasped.

"But Manu wouldn't. . . ."

"Wouldn't what?"

Pause.

"Go on, Félice."

"*Zut*. It's nothing, but. . . ." She hesitated. "Manu met me the other day, after René and I argued," Félice said. "René meant well, warning me about Manu, but it upset me. And he's right, Manu's a vicious *salaud*. But Manu picked up on the fact that René didn't like him."

"Vicious enough to get even?"

"Manu talks big, but no action. He brought over my apartment keys later. Now he thinks I'll take him back."

Aimée thought. "Does Manu know where our office is?"

"He picked me up there last week."

Excited now, Aimée grabbed a pencil and wrote "Manu" in big letters on the Nadillac case spreadsheet, the first thing at hand. He had a motive and knew their location.

"Where can I find Manu?"

"*Ça alors*, I'm shattered that René's been injured. I want to visit him."

"The *flics* have him in protective custody," Aimée said. "I just want to talk to Manu."

"Manu left a message for me to meet him at Au Chien qui Fume at the bar tonight."

"Good girl. Don't go. Let me talk to him."

Now she'd find out where Manu had been last night and whether he had a helmet like hers. The figure going into Tout-Moto was female. But if he'd enlisted an accomplice who had studied Aimée's movements. . . . She wondered if he was the type who planned in detail. But prisoners learned more about crime on the inside than on the outside.

"One more thing, Félice," she said. "Change your locks."

* * *

AIMÉE OPENED THE door under the sign of the dog smoking a pipe, Au Chien qui Fume. An inviting warmth filled the old-style brasserie lined with mirrors above the red leather banquettes. Paintings and photos of dogs decorated the walls. A low hum of conversation and the clink of cutlery came from the dining area. Ahead she saw the curved polished-wood bar taking up the rear of the room. Liquor bottles lined the shelves behind it.

She reviewed the patrons on the stools: a banker type, talking into his cell phone; two middle-aged women drinking red colored *apéros*; a bus driver in his RATP-emblazoned green-blue jacket, reading *Le Soir*. This was not a biker hangout.

Then she heard the roar of a motorcycle outside. Someone opened the brasserie door. A gust of chilled air whipped the white tablecloths. A glimpse through the door revealed that it was *l'heure bleue* twilight. Distant Pont Neuf's streetlights glowed like a string of misted pearls.

"The fog's rising tonight."

The speaker wore black leathers; longish tousled hair curled on his neck. He had a wide forehead, prominent cheekbones, and narrow lips. He was almost handsome, except for the scar running from the corner of his eye into his hairline.

He perched at the bar, his gaze resting on Aimée's legs for a second, then shook hands with the bartender.

"*Ca va,* Charlot?" he asked.

"She's not here, Manu."

"A *bière* while I wait," he said defiantly. He rested his boot on the railing below the bar.

No one paid him any attention. Neither did Charlot, the barman, once he'd set the foaming beer on a coaster before him. Not the most popular patron, Aimée could see.

"He's right, Manu," she said, slipping next to him at the bar.

"Eh, I don't know you, but we can dispense with introductions." His gaze again flicked over her black-seamed stockings.

"Aimée Leduc. But you know my partner."

He shrugged. Took a sip of beer. Then another.

"Whatever you say, *ma fille.*"

"Mind telling me where you were last night?"

"Funny." He shook his head, caught the barman's attention. "She doesn't look like a *flic,* does she, Charlot?"

Charlot averted his eyes. In the mirror, she could see Charlot's bald spot.

"Weren't you on rue du Louvre, in our office?"

"Do you have a problem with that, *ma fille*? You don't look the type to pick a fight."

"But you do. Jealous, vindictive, a grudge-bearer. You locked Félice out."

"So Félice sent you?" He took another sip, then slammed the glass down. Foam dripped down the sides.

"She told me you'd be here. But I'm here about René Friant, my partner."

The banker set down some francs, then edged off his stool, which scraped the mosaic-tiled floor as he left. Charlot wiped the inside of a wine glass with a towel until it squeaked.

"Your partner . . . the dwarf?"

"You had a grudge against him, so you shot him."

"Shot him?" Surprised, Manu set his *bière* down, then threw back his head and laughed. "You think I shot that dwarf? Why?"

"You're the jealous type, Manu," she said. "You were angry about Félice."

He pushed his hair back from his eyes. "I was at Place de la Bastille last night."

"Quick thinking, Manu," she said. "But I bet there's a Blue Fever helmet in your motorbike's compartment."

"Charlot, put this on my tab." Manu reached for his glass.

But Charlot took the half-drunk beer and dumped the glass in the sink. He motioned to the manager. "First, settle your old tab, Manu."

Manu's thin lips pursed. "No family feeling, eh? No wonder my sister left you, Charlot." He straightened, reached into his pocket, and threw fifty francs on the bar.

Now that he stood, she saw that Manu was short; he didn't even reach her shoulders.

"René's a black belt; you wanted to avoid a confrontation you'd lose," she said. "So you got some girl to impersonate me. Why?"

"All that, for Félice?" He snorted.

She followed him out the door. Mist enveloped the rue de

Rivoli, drifting through the colonnades, blurring car headlights.

As he took his white helmet from the motorcycle compartment, she peered in. The end of a baguette, a can of motor oil. No Blue Fever.

He keyed the ignition, shaking his head. "Hire an assassin on the installment plan to shoot a dwarf?" His laugh echoed off the stone.

"Don't tell me people don't owe you favors, Manu."

"You don't quit, do you?"

"Convince me, Manu."

"Like hell I will." But his shoulders sagged. Resignation showed in his eyes. "I'm broke. I just spent my last fifty francs."

She believed him.

"That dwarf didn't change Félice's feelings for me," he said, grabbing her sleeve. "You did, Aimée Leduc, sticking your nose into my business. You scared Félice away, didn't you? You persuaded her not to come."

His arm went around her neck, snapping it back, choking her. She felt a sharp point raking her skin under her sweater. Terrified, she tried to speak, but no words came out. Manu pressed the knife deeper against her rib. Choking, her air cut off, she struggled as the knife point went deeper.

Then he let go. The motor revved and he roared away. Gasping, she stumbled against a topiary tree, rubbing her side. And when she looked up, he'd vanished in the mist.

It had been stupid to accuse him outright. She was losing her touch. Losing her grip. Her shaking fingers were smudged with blood.

* * *

WHAT HAD SHE accomplished? She no longer thought Manu had bought the helmet or shot René. He seemed too petty a crook to have hired someone. Apart from making him her enemy, and needing a Band-aid, she'd gotten nowhere. She had to think more clearly and get some sleep. The twelve-hour kind.

Her office was only two blocks away. Shakily, she made her way beneath the rue de Rivoli arcade. At her corner café, she stared at the steamed-up windows. Zazie, the owner's young red-haired daughter, sat doing her homework on the counter. The scene was familiar and inviting. But she couldn't face Zazie, or anyone else, right now. She had work to do.

* * *

UPSTAIRS, SHE UNLOCKED Leduc Detective's door, and again faced a dark, chilly office. She closed the window, then kicked the radiator until it rumbled to life.

The chandelier illuminated the marble fireplace, the beveled mirror over it, the recamier piled with folders, the emptiness. She found the first-aid kit, left the door ajar, and went down the hall to the WC. Viaggi Travel was still dark. The other offices, too, were closed.

In front of the tarnished mirror, she lifted her worn cashmere sweater and dabbed antiseptic on the tiny slit over her rib, and covered it with an Asterix Band-aid.

Back at her desk, she checked for messages and found one.

"Sophie from Cybermatrice returning your call. No hard feelings, I hope, but we got the Ophatrix contract. That's what this is about, right? I'm dating the coordinator, FYI. Better luck next time." Then, a click.

Talk about rubbing it in. René had offered the same terms to Ophatrix; but if Sophie "dated" the coordinator, no wonder she'd obtained the contract. But if Sophie slept her way into contracts, she wouldn't have to threaten René, much less injure him.

His cell phone. Why hadn't she thought of trying that before? She could speak to him directly and find out where—and how—he was. She hit René's number.

A moment later, she heard its distinctive Chopin sonata ringtone. René's cell phone was still on his desk under some papers. Disappointed, she clicked off. Her phone rang the very next second.

"Aimée," Saj said, his voice hesitant. It was their permanent part-time hacker. "You're in New York?"

"I cancelled my trip. I'm in the office." She sensed something in Saj's voice. "What's wrong, Saj?"

"What's *right*? The *flics* questioned me this afternoon. Why didn't you tell me René had been shot?"

"Forgive me, Saj," she said. "I've had no sleep. I spent the night at the hospital, and then with the police. And the *flics* suspect me of shooting René."

"You're kidding."

"If only I were." And she told him all, from the beginning. "Can you think of any disgruntled client, or jealous hacker, who may have it in for René?"

"René's diplomatic," Saj said. "He's professional with clients and respected among hackers, Aimée."

"I know." Was he implying that she wasn't?

There was a pause.

"I'm monitoring the daily updates and pursuing the Nadillac investigation as planned," Saj said. "But Nadillac's keeping tight; it's like shaving an egg."

She couldn't worry about that. Right now, she needed Saj's help. Apart from René, no one hacked computer systems better.

"Delve into our bank account," she said. "There's been a

wire transfer to us of a hundred thousand francs. A mistake, I'm sure," she said. "Use our access code. 09AS876. No fancy footwork, keep it low-key, and sniff the site. I'm waiting for the bank manager's explanation."

"I'll try."

The distance in his voice bothered her. "Don't you think I'm upset? René's right lung was punctured. If only I'd taken the bullet instead."

"Things don't look good, Aimée."

"Tell me about it, Saj. I need your help right now so I can find who shot him and why."

"Aimée, René's blood is still staining the floor," Saj said. "I saw it today. I can't enter the office any more."

The sight of the reddish-brown stain where René had fallen made her stomach churn too. The crime-scene tape was still draped over René's chair.

"Can't you get the woman who cleans at night to remove it?" Saj asked.

"Véro?" She considered. "Why didn't I think of her? She was working last night; she may have seen something."

"The *flics* will have questioned her," Saj said.

If so, Melac hadn't mentioned it. But she hadn't seen the report. Maybe she was clutching at straws, but right now that's all she had.

After he hung, up, a bad feeling dogged her. Did Saj doubt her?

She grabbed her leather coat, knotted the wool scarf around her neck, and ran down the stairs.

* * *

AIMÉE PEERED INTO the ground-floor concierge's loge.

"Véro?"

But it was Anna, the building concierge, a short Portuguese

woman, who frowned back. Her black hair, streaked with premature gray, was pulled back from her lined face. "Véro's off tonight."

Aimée clenched her fist in disappointment. In the small loge, Anna's two young children argued about whose turn it was to feed the caged parakeet in the window.

"Véro worked last night, *non*?"

Anna shrugged and consulted a sheet on the wall. "It says so here. Not my responsibility; my job starts in the morning."

"Do you have Véro's number?"

Another shrug. "She works sometimes for her sister at another job."

"What's her sister's number?"

"It's here somewhere. Hold on." Aimée heard the children's shouts, then the parakeet's feathers flew in the air as birdseed sprayed on the floor.

Before she could ask her to hurry, Anna had rescued the squealing parakeet in the cage.

Aimée scanned the sheet on the wall herself, found Véro's number, wrote it on her palm with an eyeliner pencil, and closed the door.

* * *

THERE WAS NO answer on Véro's cell phone, so she left a message. Hunger gnawed at her. If the woman was asleep or had gone to her other job, she'd grab something to eat, then go back to the office and hope it wouldn't take hours before Véro returned her call. But by the time she'd paid the man at the charcuterie on rue du Louvre and clutched her takeout, her phone was vibrating in her pocket.

"Aimée, I'm sorry," Véro's voice boomed over the line. "I should have called you."

She pictured the dark-haired thirtyish Véro, a woman with pulsating energy, a sure touch at cleaning and the gleam mistress of crystal chandeliers: "Vinegar, that's my secret."

Might she have information about René?

"Let's meet, Véro."

"I'm sorry, I can't. I'm subbing at my sister's job tonight."

Blocked at every turn, Aimée thought.

"What time's your break?"

"Look, I meant to drop the letter at your office, I'll bring it tomorrow."

"What letter, Véro?"

She heard voices, then the roar of a machine. "My supervisor. Got to go, Aimée."

"Forget the letter. Haven't you heard? René was shot last night, in our office."

She heard Véro's gasp. "*Nom de Dieu*. Let me ask the supervisor to switch my break."

"Where are you, Véro?"

"Just five minutes away from you. Hurry."

"Eh?"

"Porte de l'Oratoire. The Louvre's staff entrance, on rue de Rivoli."

* * *

AIMÉE STOOD AT the inconspicuous staff entrance of the Louvre. There was nothing to indicate that more than a thousand employees filed through this stone-framed doorway, day and night, into the offices, galleries, and fifteen kilometers of corridors under the Louvre. Curators, museum admin staff, historians, archeologists, electricians, guards, glaziers, exhibition hangers, carpenters, cleaners, and chefs. Like a small contained city, the Louvre operated its own medical center, staff cafeteria, gym, painting and sculpture restoration studio, and library. Plus three hundred thousand works of art, not all of them displayed.

A guard ground out his cigarette on the gravel of the walkway, then shoved it into the drain with his shoe. She couldn't count the many times her grandfather had taken her here to visit his friend, Donnac, a guard. Donnac would sit her on his knee in the narrow guardroom while sharing a bottle with her grandfather. But she didn't recognize this guard.

"Lost, Mademoiselle?" the guard asked. "You'll find the main entrance near the Pyramid at the center of the Napoléon courtyard."

"*Non*, Monsieur. I'm meeting Véro. She's on her break."

His eyes narrowed. "No one told me."

Times had changed.

"Véro forgot her dinner." Aimée held up the *charcuterie* bag.

A woman, dark-haired, a shorter version of Véro in a mustard-colored cleaning smock, appeared, breathless, at the door. She shot Aimée a look.

"Véro's not on break yet," she said. "*Et voilà*. Véro—my sister—would forget her head if it weren't on her neck."

"Then you can take this for her," the guard said, blocking the door.

All this for nothing?

Véro's sister took the charcuterie bag and pecked Aimée on both cheeks. "Got time for a coffee? We've got a new machine." She rolled her eyes. "Better brown piss."

"You need to clear visitors beforehand, Sylvie," the guard said.

"*Alors*, Renutti, let me offer her a coffee. It's the least I can do after she made this trip."

He shrugged. "Like I said, visitors need authorization."

"But Donnac never had a problem," Aimée said.

"Donnac retired. Rules have been tightened up. We have new security directives."

A small Corot and medieval sculpture had been stolen in broad daylight recently.

She handed the guard her ID, her card from Leduc Detective Privé. "My office is just there on rue du Louvre." She stuck fifty francs in the guard's jacket pocket. "Something for your trouble, Monsieur." They didn't make much and an imminent guard's strike loomed.

He glanced around the courtyard. "Leduc? I knew one. We called him *Le Vieux*, tall, thick moustache, broad shoulders."

And warm arms that held her when she'd been bitten by a dachshund in the park. Who took her to piano lessons; then for a hot chocolate afterward.

"My *grand-père*."

The guard drew a breath. "Just this once. Don't ask me again."

Inside, Sylvie pointed her toward the staff locker room. When Renutti looked away, she pulled Aimée's hand down the hall. Several pairs of rollerblades waited near the lockers. "Put these on."

"Now?" She'd skated as a child, but never rollerbladed.

"How else do you think we navigate this place in a hurry? Véro's waxing in the Sully East wing and I'm in the other. I have to get back."

Aimée slipped off her boots, wedged her feet in the rollerblade boots, and laced them up. Wobbling, gripping the wall, she followed Sylvie into a dank corridor threaded with ventilation pipes under the Louvre.

Soon she was taking long glides to maintain her balance and keep up with Sylvie. Flying. Cold stone-scented air hit her face; her calf muscles strained with each glide. The whooshing of their rollerblades competed with beeping from a motorized baggage-carrier-like cart with a flashing orange light.

She wanted to talk to Véro, not exercise in the long cold corridors under the Louvre.

A sharp right! Double doors. Another corridor leading to the sculpture and restoration studios. Four workmen in short blue jackets wheeled an open wooden crate containing a massive painting. Riding by, she glanced at the painting, a Madonna, her enigmatic smile distorted by the crackled and peeling patina of the wooden panel on which she had been portrayed.

"Quick, up here." Sylvie pointed to a narrow wooden stairway that twisted like a corkscrew. Aimée unlaced her skates and looked up, but before she could ask any more questions, Sylvie had glided away with a whoosh.

At the top, winded, Aimée caught her breath, then pushed open the door. She found herself in a long gallery under a skylight, facing floor-to-ceiling paintings. It was deserted except for Véro, in a mustard-yellow smock, and her waxer machine. Crackling sounds came from the walkie-talkie clipped to her hip.

"We won't be disturbed here for a few minutes. And they won't mind." Véro jerked her thumb at walls filled with what Aimée assumed were Italian Renaissance masters, by the signs, of the School of Raphael.

"The supervisor wouldn't switch my break," Véro said. The waxer thrummed as it crossed the herring-bone-patterned wood floor.

"How's Monsieur René? I feel terrible."

"He's stable," Aimée said. "But haven't the *flics* questioned you?"

Véro's eyes crinkled. "Why would they?"

And then, keeping pace with the waxer, Aimée told Véro what had happened.

Véro's eyes widened. "But *you* wouldn't shoot Monsieur René. I'm so sorry, Aimée."

"Think back to last night, Véro. It's important. What do you remember?"

"You mean this?" She pulled a folded envelope from her jeans pocket, addressed to "Aimée Leduc."

A letter from the shooter? Before she could open it, a voice came from the walkie-talkie.

"Véro, have you finished the east gallery?"

"*Oui*, Monsieur," she said. Véro tugged at Aimée's sleeve.

"Shhh . . . walk with me as I work. The supervisor will return and check." Véro continued pushing the waxer, leaving a gleaming sheen on the floor. "Hurry."

Aimée kept pace with Véro, who was now heading into the next gallery and another wing. Greco-Roman marble statues stood poised on pedestals, as if caught in flight.

"Who gave this to you, Véro?"

"Your office door was shut," Véro said. "After I finished mopping, I did the other floors. Mondays I only do touch-ups, two hours max. A young woman buzzed the door. She wanted to give this to you. But when I said you'd gone, she didn't want to leave it in the mailbox or for the concierge."

"Was she wearing a raincoat and a motorcycle helmet?"

Véro shook her head. "Pitiful, I thought. She was shaking, nervous. Upset, I could tell. Not even a warm coat, just a thin sweater. Young, too, a small washed-out blonde."

Aimée wondered who this could be.

"But René was working; didn't she ask for him?"

"*Vraiment?* The office looked dark, so I thought only those Italians were upstairs. They made enough noise! She gave this to me. Told me to put it in your hands."

"What time was this, Véro?"

Véro kept the waxer moving back and forth on the parquet floor. "Say nine or so. I left before ten."

So Véro wouldn't have seen the shooter. A shame, given her powers of observation.

But Aimée still didn't understand one thing. "Why did she give it to you, Véro? After all, I don't often see you."

"Anna, your concierge, *alors*, she's not on top of things, to tell you the truth. She loses mail, I've seen her forget things. The girl seemed nervous, distressed, so I said I knew you." Véro shrugged. "I went to work here after that, put the letter in my pocket, and forgot it. I slept all day until they called this afternoon and woke me up. I rushed over here to work. Now that my sister has gotten me on the call roster, I have to come when they call. If you miss once, they don't try you again." Her eyes crinkled.

The walkie-talkie squawked. "Véro, I don't see your machine in the east wing."

"That supervisor's checking up on me. A real *salaud!*"

Footsteps echoed in the long gallery. "You better go, Aimée."

"*Merci*, Véro. How can I get out of here?"

"Go out the Richelieu wing; there's a reception tonight," Véro said. "They check who comes in, not who leaves."

And with the letter burning a hole in her pocket, Aimée sneaked out behind two revelers leaving early.

* * *

"ENCLOSED FIND YOUR *visiting hour confirmation to visit prisoner #1387 Nicolas Evry Tuesday 4 p.m. Bring this confirmation with you to La Santé Prison, visitor entrance rue Jean Dolent.*"

With a start, she recognized the name. Nicolas, the neo-Nazi member of *Les Blancs Nationaux*, who had torched the

Marais synagogue. Four years ago, her testimony had put him in prison.

A scribbled note had been added: "Nicolas must talk to you. It's vital. You're in danger."

No signature.

In danger? Did this involve René? Her mind spun, wondering why Nicolas needed to meet her. And why now? He must be up for parole.

Had a threat meant for her been enacted with René as its victim?

Yet a woman wearing a raincoat and helmet like hers had shot René. That was not a coincidence.

The appointment at La Santé had been scheduled for today. She'd already missed it.

As she walked down the quai, fatigue weighted her shoulders. She crossed the Pont Marie, veiled in mist, to Ile Saint-Louis.

In her building courtyard, Chloë wheeled a green garbage bin by the pear tree, bumping and scraping the stone wall as she tugged it forward.

"*Alors*, you're giving the concierge ideas, Chloë," she said. "That's her job."

"Madame Cachou's bursitis acted up." Chloë smiled. Her round glasses and the thin metal curlers in her hair gave her an old-fashioned look. Yet Aimée figured she was only in her late twenties. "It's no problem helping her out. I walked Miles Davis earlier."

Madame Cachou's bursitis flared up on a consistent basis these days, Aimée thought. More often than not, at the evening trash collection. Or had she grown too cynical?

"*Merci*, Chloë, don't mind me." Her body ached and she didn't relish the climb to her empty apartment.

Chloë gave a low whistle as she shoved the garbage bin in place. "Talk about a hunk, Aimée!"

She meant Mathieu. Chloë had lent her the *Elle* article. Of course she wanted to know how their dinner turned out.

"Him? I found out he's married with a kid. Next time I'll put nettles in his Speedos."

Chloë gave her a hug. "*Quel dommage.*"

Chloë taught adult literacy and worked part-time at Gilbert, the used-textbook annex on Boulevard Saint Michel. She scraped by and referred to her fifth-floor sublet garret as "romantic" and "living an adventure." Aimée wanted to hear her verdict after a bone-chilling winter in this seventeenth-century building with temperamental heating.

"So it's like they say, Aimée? That all the good ones get married, eh?"

"Good? A centimeter less and he'd be a girl."

"Bazar Hotel de Ville's the new place for meeting men."

Chloë waited.

"A department store?"

"In the hardware section." Chloë nodded. "It's *the* place on Friday nights."

Over tool sets? Not her scene.

Chloë paused on the black-and-white-tiled entry hall outside Aimée's apartment. "What's the matter, Aimée?"

Not intending to, she opened up, telling Chloë what had happened as they mounted the stairs. It eased her to confide in someone. She had always confided in Martine, her best friend since the *lycée*.

Too bad Martine was traveling in the Camargue salt marshes in a horse-drawn Gypsy caravan, following the wild horses with her boyfriend Gilles and his children who had taken early leave for the October school holidays. And, for once, Martine had left her cell phone behind.

What Aimée told Chloë was in edited form, since her eyelids were drooping and her shoulders sagging in tiredness.

Chloë hugged Aimée again. "But the *flics* can't think *you'd* shoot René. What does the doctor say?"

"That's just it. They moved him." Aimée pictured René in the hospital bed, the tubes, his wound, and suppressed a shudder.

"Where?"

"I don't know."

Chloë flicked her thumb up, toward the stairs. "Count on me any time you need help."

"*Bonsoir,* Chloë." Aimée picked up her pile of mail and got out her keys. The timed light went out. She stood in thought on the dark landing, the echoes of Chloë's footsteps trailing up the stairs, wondering what the prison letter meant. But by the time she unlocked the front door to her musty, cold apartment, and Miles Davis's wet nose nuzzled her legs, her only thought was of sleep.

Wednesday Morning

AIMÉE BREATHED THE close prison air edged with flaking rust, testosterone, and the perspiration of too many bodies in this narrow visiting room. She hated prisons and flinched at the sight of jumping lice on the jumpsuit of the young man opposite her, visible through the glass partition. No doubt he hated it more. *Maison d'Arrêt de la Santé,* the nineteenth-century prison on the Left Bank, built to house over a thousand, held a population closer to double that now.

She'd talked her way into the warden's office, showed him the confirmation letter, and with abject apologies explained she'd had a abscessed molar pulled. But could the warden, just this once, allow an exception? Of course, it was all her fault and yet so very painful, this tooth. By the time the warden relented, she'd missed three quarters of the morning visiting time and had to put her bag through the metal detector twice. All that, and then she still had to store it in the locker.

Nicolas Evry leaned into the dirty chrome speaker bolted to the smudged glass cubicle. Older now, his cheeks had hollowed. His dark red hair clumped in greasy tufts behind his ears; rough pinkish scales that he scratched non-stop were visible on his neck. Lice were not the only thing shared among the inmates: drugs, the domination of the strong over the weak, rape. She didn't like to think about it. Or that it was her testimony that had put Nicolas here.

"Nicolas, do you have something to tell me? We don't have much time." She tugged her agnés b. short black pencil skirt to her knees, aware of the looks from the guards. One, stout and sallow-faced, kept his eyes focused on her black-stockinged legs.

"Rats nibbled my thumb last night," he said, holding up a bandaged finger.

She frowned. "You must be up for parole by now."

"My lawyer's sailing vacation got in the way."

A sinking feeling hit her stomach. "Look, what's so vital that we need to talk? What's put me in danger?"

"Danger?" he said, his dark brown eyes intense, glancing at a notebook under his fist. Then he looked up at the guard, who'd bent to tie his shoelace. Nicolas stuck a piece of paper to the glass reading "Wait at the south wall, 10 A.M."

Then he stuck the paper in his mouth, chewed, and swallowed.

"At least you came." A flicker of a smile, an expression that could pass for gratitude, crossed his face. "Clémence, my ex, won't visit me any more."

"Did she arrange this and send me the note?"

He nodded.

Strange, she thought. "Why?"

"My parole hearing's been postponed," he said, shouting so he could be heard over the din of the twenty or so visitors, mostly women with crying infants. "Now it could take months. You've got to get me out."

"So that's what this is about? Some ploy to speed up your parole?"

Loud buzzing in the mike drowned out the rest of her words. The overhead fluorescent light dimmed. "Visiting hour ends in five minutes," announced a voice over the loudspeaker.

"I did my time. You're responsible," he said.

"Responsible?" she stood up. "You torched the synagogue." Four years ago in the Marais, Aimée had found the videotape, the proof that had put Nicolas, then eighteen years old, in here. "What does this have to do with me?"

Fear flooded Nicolas's eyes. And for a moment he looked like the scared, adrift twenty-two-year-old that he was. "I was covering up for the rich *salaud*. This proves it."

He raised his notebook.

"But it's a little late, Nicolas," she said. "The Tribunal convicted you, not me. Now it's your lawyer's job to get you out."

"Don't you understand? I can't take any more. These four years have been hell," he said. "There are fights every day. I've got two broken ribs."

"Deal with your lawyer, Nicolas."

His eyes swept the visiting room, the women and children at the cubicles, the guards.

"They're in this together."

"Who?"

"They're all against me."

Paranoid now, too. She'd had enough. This was leading nowhere.

"I tried to send this to you." Nicolas's voice faded in and out over the crackling microphone. He lifted the brown notebook again. "Take it. Read it. You'll know what to do."

He flipped the notebook open and pressed it against the glass between them. All she could make out were numbers that didn't make sense.

"'Know what to do'?" she asked.

Nicolas cast a furtive glance at the guard. What was he trying to tell her?

A deafening alarm sounded, shaking Aimée's feet on the floor, sending a reverberation up through her high heels, signaling that time for visiting was over.

"*Bon*, go ahead push it through," she said. "Quick."

But the handle in the small revolving window Aimée reached for didn't move.

Nicolas was arguing with a guard behind him. "'Application'?"

The guard shook his head. "Four years here and you don't know the rules? Go through the proper channels, Evry. You need twenty-four hours to clear personal items." The guard pushed Nicolas's hand down.

"Since when did the regulations say I can't give this to her?"

"Can't you read?" the guard interrupted, pointing to a sign. "See, it's all there. Time's up. Get going, Evry."

"Mail me your notebook, Nicolas." That's all she could offer.

The guard pulled Nicolas to his feet.

"They denied my mail privileges. They know about you."

Her body went cold.

"Who?"

"They're watching."

A horrible fear overtook her.

"Is that why my partner was shot?"

Panicked, he slammed the glass. The guard grabbed his arm.

"They think you know who paid me off." He stopped. Hesitated, looking at the guard, then back at her and mouthed "wall."

"Visiting hour's over." The sallow-faced guard grabbed her elbow. She flinched. "That means you, Mademoiselle. Time to file out. One by one."

The last she saw of Nicolas before the guard dragged him away were his intense, pleading eyes.

* * *

Aimée's hands shook as she stood outside the high stone wall of La Santé on tree-lined Boulevard Arago. She didn't like thinking of the public guillotinings that had taken place here, outside these walls, until the 1930s.

She saw the heads of prisoners, visible at the top of the wall. But no Nicolas. A petite woman on the pavement near her took aim and lobbed a cell phone upward. The phone's metal case glistened as it sailed in a high arc. A small shout from above signaled the phone's arrival.

She figured the fracas with the guard was Nicolas's ruse to deflect him from his intention to toss her the notebook. Again she surveyed the prisoners' heads. No Nicolas.

Brown-yellow leaves rustled underfoot. A squirrel nibbling the shell of a split chestnut darted up the tree trunk at the rumble of the approaching Number 21 bus. The everyday world surrounded her: an old man held his grandchild's hand; a woman sat in the bus shelter with a shopping bag on her lap; the autumnal orange light fell on the cinnamon-stone buildings.

After twenty minutes, the prisoners disappeared. She waited

ten more minutes. Only black crows strutting on the parapet now. No Nicolas. Frustrated, she caught the next bus.

She wondered who knew about her and what they knew. Nicolas had said "They think you know who paid me off." How was it all connected? She hadn't seen Nicolas or heard from him since that day in court four years ago. She tried to shake off a clinging miasma of guilt: first René and now Nicolas. But it didn't go away.

Wednesday

"BONJOUR, MONSIEUR ROBARD." Clémence kissed the antiquarian bookseller on both cheeks. The old man's sagging skin and his discolored teeth repulsed her, reminding her of her uncle's grinning yellow teeth and those afternoons when he'd taken her under the pines, the pine resin clinging to her skin. He'd told her to keep it their secret. Older men liked her. And after her uncle, Clémence wised up and used it.

"Aaah, *ma petite fleur*," Monsieur Robard said, his rheumy red-rimmed eyes lighting up, "you brighten my day."

Still, she liked his bookstore, a musty place piled with leather-bound volumes and smelling of old paper. Monsieur Robard had jumped at her idea to use his shop for a "letter drop," something he'd said he'd done during the Resistance, implying danger, passwords, and meetings in dark alleys.

"You appeal to the romantic in me, *ma petite fleur*," he'd said. Of course, Monsieur Robard thought an affair with a married man was involved. Not blackmail.

Clémence grinned, handing Monsieur Robard his customary demitasse, which she delivered from the bistro to him each morning. A lip of tan foam on his espress, a curled twist of lemon skin, one white sugar cube on the side, just the way he liked it. She smiled. An old man with a faint vetiver scent clinging to his ancient wool suit. And he hadn't pinched her once.

"*Parfait*, as usual." He downed the espress and with trembling hands patted the corners of his mouth with a handkerchief.

"Did you receive the envelope, Monsieur Robard?"

"*Ma petite fleur*, I hope you'll forgive me?" he said. A melodramatic tone in his voice, one arm raised in supplication, the other on his heart. "A little chest pain here, so I went to the doctor. I closed early yesterday."

Clémence's hopes sank. No fifty thousand francs. She scanned the slanted wood floor in case the envelope had been slid under the door and saw only dustballs.

"But I'm sure he'll write today." Monsieur Robard patted the self-addressed stamped envelope she'd provided him with on his desk. "When it arrives, I'll take no chances and do as we planned." He winked. "I'll slip it into your envelope and mail it on rue du Louvre. And tonight you'll find it at Poste Restante."

But if she didn't? She'd left her roommate her share of the rent, packed her bag, and bought a train ticket with the last of her money.

She had to find Aimée Leduc, hoping to God the detective had visited Nicolas in prison and gotten his notebook.

Now she had to leave, in case anyone was watching the bookseller's shop.

She set Monsieur Robard's empty demitasse on her tray, slid his two-franc tip into her apron pocket, and left him with a smile. She walked under the shaded canopy of lime trees lining the Palais Royal quarter, looking neither left nor right.

Wednesday

A YELL ERUPTED near the pots of lamb shanks boiling on the industrial stove in La Santé prison's underground kitchen. Trays clattered on the stone floor, food spilling everywhere. The rising steam created a fog with the sweltering aroma of bay leaves.

"Not again!" Alphonse, the red-faced cook, wiped the edge of his white apron across his brow. "Can't you *auxi's* serve the C-block meal trays right? How simple can it get?"

C block, the VIP wing, held convicted ministers and corporate heads, along with Carlos the Jackal and wealthy terrorists who enjoyed room service and a cognac after supper. An elite group dubbed by the prisoners "the mighty."

Two *auxiliaires*, prisoners with the coveted job of serving meal trays to C block, backed away from the pantry door.

"Alphonse, look. . . ." said one.

The body of a man was suspended from the meat hook on the old pantry door. His bare toes hung centimeters off the flaking stucco floor.

"*Nom de Dieu*." Alphonse crossed himself. He batted away the vapors. And gasped.

A cockroach scurried into a hole under the sink.

Socks knotted together formed a noose around the man's neck. From the deep groove worn in his flesh, it had taken him a long time to die.

"It's a curse! A curse on my kitchen." Alphonse's jowls shook. "Damn him, damn whoever did this."

By the time the duty guards appeared in the humid, narrow cellblock corridor, hoarse shouts accompanied muffled banging on the thick metal doors. The prisoners in the exercise yard, the one hour in twenty-four that they were let out of their crowded cells, jammed against the windows of the sweating, moisture-clad kitchen walls, trying to see inside. Scummed greasy water, drained from the lamb shanks, trailed over the cracked concrete floor. Laurel and bay leaf smells rose through the steam vents.

The first guard shook his billyclub. The second, armed with a taser, stepped inside. "By the wall, you lot. Now!" he ordered.

"We found him like that. And in this heat . . . still warm."

"Parboiled more like it, eh, Alphonse?" said the other *auxi*. "Second one this month. It's quite a comment on your cuisine." He cleaned under his fingernails with a matchstick, a studied look of indifference on his pale face.

"Shut up, Sicard. Leave Alphonse alone." The guard edged closer with his taser outstretched. Alphonse, oblivious, stirred the simmering pot of lentils, his thick lips moving in silent prayer.

The guard flicked the taser against the stainless steel counter. "Cut him down." He motioned to the other guard. "I'll call the chaplain."

"Doesn't make sense," said Sicard.

"Makes every kind of sense in this hellhole." The guard shrugged. "Then again, no one comes here for gourmet cuisine."

"Why the hell in my kitchen?" Alphonse asked no one in particular.

The guard waved the vapors away and turned over the body. They saw the face.

Nicolas Evry's bulging vacant eyes were webbed with thin red veins. His swollen tongue hung over his blue lips.

"So young," said Sicard, his voice thick.

"Won't do him much good now."

"But he was scheduled for the review board," said Sicard. "I don't get it."

"Don't you have work to do, Sicard?"

Sicard bit back his reply. He was due to be released in two days.

The guard hefted Nicolas's body and he saw the clean, pale soles of Nicolas's bare feet. Too clean for this dirty floor. "What are you looking at?" he snapped.

Sicard grabbed the mop, averted his gaze, and lowered his head. He knew what he'd seen. And he wondered what it would be worth.

Wednesday

"It's urgent, Monsieur Guérin," Aimée said, over the phone. "There's a wire-deposit mistake in our account."

She'd tried to reach the banker all morning. Finally, she got through to him after lunch. She imagined Guérin at his desk upstairs in Paribas. He had a corner office replete with mahogany desk, leather armchairs, and private bar concealed in a matching console, and a highly polished parquet floor. His plump cheeks, little moustache, and rotund body were almost comical. His little feet, supporting such a big girth, fascinated her.

"There's no mistake, Mademoiselle Leduc," said Guérin.

"Bookkeeping recorded a wire deposit of one hundred thousand francs." He cleared his throat.

She'd known Guérin for years. After her father's death in the Place Vendôme explosion, he'd guided her through shock and grief, through the intricacies of the inheritance laws, and her reorganization of Leduc Detective from criminal investigation into corporate computer security, advising on streamlining their antiquated accounting and bookkeeping systems used since her grandfather's time.

"Monsieur Guérin," she said. "Data entry should have alerted you. I'm sure there's been a simple bookkeeping error."

"'Error,' Mademoiselle?"

Frustrated, Aimée tapped her heels on the parquet floor of her office. On her laptop screen, she scanned Leduc Detective's bank account display. Beside her, client records and bank statements were piled on her desk. Sunlit limestone Haussmann buildings caught the early afternoon light outside her window on rue de Louvre.

"No client owes my firm anywhere near this amount, Monsieur Guérin. There's some error."

"Given your long standing as a customer, of course I meant to call you," he said. He gave what sounded like a short, embarrassed cough. "You have beat me to it, as they say." He paused. "But I've been at La Defense all day. I'm sorry, an inquiry has started."

"An inquiry?"

"With a sum of this size, originating from a Luxembourg bank—"

"We have no clients in Luxembourg."

"As instructed by my chief, I filled out the regulation paperwork."

De mal en pis, from bad to worse. "Paperwork" meant a

SAR—a suspicious activity report—kicking off Treasury alarms. This would entail forms, certificates, and affidavits to unravel the bureaucratic quagmire.

"Please, let's correct this right now."

"Mademoiselle, the Luxembourg bank wire-transfer deposit is a *fait accompli*," Guérin said.

A frisson passed through her.

"Which bank wired it, Monsieur Guérin?"

"The bookkeeping report only indicates a Luxembourg origin."

This wasn't the helpful Guérin she knew. Why couldn't he answer a simple question?

"I don't understand," Aimée said. "You're my banker and I want to know the bank origin of the funds sent to our account. More to the point, I need to *see* this wire transfer record."

"Mademoiselle Leduc, I'd like to help you, but the report contains no more information. The inquiry's out of my hands; it's been routed to the department that deals with these matters."

The tax man? Or a criminal fraud investigative unit?

No one in their right mind would wire her a hundred thousand francs. Even a money launderer knew better than to attempt a transaction of over fifty thousand francs, the sum that triggered an automatic inquiry.

"Can't you send back the wire transfer?"

"The bank processed the deposit in accordance with procedure. It's too late, Mademoiselle."

"But Monsieur Guérin, we've been customers for a long time."

"Correct. We have a long history, Mademoiselle."

Her grandfather had opened a bank account with Paribas's predecessor when he founded Leduc Detective. As a little girl, she'd accompanied him to the Place de l'Opera branch. She recalled trying to keep up with his long strides over the cobblestones.

"Whoever wired the deposit must have showed photo ID and proof of the existence of the transferee's bank account with Paribas?"

"Again, the details. . . ." A sigh. "Financial regulations forbid me even telling you this much, once this inquiry has started."

This wasn't like Guérin at all. He talked like a bank *fonctionnaire*, not the man who sent her a fruit basket at Christmas, a card on her birthday, the occasional note with a biscuit for Miles Davis. Was he trying to tell her something in an oblique way?

"It's out of my hands. I'm so sorry."

She wouldn't give up. "Then who can I talk to, Monsieur Guérin?"

"It pains me to tell you that I can't help you, Mademoiselle."

She doubted that. More like he wanted to keep his job.

"What's going on, Monsieur Guérin?"

There was a pause.

She continued: "Listen, you know Leduc's finances, know this doesn't make sense. It's like someone's framing me. A name, Monsieur Guérin?" she said. "My grandfather and my father valued your advice, as I have. We've trusted you."

Another pause. "Fine men, your grandfather and your father."

"So *entre-nous*, eh? That's not breaking rules. Just a name, Monsieur Guérin."

Another sigh. "Just a moment. I have another call."

But she heard no click of another call on the line, just what sounded like creaking wood, like the creak Guérin's ancient leather chair made when he shifted his weight.

"Tracfin," he whispered.

And he hung up, but not before she registered the sound of footsteps. Had someone else been sitting in his office?

Wednesday

"WHY BLACKMAIL US now?" Gabrielle asked.

She stood next to her husband, Roland, on the Savonerrie carpet in her office. The caw of crows and the scent of crisp, cold air drifted in from the tall window overlooking the Palais Royal. "I thought all this was past. Over."

"Why didn't you tell me at once, Gabrielle?" Roland, all six feet of him in a navy pinstripe suit, held the blackmail note, his brow furrowed.

"You were in Versailles at meetings," she said. "By the time I arrived, the bookseller's was closed."

"Closed? You mean you intended to pay?"

"Nothing must jeopardize your posting, Roland. Or hurt Olivier," she said fiercely. This wasn't putting out fires in the Ministry; this was her family.

Concern washed over Roland's face; he took her in his arms and held her tightly, protectively. "Always a fighter, my Gabrielle. But blackmail never ends. It's a stranglehold that will be pulled tighter and tighter."

He tore the note and newspaper article into little pieces, letting them drop like confetti into the trash. "I can't let you do this. Not for me."

She watched Roland. A dreamer, a poet and brooding rebel when they'd met; but now seeing his graying temples, the upright posture, that controlled expression, she thought of him, these days, as a stoic. There was something unfamiliar in his expression. Like many of the 1968 generation protesters, he'd joined the government they'd vowed to tear down. The burden of the secrets he carried, ones they all carried in this milieu, had altered him.

"What's the matter, Roland?"

He shrugged. Where had the lean aristo rebel she'd fallen for in '68 gone? She still searched for a glimpse underneath the politico façade; every so often it appeared. More and more rarely these days.

"Everything's changed now," he said. "Nicolas Evry committed suicide in La Santé."

"Suicide?" She stepped back, horrified. Nicolas had been so young, so pathetic. But willing to keep quiet over Olivier's involvement. "How do you know?"

Roland rubbed his forehead. "Not a nice story. My thoughts are with his family, if he had any."

"Terrible. I'm so sorry." Her thoughts sped through the implications. "But who wrote this note, and what proof do they have? It can only mean that Nicolas revealed Olivier's involvement."

"There's no proof. Nothing specific in the blackmailer's note. Just an old newspaper article."

"What is the worst-case scenario?" she asked.

As she always did; it was her training. A gurgling sound came from the fountain in the center of the Palais Royal garden. Sun glinted off the sundial, a small beacon amid the rose bushes.

"It's over, Gabrielle."

"You can't think this will simply go away," she argued.

Roland gripped his briefcase. His mind was elsewhere now as he gave her a small smile. "I'm due to present a report in thirteen minutes next door in the Ministry."

He paused. "It's terrible about that boy, Gabrielle, but that finishes it."

"A 'boy'? Face it, Roland, they're men. Our son Olivier's a man."

A long sigh escaped Gabrielle. No use arguing with Roland now.

He reached for her hand. "I'm worried that Oliver will feel responsible for this suicide," Roland said. "It could haunt him, scar his psyche."

Roland's insight amazed her sometimes. Still. She stood in her stockinged feet, pulled Roland close, inhaled the traces of his citrus shampoo. Of course she would take care of this, and much more. She'd alerted her contacts. Roland would never know. She'd already taken the money out of the bank. Then, once and for all, it would be behind them. But first she'd wring the truth out of Olivier.

"I'll talk to Olivier," she assured Roland. Somehow she'd manage it, along with defusing a major scandal, before the 8 P.M. news show.

* * *

GABRIELLE PRESSED THE carved woodwork panel in the wall which was a camouflaged door opening to the next office, deserted now except for hot tisane herbal tea on her secretary Jean-George's desk. With fifteen minutes until her next meeting, she hurried into the hall, up the rear stairs two flights into a narrow top-floor corridor punctuated by skylights. In the late afternoon sky, cloud clumps cast shadows darkening the interior passage which wound to the Galerie de Valois bordering the western wing of the Palais Royal. The passages all connected but from the exterior no one would have known this.

"Bonjour, Madame de la Pecheray," said Polivard, a wizened older man, white hair combed neatly over his balding pate.

Gabrielle nodded at Polivard, an octogenarian, entitled by former service to rooms in this wing reserved for the Ministry of Culture and Council of State *hauts fonctionnaires*. He was one of the few surviving relics of the "*ancien* regime," the Vichy government.

"I knew your father, Madame." Polivard leaned on his cane, expectant. No doubt it was a highlight of his day to catch someone in the hallway and converse about the old days.

"*C'est vrai,* Monsieur Polivard?" She gave a strained smile. "We must catch up one of these days." She smiled again and edged past the old man.

"He was one of us, you know." Polivard winked.

She suppressed a shudder. Her father's ties to the corrupt Vichy government, his anti-Semitic leanings, were the last thing she could deal with right now. Or Polivard's old-man smell.

"A fervent follower of Marshal Petain," Polivard said. "Fine articles your father wrote. Laval quoted him, you know."

Her father's infamous phrases had been used in Laval's Jewish Deportation Directive. The shame of the past haunted her steps, always. Could she never get away from it?

"A *bientôt*." She hurried around the corner.

Nowadays, many high-ranking administrators used their elegant, spacious *appartements de fonction*, common perks for officials, as *pied-à-terre* for liaisons, preferring to save on hotel rooms. The higher up, the more frugal, she thought. All on the ministry franc.

Gabrielle stayed here only if meetings kept her past midnight and Roland was working out of town. They maintained the family flat she'd inherited on nearby Place des Petits-Pères. But now this apartment presented her with a perfect place from which to call Olivier undisturbed.

She turned the key, an elongated antique, opening the door to the high-ceilinged eighteenth-century suite of rooms.

An eclectic mix of furnishings had been provided, courtesy of the State: bulbous inlaid-wood chests, rococo beveled mirrors, delicate Louis XVI upholstered chairs, and more armoires than she could shake a stick at, all smelling of other people's lives.

Then an acid sweet odor overlaid with that of malt scotch met her nostrils. Shocked, she saw her son Olivier sprawled on the bed's duvet beside his own vomit, passed out. His jeans and rumpled suede jacket trailed off the chair; his billfold lay on the floor.

"Wake up, Olivier!"

A groan answered her. She could only stall fifteen minutes at most; she still had to revise the script yet again for the minister's approval. Instead of telling her son about Nicolas's suicide, holding his hand, calming him down, she'd have to get him into the shower.

A chirping beep came from somewhere near Olivier's head. His long tanned arm reached for his cell phone.

"No, you don't." She grabbed the cell phone. "Get up. What are you doing here?"

"*Maman*." His eyes opened. Those long lashes, the pout of a mouth, that slim jaw. Just like her father.

Her baby.

"What time is it?" He yawned, stretched, and then winced. "Bang-up rave last night . . . this morning . . . whenever."

"But you have class. Since when do you lie in your own spew?" Disgusted, she stood with her hands on her hips for a moment, then opened the window. "Now clean it up."

The breeze scented by flowering lime trees lining the Palais Royal garden below wafted inside. The waters spouting from the central fountain into the circular pool glinted in the fading light. The quadrangle was like a private garden in the center of Paris. And with the gates locked at night, it was a garden just for the elite.

"Don't worry, *Maman*. The maid. . . ."

"And let talk begin, Olivier? You're not allowed to use this apartment. How long before the staff leaks that my spoiled playboy of a son—"

"You'll get around it, *Maman*, you know how."

She'd spoiled her only child. Gone wrong a long time ago, letting him getting away with things because of her guilt for working late hours. Or was it his inborn charm that got around her?

"And abuse this privilege? My work, my service to the Republic, is what earned this. It's part of my compensation."

"Save that for the earnest interns, *Maman*."

"That's enough, Olivier. I want your word that you'll never use this suite again."

He nodded. She noticed all the messages on her cell phone. But she had to deal with Nicolas's suicide before she ran back to deal with the ministry crisis.

"We have to talk about Nicolas Evry."

Ready for tears or remorse, she watched him.

"That loser?" He exhaled in disgust, then sat up and shrugged. His boxers lay low on his hips. "You paid him off, right? History, far as I'm concerned."

She stepped back, shocked at his coldness. "How can you say that? You're damn lucky he took all the blame."

"For a price."

She shook her head. "I can't stomach this."

Olivier crinkled his nose. "I agree. Pretty rank." He balled up the duvet, shoving it into the corner. He scratched his crotch. "I'm taking a shower."

"Here your father and I were so worried how you'd take the news, that it would scar your psyche."

"Quit the New Age stuff, *Maman*." With a bored expression, he paused at the bathroom door. "And no more martyred looks. I'll go to class. Promise."

"*Bon*. I should get down on my knees and thank you for that, eh? The boy's dead, you don't give a—"

"Who?" Surprise painted his face.

"Didn't you know?"

"Stop the riddles, *Maman*."

And she realized Roland had passed the awful job on to her. Angered, she inhaled, trying to control herself, wondering how to word her news.

"Nicolas died in prison," she said unable to say "suicide."

Olivier shook his head. "A tough place. So, he got a shiv in his back from a cellmate?"

"This isn't American *télé*, Olivier. He committed suicide."

A blank look filled Olivier's face, then he averted his gaze. Was he remembering?

She'd never forgotten her six-year-old son tugging at her skirt in their country-house kitchen that scorching hot day. "Why's *grand-père* hanging from the tree? He told me I couldn't climb it. And he's sticking out his tongue at me. It's not nice." She'd found that her father had hanged himself from the pear tree in the garden. Again she felt her searing pain. She'd tried to shield Olivier in her arms, tried to block his view. Mimosa scent wafting in the heat from the bush near her father's dangling foot, she recalled. She stifled a sob.

Where was the six-year-old who'd clutched a fistful of mimosa behind him, dirty streaks from tears running down his cheeks? "I'm sorry, *Maman*. Are you mad? Did he make a mistake? Won't *grand-père* come back when he's better?"

There was an apologetic tone in his voice, as if he'd done something wrong. Her own father, the grandfather Olivier had looked up to.

What had happened to her beautiful boy?

Money in the right hands went only so far. What if Olivier was implicated, his onetime white supremacist affiliation discovered? With a Vichy-government, Nazi-sympathizer grandfather, the old stories would get raked up.

Olivier put his arm around her shoulders and hugged her. She had to snap out of it and deal with the present. Instead of comforting him, he was cradling her in his arms.

"Don't cry, *Maman*."

"Is there something you didn't tell me, Olivier? Something I should know?"

"Nicolas was a strange *mec*. Moody."

"Did he tell anyone, Olivier?"

"He liked money too much. And I told you, I hardly knew him."

"Madame de la Pecheray?" It was Jean-Georges's voice.

"*Un moment*." She blotted her eyes with the towel.

"It's all right, *Maman*." Olivier lifted her chin. "Believe me. Listen to Papa."

She hoped he was telling the truth. And she hoped she hadn't heard that cold tone in his voice. Just imagined it.

"*Alors*, I'd never disturb you, Madame," said her secretary through the closed door, "but the minister's en route here."

Jean-Georges watched her back. A jewel. But then watching Gabrielle's back was his job in the Ministry of Culture.

"Hurry, clean this up, Olivier. Hide your things."

Clean up, hiding. Wasn't she always cleaning up and hiding something?

Wednesday

AIMÉE SAT ON their hard office floor across from Saj, who was crosslegged on the tatami. Sunbeams caught reflecting gleams from the chandelier's prisms. Outside the window, the hum of afternoon traffic was punctuated by the blasts of a horn, the rumble of buses.

Saj liked spreading out on the floor. A bamboo curtain, a tatami mat, and a surge protector were all he required. He leaned over his laptop, long dirty-blond dreadlocks cascading down his back over his cotton muslin shirt. A leather strip held coral and turquoise beads, from his recent ashram stay in India, around his neck.

"Sounds like you want the pedigree," he said.

"Whatever you call it. Hack into the bank, Saj."

"That's René's metier."

"Right, but René can't help us," she said. "We have to get to the bottom of this. This amount tripped off the alarms," she said. "You know what that means."

"Inquiries, freezing the account, tax audit, the usual?"

"Not that bad, I hope."

No one knew Ministry systems and networks like Saj, or how to hack into them. The Ministry had intervened to commute Saj's prison sentence so that he would patch the holes he'd hacked. They'd even kept him on call as a consultant.

"My banker was guarded, Saj," she said. "I'm sure someone in his office was listening to the conversation."

Saj stretched, brown prayer beads clicking around his wrists, still tan from India. He reached for his tea. Steam rose curling in a lazy spiral. The only reminder of René's bloodstain was a pale circle on the wood floor that she'd scrubbed this morning.

"I've known the banker for years," she said, shifting on the hard floor. "He wouldn't tell me anything, but before he hung up he whispered 'Tracfin'."

Saj sat up. Whistled. "Tracfin, the money-laundering investigators?"

"You know it?"

"Tracfin stands for *Traitement du Renseignement et Action Contre Les Circuits Financiers Clandestins*, Treatment of Information and Action Against Illicit Financial Circuits. Sounds bland, but I'd say your banker pointed you to what used to exist in a subbranch below the normal radar. Initially with customs, Tracfin's now the financial intelligence unit of the Ministry of Economy. They investigate and decide whether to alert the judicial authorities to prosecute. Kind of *über* investigators."

Aimée pushed the demitasse of now-cold espress away from her feet toward Saj's tea cup of Rooibos, red bush tea. This didn't sound good.

Saj typed, his fingers flying over the keys. Then he turned the keyboard in her direction. On the screen she saw a grid of numbers and columns of acronyms. One was TRACFIN.

Saj clicked on the acronym, and reams of code came up.

"Irritating, too," he said. "Now they're official and part of a European network-sharing and regulatory system."

"Can't you wiggle in?"

"We're talking big boys with big resources, Aimée. This takes work. There are new EU banking-compliance safeguards against money laundering. Now if René were here, together we could worm in."

Saj cocked his head. His gray-green eyes clouded. Did even Saj distrust her?

"You can't think *I* shot him? Or that I know about this?" Aimée asked.

He stared at her. "You did something."

"I went from René in the hospital to the *flics* dogging me. So far, it's the worst seventy-eight hours of my life."

Apart from finding her father's charred remains on Place Vendôme's blackened cobblestones.

"Feels like a kick in the gut from nowhere," she said.

"In the stream of life, all is relevant," Saj said. "Witness the Sanskrit term around my neck, *Sita:* a furrow for planting seeds."

What did that mean? But if she didn't convince Saj and get him on her side, she faced big trouble. She gave him a quick account.

"So the bad boy Mathieu's married and wouldn't give you an alibi?"

She nodded.

"A typical piece of media fashion fluff," he said. "Meanwhile, someone posing as you shot René, and the video you showed the *flics* led them to the taxi dispatch and straight to your door."

She nodded again. "Cold and calculated."

"Then the skinhead you put away four years ago cries 'coverup,' implying he's put you in danger. And you think, somehow, that's why René was shot?"

The wind chimes tinkled from his bamboo curtain.

"And now you want to get me implicated too?" he said.

Her shoulders sagged. Even if she lost the business her grandfather and father had founded, she had no right to pull him down with her. "You're right, Saj. I've already led to René being shot. I couldn't stand it if you got hurt too. "It's not fair to put either of you in more danger." She started to get up.

Saj was hunched over his keyboard. "It's your aura, Aimée,"

he said. “A clouded blue. Indicative of disharmony, disturbed cosmic connections.”

Now he was blaming her on a karmic level. “Another nail in my karmic coffin, Saj?”

Nicolas’s pained pleading eyes and the crowded visiting room in La Santé passed through her mind.

“Straighten your back and we’ll try the lotus position.”

“Not now, Saj.” With so much hanging in the balance, Saj wanted her to meditate!

“This will help,” he said. “It will liberate the chakras and life force.”

“Espresso does that for me.”

Saj draped an orange prayer scarf printed in Sanskrit with “*Om Mane Padme Hum*” over her shoulders. “I received this from my Guru in Varanasi and dipped it in the holy Ganges. Three times.”

No doubt it was a living, breathing laboratory of imported bacteria. Then she brightened. “You mean you’ll help?”

“I’m implicated already, Aimée, just by working here.” He inhaled deeply, letting his breath out with measured puffs. “And with that aura, you *do* need all the help you can get. Me, too. Now, try cleansing deep breaths. Tracfin’s sophisticated; requires work.”

She set her Valentino boots to the side, straightened her spine, breathed, and closed her eyes. Tight.

* * *

AN HOUR LATER, chakras aligned, Aimée pressed the button and the door buzzed open to rue du Louvre. Saj waved and headed to the Métro to meet a contact who’d dealt with Tracfin.

“Aimée Leduc, *non?*” said a woman.

Blond, in her early twenties, the woman wore a short black skirt, low black heels, and a long cardigan sweater that fell to her knees. With a nervous movement, she pulled her sweater tighter against the rising wind. On closer inspection, black roots showed in her limp hair.

"*Oui?*" Aimée was confused. She'd cleared her calendar and wasn't supposed to be here. She was supposed to be in New York with her brother. Who would look for her here?

"I need to talk to you," the blonde said, a strong Occitan drawl to her words. From somewhere in the southwest, Aimée thought. Toulouse? Wary, she hesitated to take this woman upstairs to the office.

"Did we have an appointment?"

"I'm Clémence."

So this was Nicolas's ex. No *bonjour* or introduction. But there was a panicked look in her hollow eyes and pale face that excused this.

"You left me the appointment notice for La Santé?"

Clémence nodded.

"You're right, we need to talk. And you need to explain. I visited Nicolas in La Santé. He's gotten me in trouble, hasn't he?"

Clémence clutched her stomach. She leaned against Aimée's fawn-colored stone building. Passersby, bundled against the rising chill, stared.

"Something wrong?" Aimée asked. She took Clémence's arm. "Can I help you?"

Clémence shivered and shook Aimée's hand off. "You don't know, do you?"

"'Know'? I think you've got things to tell me. Nicolas and I never finished our conversation. I waited under the prison wall, too, but he never appeared. I want to know why he was afraid."

"Too late." Tears brimmed in Clémence's mascara-smudged eyes.

Concerned, Aimée gestured to the red-awninged café on the corner.

"Let's talk in there." The canvas awning's scalloped edges flapped in the wind rising from the Seine.

Inside the café, wisps of cigarette smoke spiraled in the close air. Virginie, the owner's wife, chatted with a man in overalls at the zinc counter and nodded at Aimée.

"*Bonjour, un espress et une Badoit, s'il vous plaît*, Virginie," Aimée requested.

"Sit down, Clémence," she said, pointing to the round marble table in the corner. "Now you can tell me why I'm in danger. Who 'they' are. Why Nicolas said he'd throw me his notebook over the wall, but didn't."

"Look, Nicolas insisted he had to see *you*." Clémence pulled her sweater tighter around herself, sniffling. "They just called from La Santé." She paused wiping her nose with the back of her hand.

What had happened? Aimée wondered. She searched in her bag for a tissue and came up with her LeClerc mirrored compact. "Here, it's not that bad. Wipe your eyes. Check your face."

"Nicolas hanged himself."

Aimée dropped the open compact. The round mirror fell, shattering on the table top. Sharp glass shards gleamed in the sunlight. Clémence's sobs mingled with the *whoosh* of the milk steamer. Seven years of bad luck, and more bad karma.

"But I just saw him." Aimée's mind went back to Nicolas's last look, the fear in his deep-set eyes. Her insides went cold. "Do you think he was really murdered?"

Virginie appeared and wiped up the sparkling sharp mirror bits with a damp rag, then set down the espress and bottle of

Badoit mineral water beaded with moisture. Without a word, she left, having read Clémence's stricken face.

Clémence pushed the bottle away. "You were supposed to find out what he wanted. I'm four months pregnant." Clémence stared at Aimée. "It's Nicolas's baby."

"Don't con me, Clémence." Her shock was replaced by disbelief. "La Santé doesn't have conjugal visits. And he said you wouldn't even come to see him."

Clémence grabbed her arm. "He lied. Even after we broke up, I visited him. I felt sorry for him. We went to the *parloir des bébés*."

"What's that?"

Clémence said, "Those cloakrooms off the lockers."

"So?"

"Didn't you see the women and all those babies?"

Of course she had. "You're saying the guards look the other way?"

"Where do you think the babies come from?" Clémence didn't wait for her answer. "The *parloir des bébés*. The guards take a little cash and pretend not to know what's going on. They call the kids 'stairsteps,' one for every year of their father's stay."

Aimée knew the guards would look the other way for a price. But she'd never heard this. Then again, what woman would take someone else's baby to visit her man in prison?

"So Nicolas knew about the baby?"

"We had history, but I knew it wouldn't work. After all, you don't need a man to raise a kid, eh? And Nicolas. . . ." She shrugged. "Brilliant, but always a *dépressif*, and then his white supremacy talk. I don't know how much he'd changed. He had a good job in the kitchen, too. His cellmate Sicard helped him get it."

Why would Nicolas, about to become a father and up for parole, hang himself? Aimée wondered.

Clémence accused, "He wanted to talk to you. You're the last person from outside to see him. You could have saved him."

"Me?" Aimée thought about the way he'd looked, what she took for his paranoia. Had she caused his death? Had it been murder? "The only thing Nicolas had time to mention was his lawyer saying 'they' were in this together against him, he wouldn't cover up for a rich '*salaud*,' and 'they' knew about me. That's all."

"See, he tried to explain," Clémence said. "Now I have nothing."

"He said he had the proof in his notebook. Visiting hours ended. Then, when he didn't appear to throw it from the wall, I finally left."

Clémence covered her face with her hands.

Aimée stirred her espress. She suspected Clémence knew more than she was letting on. Time to stretch the truth. "Nicolas said to talk to you."

"Why?"

"Didn't information about this coverup get him killed?"

Clémence bowed her head, then looked up, pushing her hair back. Her fingernails had been chewed to the quick, Aimée noticed, as Clémence gripped the bottle of Badoit.

"My partner was shot in our office. Nicolas implied there was a connection between that shooting and his 'proof.' I need to know what it was, Clémence."

She blinked. "*C'est vrai?* What should I say? He talked big, but it was always vague, nothing specific. I hadn't even seen him in four months."

Clémence's surprise seemed real.

"Hadn't he said anything that might point to what he knew?" Aimée asked.

Clémence thought. "It seemed strange," she said, pausing. "I threw him cell phones over the prison wall—that's how it's done—he sold them to other prisoners. Even with that, and the credit he earned in the kitchen, it didn't amount to much. Still, he sent me money until last month."

Dust motes swirled in the weak autumn light slanting through the café window. A crisscross pattern of shadows covered Aimée's boot.

"Where did the money come from?"

"Who knows? But it stopped. And I'm broke." Clémence shrugged. "I've got to go. Before I return to work, I need to sign some forms and pick up Nicolas's belongings."

"You're going to La Santé? I'll go with you, Clémence."

"Why?" Clémence slung her bag on her shoulder.

"Don't you realize Nicolas may have been murdered?" she said, desperate now. "His notebook might indicate why my partner was shot. While we're there, we'll arrange an appointment with his cellmate."

"You think someone killed Nicolas?"

"It's possible."

Clémence averted her eyes. "Like I said, he talked big. He thought you could speed up his parole. Why would they kill him?"

Aimée had no answer.

"I don't need your help," Clémence said.

Odd. Aimée had thought she would welcome it.

"Stupid to think you could've helped him. Anyway, he's gone. He was a *dépressif*, I told you." Clémence sighed. "So he killed himself, who knows why. I'm quitting my job and going home."

"But what if Nicolas was murdered?" Aimée asked. "You may be needed in the investigation."

"I won't raise my baby here." She pulled her sweater around her. "Four long years, and I still have to struggle to make the rent."

"Let me help, Clémence." She needed Clémence to claim the notebook.

Clémence slapped a franc down next to the Badoit bottle. "And ruin your record? Forget it."

"How can I know what Nicolas meant unless I see this notebook?"

Fear flickered in Clémence's eyes. And then it was gone. "Nicolas liked to talk, and prison walls have ears. If I were you, I'd watch my back."

The café door slammed behind her.

Aimée threw a few francs on the table, grabbed her bag, and stood, but an old woman with a cane blocked her way. By the time she reached the bus stop, the Number 85 bus had left. There was no sign of Clémence; she must have gotten on it.

Aimée didn't even know Clémence's last name or phone number. She ran to the taxi stand. A long line waited. Frantic, she ran a block and raced down the Métro steps.

* * *

"I'M SORRY, MADEMOISELLE." The gate guard at La Santé shook his head. "I haven't seen the woman you describe."

"But she came to pick up Nicolas Evry's belongings."

"His ex, you said? Then she's the only one who's certified to enter."

She handed him her card. "If you see her, would you give this to her, please?"

"We're not a message service, Mademoiselle."

"I realize that, Monsieur. But she was so distraught over Nicolas's death. I should have accompanied her. Now I feel terrible."

"Nothing you could do, anyway," the guard said. "Only family and relations are allowed."

"But as a small favor, can you give her my cell phone number, ask her to ring me? I want to help."

"In these difficult times, we do try to help the family," he said. "I'll do my best."

She figured he'd throw her card in the trash as soon as she rounded the corner.

Now it was out of her hands, she thought; not that it had ever been in them.

* * *

SHE TOOK THE Métro back to Louvre-Rivoli, back to where she'd come from.

Her feet carried her down rue du Louvre in the dusk, threading a path among the hurrying pedestrians. Past the boutiques and travel agencies whose once-wooden storefronts were now gentrified, whose courtyards contained remnants of the thirteenth-century wall enclosing the Louvre. Even the vestige of a tower, a semicircular trace left, fossil-like, indented in stone.

She tried to clear her mind. In the crisp air brown leaves rustled, a siren wailed in the distance—the usual street symphony—accompanied by the smoky smell of roasting chestnuts. She bought a few francs' worth from the street vendor. The hot chestnuts in the paper cone warmed her hands. She split the chestnut shells, crunched the sweet nuts, and thought.

Surely Clémence would contact her again. She hadn't heard the last from her. Clémence wasn't telling her something.

Right now, Saj was meeting with his bank contact. There was nothing more she could do there.

Mathieu still hadn't returned her phone calls. And unless he changed his statement, she had no alibi.

The fleeting thought that Mathieu had been in league with the shooter surfaced.

Had Nicolas's paranoia rubbed off on her? She crumpled the empty paper cone, thrust it into her pocket, and hurried up the street.

There was only one way to find out.

* * *

AIMÉE CHECKED MATHIEU'S business card for his address when she reached Place des Victoires. It was a glorified roundabout, she thought, with its starlike profusion of six radiating streets. Designed by Mansard, the seventeenth-century pale honey-colored stone façades were supported by high pillars capped by sloping slate mansard roofs. The circular Place lay deserted, apart from the equestrian statue of Louis XIV. His original statue was torn down in the Revolution. The saying went around that *Henri IV gave his people the Pont Neuf, Louis XIII gave his nobles the Place des Vosges, and Louis XIV gave his tax collectors the Place des Victoires.*

The Place des Victoires was *the* address for fashion houses and designer-label shops. And the best shoe shop, Aimée had found, for discards from the runway fashion shows. But she wasn't here to shop.

She entered a corner building and climbed a flight to the couture house of Soutien, where Mathieu worked. Occupying the whole floor, the decor harkened to Louis XIV with huge crystal chandeliers floating in the entrance and low bergère chairs covered in a pastel brocade in the waiting room. Already, Aimée wished she'd worn a better jacket.

The designer, she read on the framed two-page *Vogue* article above the reception desk, was the son of a shoemaker, had graduated from the École des Beaux-Arts and introduced his own collection in 1987, proclaiming that his inspiration came from the wind blowing through the hair of a woman on a motorcycle, the smell of a ripe pear, and the old dancehalls where dancers only wore feathers and heels.

As pretentious as Mathieu, who was employed in their media department. Clumps of blue hydrangea, dozens of them, stood in clear glass vases everywhere in the white-carpeted salon. The vegetal scent mingled with the sweat of stylists hovering under heat lamps, draping models in scraps of lime-colored fur. A low techno beat thudded from large speakers. She picked Mathieu out of the huddle of mediatheques and business types bent over an oval wood-inlaid table.

"No press yet," said a breathless, flush-cheeked woman with black bobbed hair. "For pre-show invites, give us an hour." The woman waved Aimée to one of the chairs. She held multicolored wool samples in her hand and wore a three-quarter-length frock coat cut from an eighteenth-century floral tapestry. Trim, tapered, and unique. Aimée figured that with several more zeros in her bank account, she could have one too.

"Just give me your press card," the woman said, in her breathless way. "I'll put your name on the *défilé* list tomorrow. Save you time and spare you the rush."

Fashion Week, of course. She'd forgotten.

"I'm here to see Mathieu Albret," she said.

The woman's gaze traveled to Aimée's boots, the cut of her little black Chanel under her denim jacket, the cashmere scarf. All courtesy of the flea market.

Did she pass inspection? Aimée wondered.

"Retro and classic, you put yourself together well," the woman said, her voice soft like the purr of a cat. "But he's busy."

Like a cat with claws outstretched.

"Sabine! We need the Milan color swatches."

Mathieu stood with his back to her, riffling through fabrics on the glass table.

"Sabine, don't tell me you didn't find the swatches!" Mathieu looked up and his gaze locked with Aimée's. His eyes widened in fear.

"*Voilà*, you wanted to talk with my husband?" the woman asked.

Mathieu's mouth pursed, and he walked over and put his arm around Sabine's shoulder, pulling her close.

Given the body language, she'd forgo confronting them united as a couple. Sabine would lie. She would have to get Mathieu alone.

"You know her, Mathieu?" Sabine moved a fraction of an inch away from his embrace.

"Of course," he said, a weak smile at the corners of his mouth.

Sabine's eyes narrowed into slits. Aimée doubted she'd been the first woman to appear here with a story.

"But I thought you'd come earlier, Mademoiselle," he said, recovering. "With the collection tomorrow, I'm swamped, but I still need the textile list. You have it, *non*?"

She could lie too.

"*Bien sûr*," Aimée said. "I've got the list and corrections. Over there?"

She pointed to the door.

"*Bon. Chérie*, bring the swatches to the team, please." He kissed Sabine.

Aimée wanted to sink into the carpet.

"Join you in a moment," Mathieu said.

Sabine rolled her eyes and walked away.

He grabbed Aimée's elbow and steered her toward the bergères.

"Never come to my work," he hissed.

"I'm not interested in your marital situation, Mathieu," she said. "Rescind your statement to the police. Tell them the truth."

"Forget it. I love my wife."

His hostile look flickered with something else—guilt or shame.

"Admirable," she said. "Hard to tell from the way you act, but that's your problem. Mine is that I'm under investigation. I'm a suspect, and you could clear me."

His voice changed. "Can't you see this is the worst time? The collection previews tomorrow, a year's work."

"Funny, you had time to come to my place."

He shrugged. "I'm attracted to you."

"And that explains it? Call the Brigade Criminelle. Here's the number."

She passed over Melac's card.

The techno beat volume increased. Reverberations pounded in her stomach. Aimée could have sworn the hydrangea vibrated in their vases.

"I can't. We're in couples' counseling. I won't ruin my marriage or hurt my child."

"Shouldn't you have thought about that before?" She shook her head. "It's not my problem. But the *flics* don't care about that. None of it pertains to your wife or your marriage. Your wife doesn't even have to know."

"Sabine . . . well, she's sensitive. . . ."

Sensitive like an attack dog.

"You've done this before, it's obvious. She's wise to you, Mathieu."

"That's why I can't endanger our relationship further. I want to save our marriage." He folded his arms across his chest. "You know the way out."

She planted her feet.

"Cut the clichés, Mathieu. Want me to tell Sabine about the birthmark on your hip?"

Taken aback, he shook his head. Then shrugged. "I love women. It complicates my life."

"The video surveillance camera at my apartment building doesn't lie."

"What?" His eyes batted in fear.

"You're caught on tape visiting my building."

Too bad the video camera, just installed, hadn't been hooked up yet. But he didn't have to know that.

"So, shall I show the tape to Sabine?"

"How can you threaten me? After how I made you feel, don't you care?"

"Fool me once, shame on you; fool me twice, shame on me," she said. "I give you credit. I haven't fallen for a married man in years; I thought I could tell."

"The collection sales depend on this show. It will make or break our fashion house. I can't leave."

"Up to you, Mathieu."

He stepped back in alarm. Then something in his face changed. "But you have the tape; you don't need me to talk to this *flic*."

He was calling her bluff. Shafting her again. She had to get him to cooperate. What more could she do?

"Let me put it this way. I can't change your statement. But you can," she said. "And I'm sure you will. The *flics* will check whether your wife was in Milan Monday night. Once you lie, it spins out of control."

Mathieu backed away. "Leave us alone."

Now a man in a velvet-collared smoking jacket and slim black trousers beckoned to him. And he left.

Mathieu loved his wife, no doubt the classic case of a husband fooling around on the side to obtain the spice and excitement he felt entitled to. Typically Gallic.

A good lover. But like everything else, too good to be true. Time she forgot bad boys; they never worked out.

Inside the shop on Place des Victoires, the shoes were displayed on low tables and in display cabinets along the back wall. Like a museum. These were shoes that had been worn once, on the runway. A pair of bronze leather strappy sandals with their glossy nail-varnish-red soles beckoned, a trademark of Louboutin. And half-price.

Even with all those fantasy new zeroes in the office's account, she couldn't afford these. Her spirits dampened, she tightened her grip on her bag.

Her phone beeped in her jacket pocket. A strange number was displayed on it.

René? Her hopes were high.

"*Allô?*"

"Look, lady!" A male voice with a strong New York accent came through the buzz of static. "What's with the no-show?"

Jack Waller, the retired NYPD detective turned missing-persons hunter. She'd arranged to meet him at JFK.

"*Désolée.*" How did you say that in English? "I mean so sorry, Monsieur," she said. "But I tried to reach you. Your voicemail's full."

"I waited for the next flight as well," he said angrily. "Then another, when I heard some Air France flights were delayed. Do you operate under different standards over there?"

"There was an emergency with my partner. *Alors*, please understand. I still need your help to find my brother."

"Lady, I'm busy. I wedged you in as a favor," said Jack Waller.

"You're getting a bill for my time." His voice sputtered. "Plus the time I spent in traffic on the Brooklyn Bridge, and then circling at JFK."

"*Bien sûr,* I mean, of course. My plans changed and I called but you didn't pick up, your voicemail was full."

"Try another one, lady."

"Monsieur, please investigate as planned. Check out that address for me."

"Do you think I have time to waste?"

"But Monsieur, I'll pay you."

"Forget it. I'm booked for the next two months, on a high-paying investigation. Another thing, lady: the favor I owed Morbier, consider it paid. I showed up, you didn't. And good luck with a peanut-sized case. Finding long-lost relatives isn't worth the time. Save your money. Apart from my bill."

Her phone went dead. Then bleeped. The battery had run out.

Her heart sank. At a loss, she left the shop and stood on the corner of rue Catinat. She kicked the leaves into the gutter running with water. Then, ignoring the chic displays in the shop window and the chauffeured Mercedes cars parked in a line, she turned, her heels clicking on the uneven pavers. Alone.

JFK Airport, New York,
Wednesday

"*MERDE!*" SAID JACK Waller, closing his cell phone.

Known in other circles as Jacques Weill, he was still trim

even in his sixties, with a mane of grizzled, dyed-brown hair combed back over his large head. He reached for his wallet and made two calls from the public pay phone in the Air France terminal at JFK, using an international pre-paid phone card. The number in Lyon didn't answer and he left a message, as agreed. The other number, a message center in the Bronx from which calls were routed to Langley, Virginia, answered on the first ring.

"Worldwide Delivery Express, may I help you?" said a man's voice.

"Package delayed," he said.

Out of the corner of his eye he saw a figure, the same figure he'd noticed five minutes ago. Instead of paying attention to the flight arrival information board, he could swear the woman was watching him.

"Have you started the tracking process?" the man on the phone asked.

"That's not in my contract," he said. "Matter of fact, my contract's over."

"We'll extend it."

"Same terms?" he asked, ever alert to the business end.

"Correct. And indefinitely." Now this would turn into some God-awful mess that wouldn't end here, he thought.

"Agreed."

He hung up, frustrated. Now he'd have to call this Mademoiselle Leduc back. Come up with some story.

First he needed to think about what he'd say. He'd be more inspired over a glass of red at a nearby airport motel. He belted his raincoat, picked up the briefcase he'd stowed between his legs, and took the escalator down. The cold wind from outside the open automated exit doors ruffled the potted palms. Near the entrance to the Air France baggage-claim area, he noticed the woman again. She was standing by the baggage carousel.

Merde! He hated to think they had caught on to him this quick. A sigh escaped him. He was getting too old for this kind of thing. He edged his way toward the waiting figure. Arrivals crowded the area wheeling suitcases, clogging the space, blocking his way. By the time he reached the carousel, she'd gone.

Wednesday

"CONTINUE, GABRIELLE," SAID Minister Ney. He sat at his desk, eyes closed, pinching the bridge of his nose with his thumb and forefinger. The gilt-framed Corot landscape hung by the marble mantelpiece. Broyard, the assistant deputy who'd been caught with the hooker, sat, legs crossed, on a spindle-back chair.

"According to the police report, Broyard," Gabrielle said, "your actions—"

"Lies. All lies," Broyard interrupted. His visage flushed red. He was handsome, dressed in a three-piece pinstriped suit, a "comer" amidst the phalanx of bright, ambitious, and arrogant Grandes Écoles' alumni.

Gabrielle glanced out the minister's tall window at the dark blot of trees in the Palais Royal, then at her watch. Her secretary would have returned from his "errand." He would have delivered the money. She made herself concentrate on the duplicate of the Police Judiciaire file in front of her.

She had to word her questions with care in order to figure

out how to craft responses to the questions she'd scripted for Cédric, the *télé* host. Cédric had caved when she mentioned his drug-possession file. The things she did in her job left a bad taste in her mouth.

"Tell me in your own words what happened, Broyard," Gabrielle said. "Stick to the incident, please."

He threw his arms up. "You need to deal with this. I told you, it's lies."

"I see. So in two hours, you'll announce on the nation's most-watched evening interview show that it's lies," she said. "And it will be just your word against that of the fifteen-year-old hooker who's proving talkative to the tabloids."

The determined set of Broyard's jaw and flashing eyes boded disaster.

"Remember the upcoming National Archives ruling, Broyard." The Minister had raised his voice. "Fifty thousand sealed documents from the Occupation, a dark era. Unsealing them would expose the ministry's complicity in matters we'd prefer to remain buried. And embarrass people at the highest level of government, even destroy their lives. No one needs the past brought up. There'll be untold damage if this happens. Remember that."

Names like her father's. The minister's uncle. She had to salvage the situation and please her boss. She had to find a solution in less than two hours.

"But according to the report, you mentioned you'd stopped at the traffic light," Gabrielle said. "Did the girl—"

"The whore looked twenty."

"She's fifteen. A minor." Gabrielle kept her voice even. She'd had an idea. "Would you say she could have been arguing with another prostitute? Could she have been escaping from a quarrel, or that you thought she'd be attacked?"

Weak, but a start. She glanced at Ney, saw him straightening his shoulders.

"Broyard, could she have jumped into your car to escape? Could you have thought she'd be attacked? And, not knowing she was a prostitute, you offered her help?"

Broyard ran his hand through his coiffed brown hair. "I'm the victim. It's a plot to sabotage my career."

He sickened her.

"Not so fast," Gabrielle said. "Didn't you insult the *flics*, and I'm quoting here, tell them 'Don't forget that your jobs depend on me'?"

Minister Ney said, "Keep going, Gabrielle. Details later."

"Maybe the officer misunderstood your words? Maybe he misquoted you, when you meant to say 'So much depends on my job. . . .' Her voice trailed off.

"Exactly!" Broyard said. His eyes lit up; he was catching on. He took off his jacket.

Gabrielle nodded. "*Alors*, let's go back over this."

Ney needed him until the resolution to unseal the National Archives was defeated. After that, Broyard's resignation, worded in such a way as to not admit guilt but to protect the junior deputy from further malicious allegations, et cetera. A little time in the country, working with his constituents to create a groundswell of support. Another year, or two or three, and Broyard would be appointed to another post in Paris. The usual.

How many times had she done this? And not for the first time, she wondered how many more there would be.

"We'll return in a few minutes, Gabrielle." Ney motioned to Broyard to join him in the antechamber.

Gabrielle waited until they'd left, then slipped into her secretary's office.

"Mission accomplished, Jean-Georges?"

Jean-Georges looked up from Gabrielle's appointment calendar. He handed her back the envelope that she had asked him to deliver to Robard. "I regret that, according to the florist next door, the old man suffered a heart attack. The shop's closed indefinitely."

Gabrielle's smile froze. Her second attempt . . . would the blackmailer lose patience?

Years of training kicked in. She had to buy time. Dodging mines was in her job description, as well as navigating the ins and outs of the Ministry. She made her feet move and walked to the water cooler, leaned down, and took a sip. Broyard's loud laugh echoed down the carpeted hallway.

"Your son Olivier left a message," Jean-Georges said. "But I didn't want to disturb you."

Gabrielle looked up.

"It sounded urgent. He said. . . ." he hesitated. "He'd seen a ghost."

Wednesday Evening

THE PHONE WAS ringing as Aimée unlocked the frosted glass door of the office of Leduc Detective. She caught it on the fifth ring.

"Leduc Detective," she said, breathless, hoping to hear René's voice.

"I have what you want," said Clémence. Again no greeting. In the background Aimée heard clanging, what sounded like plates clattering. The hiss of something frying.

"You've got Nicolas's notebook?"

"For ten thousand francs I do."

Aimée set her bag on the desk, threw her denim jacket on her chair. "Why should I pay for something he wanted to give me, Clémence?"

"Because it concerns you."

Aimée shivered.

"Bring cash," Clémence ordered.

"Do you think I can lay my hands on that amount? On short notice?"

"You want to know, or not?" Clémence asked. "People will pay to keep this quiet. You'll make money with this, Aimée, but I don't have time."

Blackmail. Clémence was a manipulator. It added up.

Nicolas hadn't trusted Clémence. So she'd arranged the prison visit, counted on Aimée being able to pry information from him. Did she really think Aimée would blackmail whoever Nicolas had named in this coverup?

"I'm a detective, Clémence. I don't blackmail people."

Aimée kicked the steam radiator, without result. There was no issuing warmth. Then she kicked it again. There was a rumble.

"Nicolas didn't commit suicide, did he, Clémence? He was murdered, and now this is too big for you to handle."

"I leave tonight," Clémence whispered. "My kid will grow up in the south, where it's green, not gray. You want to help me? Bring cash and the notebook's yours."

Aimée heard the clattering of plates, a muttered "*Merde*"! Then, "Table 4 wants their bill!"

"*Bon*, I guess you're not interested," Clémence said. "I thought you were sharp. Guess not." She paused. Shouts and hissing noises filled the background. "Sad, too." Her voice was now a hurried whisper. "He said you were the only one who'd be able to expose them. But obtaining justice, doing the right thing, *alors*, that's easy to promise, when you're not broke, hard to accomplish."

A little voice inside told her that if she didn't agree, Clémence would make her own deal with the devil. And then she'd never find René's shooter.

"Where, Clémence?"

"Passage des Deux Pavillons, 10:15."

The line went dead.

She reached for the spring under her desk blotter. With a ping, a slot opened, revealing the hollow space in her desk in which they'd hidden their reserve office funds. A few hundred francs. She took them, stuffing the bills into her pocket. Somehow she'd talk Clémence into it.

In her head she heard René's voice, recollecting the many times he'd called her "reckless, impulsive." He would insist she call the *flics*. But how could she tell Melac, who already thought her psychotic?

So far, her calls and messages to all the clients René had worked with in the last two years had resulted in no clue to a suspect. Not that anyone would admit sabotaging Leduc Detective by wiring the money to its account, much less shooting René.

A new message popped up on her e-mail—the sender, BRIF, Brigade de Researches et d' Investigations Financières, the financial *flics*. She hit OPEN. A curt message informed her of an appointment the next morning with a Monsieur Fressard pertaining to her Paribas account.

Already!

The old station clock in her office chimed 10 P.M. She had to hurry. Her cell phone rang, startling her.

Clémence again?

But Saj's number was displayed.

"Aimée," Saj said. "Checked the business's account recently?"

She pulled up their Paribas account on her laptop screen and scanned the balance. "Another deposit of fifty thousand! It adds up to more than a hundred and fifty thousand francs."

Where was it coming from?

"BRIF's summoned me for a meeting tomorrow."

"Did they request any documentation?"

"Not yet," she said. "But the meeting's not at the Préfecture. It looks like it's at some tax office."

"So it's an exploratory meeting," Saj said. "Ask to see what they have."

There was a silence, then she heard clicks on the other end. Was he delving into their account?

"Think of it in simple terms," Saj said. "They're looking for dirty money."

"And if I use a centime of it, then it's as good as—"

"Admitting you're laundering it?" Saj interrupted. "They don't care about ethics, Aimée; it's not a court of law."

She asked, "But why pick on me?"

"Rather than Colombian cartels or Chechen arms dealers?" Saj asked. "Who knows?"

"*Exactement.* It's deliberate. Someone fingered us," she said. "Someone denounced me."

"Don't forget, arms dealers can afford creative accounting and offshore accounts. You can't."

She pounded her fist on the desk. "Saj, did your contact know anything?"

"The Luxembourg bank that originated the transfer tops the Tracfin blacklist."

"Tops the list?"

"A behind-the-scenes financial investigative unit at

BRIF is monitoring for Tracfin," Saj said. "Tracfin's priority is investigating money-laundering. Think terrorists, drug cartels, Russian mafia money. That kind of thing, along with politicos and their slush funds after the Elf affair."

Aimée knew of the ongoing Elf oil scandal involving the sale of frigates to Taiwan with kickbacks linked to the highest echelons of various ministries. A minister's mistress, a lobbyist, dispensed bribes with a largesse likened by the press to the court of Louis XIV at Versailles.

"Small fish, big fish, it's all the same in their net," Saj said. "And it's a brand-new department."

Great.

"Look, I'll explain tomorrow. You have to tell them the truth. Better yet, find out their computer's operating system." Saj sighed. "In the best of all worlds, then I could attach a data sniffer to the input cable."

"A data sniffer?"

"The little black box that hooks on the input cables and feeds back data," Saj said. "It's basic and classic, like your little black dress."

"And as seductive?"

"Term it however you like. But it would be illegal. It's too big a risk," Saj said. "Last time, it got me in trouble."

Though instead of prison, the ministry had made him work for them to pay off his "debt to society."

If only she could enlist René.

"Let me think about this," Saj said.

"But if I could find out the operating system for you?"

"Can you perform small miracles these days?"

She hooked her toe in the handle of the bottom desk drawer and pulled it open.

"Let me see what I can do," she told Saj and hung up.

She took a box from the drawer, opened it, and rooted around among the relics of her father's old life. There were spy toys he'd used in surveillance; a fountain-pen prototype pistol, a matchbox micro-recorder. And then she found just the thing.

She shut down her laptop, put her jacket back on, and, minutes later, strode under the arches of rue de Rivoli, a street built by Napoleon in what Balzac called his Italian phase. The Louvre's façade stood opposite; the street was dim, apart from a streetlamp's sodium yellow light. She turned right. Her heels clicked on the uneven pavers entering the Palais Royal, the quartier encompassing the avenue de l'Opéra, travel agencies, hotels, and theatres, surrounding the Ministerial and former royal government buildings and garden for which the quartier took its name.

She tied her scarf tighter against the chill. Ahead, the last theatregoers spilled from the doors of the seventeenth-century Comédie Française near Place Colette. A light mist hovered, moistening her cheeks and hurrying the crowd to the Métro. Lights and laughter came from late-evening diners at a café farther down the Palais Royal. Avoiding the arcade, she wove among the black-and-white-striped Buren columns toward the garden. But the gate was locked. She'd forgotten that they closed early in the fall.

Retracing her steps, hurrying now, she reached rue de Valois, which ran parallel to the garden in the center of the Palais Royal.

Minutes later, she found Passage des Deux Pavillons, one of the nineteenth-century glass-covered passages radiating from the Palais Royal. There was a lock on its metal gate. Clémence was not there.

Had she missed her?

"Clémence?"

No answer.

The passage, wide enough for a cart and just long enough for two of them, was typical of the narrow eighteenth-century passages threading to the Palais Royal.

"Clémence?" she called again.

Her words echoed off the stone. The passage steps glistened with mist, vines crawled up the peeling walls, and the stone exuded a dampness. Uneasy, she saw the CLOSED sign in the lace-curtained window of a stamp shop. A trash can stood in front of the door.

She'd heard the background kitchen noises over the phone, someone shouting for their bill, just half an hour ago. A café or bistro had to be nearby. But around the corner on the neighboring street she found only a dry cleaner and a shuttered travel agency. And then, in the dim light, Aimée's boots landed in gurgling gutter water.

She cursed herself for not waterproofing her Valentinos.

But now she could make out the lights of a bistro under the arcades in the Palais Royal. It was within shouting distance of the Passage des Deux Pavillons and still open. She knew the place: mediocre southwest cuisine, but a pleasant place to dine on a warm evening.

Retracing her steps again, she found the bistro's rear entrance on rue de Valois. The only diners, an older couple, sat near the window overlooking the Palais Royal garden. The woman's face was webbed with fine wrinkles; a blue-veined hand twisted the pearls around her neck. The man, who had a white moustache and hollow cheeks, kept raising his shaking hand, gesturing at no one in particular. Aimée looked around. No Clémence. No one from the wait staff was in view, but she heard a loud argument coming from the downstairs kitchen.

A harried waiter wearing a long white apron and black vest appeared. He raced across to the old couple, ignoring Aimée.

"Monsieur! We appreciate your patience. Please, a brandy, courtesy of the house," he said.

After the waiter smoothed the old couple's feathers, removing their dishes, serving them two snifters of brandy, and bringing the bill, Aimée caught his attention. She stepped in his path, and his only choices were either to run into her or acknowledge her presence.

"Pardon, Monsieur."

"I'm busy." He glared.

"Sorry to disturb you, but does Clémence work here?"

"Not any more. She quit."

The waiter took off. To the right, narrow stone steps led to the kitchen. Heat, garlic aromas, and shouts came from below. The chef, in white hat and stained apron, trudged up the stairs, carrying dishes. He muttered into the cell phone crooked between his shoulder and neck. A large man, Aimée noted, clean-shaven, with a ruddy complexion and reddish blond hair curling from under his toque.

"*La salope!*" she overheard. "The bitch left me in the lurch. A whole load of dirty dishes. Didn't even clean up her station." He snorted in disgust. Then moved toward the pantry.

Aimée followed him.

"Took her paycheck and split. And to think I wanted to move in with her."

He shoved the tray onto a counter, flicking his cell phone closed. Cursing, he wiped his sweating brow with the back of his hand.

She thought quickly. "*Excusez-moi,* I need to find Clémence. I've got her keys."

His eyes narrowed. "We run a bistro here."

"But where is she? I've got to give her the keys."

"You can give her this for me." He shot Aimée the finger and pointed to the door. "And leave like she did."

Instead of retracing her steps, Aimée hurried through the shadowy arcades of the Palais Royal. She figured Clémence had left the quickest way and was waiting at the passage, and she'd missed her.

Moisture blurred the air, settling on the gold-spike-tipped fence and misting the double row of lime trees guarding the village-like enclave. Once the residence of Cardinal Richelieu and the duc d'Orleans, in the nineteenth century the Palais Royal had welcomed commerce under the arcades, with the gambling clubs and courtesans. Napoleon had strolled, wooing Josephine in the garden, and the cafés had been meeting places of the Revolutionaries. How many scenes had she read in Balzac, Zola, and de Maupassant set here?

Hanging glass lantern lights cast a dim glow. Aimée ran in the shadows past the small shops under the arcades displaying vintage Chanel and Dior. A long rectangle of darkness stretched before her.

"Clémence!"

But the stillness was broken only by the distant splashing water of the fountain.

Aimée wished there were other people strolling by, that the uneasy feeling creeping up her spine would go away. Clémence could have set her up. The hurried call, the demand for money; it didn't smell right. Too bad the *flics* had her Beretta.

Faint light emanated from Le Grand Véfour, the Michelin-starred restaurant, where Colette had kept a regular table. But ahead of her in the north corner lay crumbling, soot-stained columns, a forlorn, shabby elegance.

The uneasiness filled her. Was she walking into a trap?

She heard a dog barking. As she got closer, the German shepherd's loud, insistent barks escalated from behind the waist-high construction barrier blocking an old military medal shop. The dusty windows contained striped ribbons and tarnished silver medals looking bereft, an *ancien* regime display of faded pomp.

What was the dog barking at? He snarled at her, baring white teeth. She jumped aside, bumping into the metal barricade, and felt a sharp tug as her jacket pocket caught on wire, then a loud rip as she backed away. The dog lunged, missing her leg by centimeters.

"Gaspard! *Arrête!*" Aimée heard heels clicking over the cobbles and saw a woman running toward her, leash in hand.

The panting woman leaned down and caught the German shepherd by the collar. The dog's yelps were now high-pitched and it pawed at the barricade.

"*Désolée*, I don't know what's gotten into him. He's never like this," the woman said.

"He scents something." Aimée took out her penlight and moved the barricade aside. Her light revealed a low black heel in a pile of sand, then a woman's bare leg sprawled against the pockmarked stone and peeling wood storefront. She recognized the sweater coat, the tangled limp blond hair. Clémence's head was twisted back, resting against her shoulder. There were red blotch marks on her throat.

Aimée's heart skipped a beat. She kneeled on the coarse sand and gravel covering the damp uneven stone.

"Can you hear me, Clémence?"

But Clémence's mouth hung slack, her eyes rolled back in

her head. Aimée felt a weak, fluttering pulse in her wrist. Her forehead was warm.

Panicked, Aimée reached for her cell phone. But she'd left it in the office to charge. If this had just happened, whoever had attacked Clémence could be lurking nearby. She looked around for Clémence's bag, for the notebook, but saw only a mesh of footprints in the sand.

"Call for help. Call SAMU now!" she shouted over her shoulder at the woman with the dog.

But when she looked up, the woman was pulling the dog away. Her red-soled Louboutin heels scraped the stone.

"I don't have my cell phone," the woman replied, tugging the dog's leash. "I just took Gaspard out for a walk."

"Go to the bistro, hurry!"

The woman's loud scream interrupted her.

Frantic, Aimée felt Clémence's pulse quiver. She heard footsteps approaching. In the distance, she saw a trio of men, silhouetted in the dark. Returning to finish the job? And here she was with a screaming woman.

But they wore suits, ministry types; one carried a briefcase. "Found a mouse, Mesdemoiselles?" the younger one asked, laughing.

"Get an ambulance now! Her pulse is fading."

Aimée pinched Clémence's nose closed, raised her chin, and started giving her mouth-to-mouth resuscitation.

One man reached for his cell phone. The younger one took off his jacket and rolled up his sleeves. "I'm trained. I've just been certified in CPR for my son's swimming class."

Before she could stop him, he'd knelt down. The other men crowded near the barricade; one flicked his lighter to give more light.

Aimée smelled alcohol. Not a good sign. "You've been drinking."

"A little wine after our meeting? It's nothing."

"Have you done this before?" she asked.

He didn't reply. Intent, he crossed his hands, thrusting hard on Clémence's chest. But he was botching it.

"Stop! You're doing it wrong," Aimée exclaimed.

"I know what to do."

"Just get the SAMU here. Guide them."

Aimée pushed him aside, counted, and made quick thrusts to Clémence's chest. She kept counting, breathing, and thrusting several times until she felt a response and flicker of breath.

"Breathe, Clémence; you can do it," she whispered.

"Who attacked her?" one of the men asked. The one who held her penlight looked familiar. She'd seen his face before.

It could not be a coincidence that Clémence was attacked before she could meet her. Aimée's hands shook with fear, but she kept thrusting until she heard the whine of a siren. With the Ministry and Conseil d'Etat nearby, the area must merit priority response.

"Over here!" called one of the men. The fireman response team appeared with a yellow plastic stretcher and an orange-red canvas bag.

"We'll take over, Mademoiselle." The fireman wore the signature silver helmet and a black anorak with lime stripes and the words SAPEUR POMPIER—firemen—lettered on his back.

He took over the chest thrusts. His colleague placed an oxygen mask over Clémence's face, then clipped a blood-pressure cuff around her arm.

"How long ago did this happen?"

"A few minutes? I'm not sure."

Aimée hoped they'd reached Clémence in time. But then she saw Clémence's face, the chalk-white pallor and blue-tinged lips.

"Shock paddles! Now!" one of the firemen yelled.

She heard the thrum of the mobile shock unit, the dull thud as it hit Clémence's chest. And again. And again. The paramedic put three fingers on Clémence's neck. And shook his head. "I'm sorry."

Horrified, Aimée stepped back.

"Those marks show she was strangled," Aimée said.

"Tell that to the *flics*, Mademoiselle."

Low murmurs echoed off the stone. A few bystanders had gathered under the dark columns: the woman with the dog, an older woman in a raincoat with a clean plastic bag over her hair.

"But that's Clémence! *Quelle misère*," the woman shouted.

The crowd parted; the press had arrived. Bright lights reflected on the aluminized Mylar blanket contouring Clémence's body. A cameraman balanced a heavy video camera on his shoulder. Bursts of light flashes erupted, illuminating the scene: the body covered in silvery Mylar, the shocked bystanders under the darkened stone colonnade.

At the edge of the crowd, a reporter stuck a microphone in the young man's face. "Did you try to save her? A hero. . . ."

"I'm no hero. She didn't make it." At least he had the decency to look ashamed. "We'd finished our meeting. The ministry gates were locked. Who knew that on the way to my car, we'd find this poor young woman?"

"Wait a minute, Monsieur. You work at the Ministry of Culture? Can I get a few more comments?"

"Strike that. No comment."

Several *flics* herded the bystanders away from Clémence's body. "Now if you'll assemble over there and tell us what you saw."

Any moment, *La Proc*, the investigating magistrate, and the crime-scene squad would arrive. Aimée had to avoid the police; she was already a suspect in René's shooting. Her stomach knotted, chills racked her. Her denim jacket lay on Clémence's lifeless body. She moved behind a column and bumped into one of the men, who thrust the penlight into her hands.

Aimée caught a better glimpse of him now. Graying temples, tall, a look of concern in his eyes. He wore a tailored suit and Lobb handmade shoes which she recognized as René wore them too, and held a briefcase embossed with the Ministry of Culture logo.

"Did you see anyone running away, Monsieur?"

He shook his head. "I'm so sorry about your friend."

"Not just her. She was pregnant."

Turning, she kept to the shadows. She molded herself into a dark stone niche, straining to hear the *flics* questioning the bystanders. She couldn't leave the scene until she found out what the woman who'd identified Clémence knew.

"So you knew her. You can identify her, Madame?" a *flic* was asking the woman with the odd plastic bag on her head.

"Terrible, such a sweet girl. Clémence Touvier." The older woman clutched her purse. "She lives just by Molière's statue. We're not safe here. There are thieves everywhere these days."

"If you'll step over here, Madame." The *flic* took the woman aside to question her.

Tires screeched nearby. Orange-red lights bathed the Palais Royal façades. Aimée hid in the shadows, out of sight of the arriving Brigade Criminelle. And then she recognized Melac.

Merde! A record quick police response. She pressed herself deeper into the shadowed niche.

Melac leaned over Clémence. Then he signaled to the medical examiner. Not two minutes later, the medical examiner stood and nodded to Melac. The Mylar crinkled as the medics covered Clémence's face. On the count of three, the medics lifted her onto the stretcher.

Melac gestured to the arriving crime-scene squad, then to the blue-uniformed *flics*. "Keep the scene secured." He scanned the dark columns.

In a brief moment, she felt his eyes combing the niche in which she was hiding. She covered the silver buckle on her bag, afraid it might catch the light. But no, he'd headed under the colonnade in the other direction, toward *La Proc* huddled with the medical examiner.

Moonlight reflected on the leaves. The tree branches cast dark slanting shadows over the bushes. The damp odor of crumbling wet stone clung in the corners.

She wanted to search Clémence's apartment for Nicolas's notebook. Instead of taking it to work, Clémence might have kept it hidden there, she hoped. Unless the killer already had it.

Aimée waited twenty minutes, shivering in the shadows, her hair damp, her knees knocking from the cold, watching the woman speaking to the Police Judiciaire officer. She kept gesticulating, but Aimée couldn't catch a word.

René had been shot, Nicolas had been murdered, and now Clémence. Think like the perp, her father always said. But how could she, without a clue as to how these events were linked? She had to find that damned notebook.

The conversation over, the woman headed around the corner and entered the first door of the adjoining building. Aimée kept to the shadows, out of the *flics'* sight, and pressed the buzzer of the woman's building.

The door clicked open.

Aimée slid inside to see the woman looking down over the sculpted rosettes of the iron banister.

"*Oui?* Is that you, Officer?"

Aimée let the door close behind her before she stepped into view. "Pardon, Madame, but I need to speak with you."

"Who are you?"

"Clémence was supposed to meet me, Madame," Aimée said. "I saw you talking to the *flics*."

"But you were there. I saw you. Why did you leave the scene?" The plastic bag, beaded with moisture, was still on her head, giving her a bizarre look.

Aimée mounted the stairs two at a time to the landing.

"Clémence was pregnant," Aimée said. "You know what that means."

"I do?" An unsure look. "Aaah, *l'amour*, of course."

"*Et voilà*." Aimée nodded as if that explained everything.

"Tell the authorities."

Aimée wanted to get out of the drafty hallway and out of view from the windows.

"Madame, I told the officer what I knew."

"Eh? I didn't see you."

Aimée shrugged. "Then you missed the officer mesmerized by my cleavage behind the ambulance. Please let me explain. It's important."

"I don't understand. Who are you?"

"Clémence's friend, please."

"Just for a moment." The woman relented and gestured to her apartment door. Aimée found herself in a narrow hallway wallpapered with faded peonies from the thirties. The close air, tinged with the woman's perfume, tickled her nose. The hallway opened to a small room furnished with spindly gilt chairs and walls covered with oil paintings. A place from another era, Aimée thought. A roll-top desk baring a ledger was prominent.

A narrow, winding metal staircase led below to what Aimée realized was the military medal shop. Like many in the nineteenth-century covered passages, this woman lived above her business. A cramped life, she remembered from Celine's description in his scathing novel about growing up over a Passage Choiseul shop run by his parents.

"Autumn bites with a full set of teeth, *non*?" the woman said, using an old-country colloquialism as she disappeared behind a lace curtain.

Aimée stood, afraid to move and send a glass bibelot, one of the many paperweights on the shelf, to shatter on the floor.

The woman returned and spread plastic produce bags on a chair. She'd removed the bag from her hair to reveal blond-white waves, a hair color unique to Parisiennes of a certain age. "I am Madame Fontenay," she said. "And you?"

"Aimée, a friend of Clémence."

"And she was pregnant?" Madame Fontenay settled on a chair and leaned forward. "Clémence didn't let on. But what do you want from me?"

A gossip. Good. Aimée would use that to her advantage.

"Will you inform her mother?" Aimée said.

"Me? But I never met her mother."

"Weren't you close with Clémence, Madame?"

"It's a village here." She gestured toward the semicircular window fronting the Palais Royal. "I wouldn't say close. But everyone knows everyone else."

And their business. Aimée glanced at the escritoire. Thick, off-white stationery, imprinted "Fontenay, established 1885 in the Palais Royal."

Of course the woman knew the lives of everyone who lived here and their secrets. Aimée had to appeal to her, coax her to reveal what she knew.

"Madame, who could have done this to Clémence?"

"Not that I'd break sugar on someone's back, but. . . ."

Aimée hadn't heard that circumlocution for "gossip" in years.

Madame Fontenay leaned forward, her small made-up eyes glittering, eager to impart gossip. "Can't say I didn't warn her; I told her, 'Clémence, he's not your type.'"

"Who?"

"What do you mean, 'who'?" Her eyes narrowed in suspicion. "Wasn't Clémence your friend?"

"That's just it. I haven't seen her for a few months, then she called saying she was pregnant. We were to meet, but. . . ." Aimée sniffled.

"Her sometime boyfriend," the woman said with a self-satisfied smirk. "The chef strangled her. And I told that to the *flics*."

"The chef at the bistro? But she just quit."

"A real miser, that one. He wanted to move in with her and not pay rent."

Aimée recalled the angry chef muttering into his cell phone.

"But wasn't he busy cooking?" She stopped before she revealed too much.

Madame Fontenay shrugged. "There's ways. You don't even have to come up for air here, if you know what I mean."

Aimée didn't. "What do you mean?"

"Part of the fountain's built over an old Roman reservoir. Or what's left of it." She smirked. "It's common knowledge to the residents. Tunnels run under the buildings, crisscross the garden. It's like a maze underneath."

Could the chef have strangled Clémence and used a tunnel to escape? He'd have needed split-second timing. But she filed the possibility away.

"*Mais*, Mademoiselle, I've already told the *flics* what I know, done what I can."

"Clémence had a train ticket home tonight." Aimée shivered and hoped that sounded plausible. "But her poor mother," Aimée said, making it up as she went along. "I don't know how to contact her."

Madame Fontenay sighed. "Please give her my condolences."

Aimée shook her head. "But I don't remember Clémence's address, although I know it's near the Molière fountain."

Madame Fontenay stared at her. Her small eyes, like black beads, studied Aimée as she decided. "You don't know her apartment?"

Madame had a brain below that waved hair of hers. She liked to gossip but not get involved.

Aimée wiped her eye. "I lost it. But I lost a lot of things in Geneva at the TB sanitarium. Of course, I don't blame you if you don't trust me, Madame. But would you speak to her mother, Madame? Break the news. I don't know if I can."

Madame batted her eyes in shock. "*Zut*!" She shook her head. "But I told you, we weren't that close."

Madame Fontenay's perfume, a thick floral scent, was getting to her. She knew standard police procedure required that they contact the family for a formal identification. She had to get to the apartment before the *flics* did.

"It's so tragic, just when we were going to meet. I understand your reservations about me."

"*Non*," Madame Fontenay said conclusively, "it's better coming from you or Dita."

Who was Dita? "If you say so, Madame."

Madame Fontenay stood and glanced out the window at the dark hulk of the Théâtre du Palais Royal roof, a stone's throw away. "The last act finished an hour ago. Dita should be leaving the makeup room by now. I'll call her."

Aimée's heart sank. Dita must be Clémence's roommate. She wouldn't know Aimée.

Madame dialed. "No answer."

Aimée breathed a sigh of relief.

"So sad, *non?* It always comes down to passion or money."

Or revenge, Aimée almost added. She didn't believe the chef had strangled Clémence. This was about the notebook.

If she didn't find it, she'd question Dita.

Aimée moved, and the plastic bags crackled under her. "You're right, Madame; even though it's hard to do, it's better coming from me. And the apartment number, Madame Fontenay?"

"32, rue Molière."

* * *

AIMÉE PASSED THE fountain bathed in moonlight with its elevated bronze statue of Molière sitting in thought. Below him, the muse of drama and comedy carved in marble flanked his statue. Underneath, three lions' heads gushed water into a semicircular marble trough cornering the fork of the street. Every so often she looked back on the wet cobbled street, but she saw no one. A shudder crossed her shoulders as she stood in a darkened doorway, waiting for someone to enter 32, rue Molière. A taxi pulled up and a couple emerged. Middle-aged, the woman wore high boots and the man sported a leather cowboy vest. They entered #32. Before the door could close, she slipped in after them.

She found herself in a stone-paved carriage entrance lit by a timed light. To the left a set of stairs spiraled up, and on her right a sign read CLUB EROS.

She looked back to see a woman paused in the doorway, two

flics filling the frame. As they stood there talking, they blocked her exit.

"The third floor, *oui*. What, my roommate?" Aimée heard the woman say.

One *flic* followed the woman, who must be Dita. The other remained at the door.

Aimée lowered her head and walked as fast as she could toward the blue light and open door of the Club Eros.

Cigarette smoke, blue neon light, and the wail of a saxophone greeted her. And a doorman.

"Club member?" he asked.

"Not yet."

"A thousand francs."

"What?"

A nicotine-stained finger pointed to a sign. "Singles admission, plus membership. One thousand francs."

She backed up, casting a glance over her shoulder. Dita still stood in conversation with the *flic*. Aimée rooted in her wallet and came up with three hundred francs.

"*Alors*, Mademoiselle. You pay or you leave."

What could she do? She was stuck.

"You take traveler's checks?"

Wednesday Night

IN THE GREEN languid water, René gasped for breath. He was five years old, caught in the undertow at the beach at Biarritz. Bits of shale and sand stuck between his toes. He fought for air in a slow-motion green world. His arms flailed in the heavy water, battling to rise to the surface; but the current sucked him down deeper in the dense turgid water.

He saw Aimée's face. She looked different underwater, all odd angles, and her blue helmet was crusted with silt. Then the blast of the shot rippled the water and pain seared his chest.

"Monsieur Friant! It's all right."

René grew aware of a hovering green light. He was in a hospital room. And he gasped, trying to breathe. Sweet air. His thick tongue felt acidic, with a bad taste. His throat was on fire, but at least no tube was choking him.

"You had a bad dream. The nurse says you can communicate now." Melac, the detective, leaned over him. His breath smelled of Mentos. Dark circles showed under his eyes.

"W—water, please." His voice rasped in his raw throat.

Melac stuck a straw between his lips. Cool and wet, the water swirled in his dry mouth, trickling over his parched tongue.

"We've moved you to a secure clinic. A *flic's* posted at your door," Melac said. "No worries, Monsieur Friant; and, thanks to your physical condition, an excellent prognosis from the surgeon."

Every part of René hurt. His head pounded.

"But I don't want to tire you." Melac set the cup down on a dog-eared paperback of de Maupassant short stories. "I only need a positive identification. Witnesses saw your partner, Aimée Leduc, shoot you."

Was it a dream? Had Aimée really shot him? Why would she? Something was wrong. And then he remembered the hundred thousand francs in their bank account.

"More water, Monsieur Friant?"

He nodded, took a sip, wet his lips.

"What can you tell me, Monsieur? We need your help to

proceed with the investigation. Witnesses heard you calling her name. We identified the Beretta that wounded you as hers. Isn't there something you want to tell me, Monsieur Friant?" Melac stared at him. "No one can hurt you here. No visitors are allowed. Not even Mademoiselle Leduc."

René's head hurt. His heart hurt. He felt wetness on his cheek.

Melac looked away. "I'm sorry." He reached in his jacket pocket for a tissue, dabbed at the tears running down René's cheeks. "But I have to ask you this. Did you see Aimée Leduc, your partner, shoot you?"

"Too d-d—dark." René's thick tongue got in the way of his words. "Couldn't see."

"Time's up, Inspector." The nurse's brisk tone matched her step as she glanced at Melac. She released the brake on the hospital bed's wheels. Shot a wink at René. "Late-night MRI special, Monsieur Friant. Our tech's warmed up the machine especially for you."

The rubber wheels ground over the linoleum into the hallway, but not fast enough for René to get away from Melac's probing look. The paperback in his pocket, Melac stood watching until the bed rounded the corner.

Wednesday Night

AIMÉE LOOKED AROUND Club Eros, a sand-blasted stone-arched cavern lit by hundreds of flickering votive candles. Floor to ceiling, red silk panels billowed in the breeze of a fan whirring somewhere. A dense humidity mingled with scents of perfume, peppermint lubricant, and other odors that Aimée didn't want to explore.

"First time?"

And the last, she thought.

The voice belonged to a balding man in his fifties wearing spandex bicycle shorts and nothing else. His chest glistened with oil.

This was one membership where she wouldn't get her money's worth.

"I love to show novices the ropes," he said.

She recognized him as a well-known Left Bank literary critic; his picture appeared often in the weekly book review section René read. "I've never seen you at a Rouge et Noir night."

So they'd adopted Stendhal's title for a sex-club event. An *echangiste*, a swingers' club, with literary pretensions?

"Use a little *huile de coude*, elbow grease!" moaned a woman from a cubicle. Aimée shuddered.

"This might relax you." He offered her a black-and-white Pierrot face mask. "Join my wife and me."

Ménages à trois weren't on her agenda tonight. Or ever. She had to get out of here as soon as the *flics* left the courtyard.

A naked woman on a velvet rope swing hung suspended from the ceiling, dropping rose petals on those below . . . couples, trios, limbs intertwined, from what she could make out in the flickering vanilla-scented candle light, a scent that made her want to sneeze.

A rank of people watched from the walls as if glued there. Voyeuristic kicks, she assumed, as some watched and some performed. People from the suburbs, or offices, or a smattering of the elite. The age range varied.

"Call me Xedo. Like to whet your appetite at the buffet?"

Buffet? He gestured to a banquet spread out on a table piled with food. They ate before they got down to business, as if to store up energy for an athletic event. A do-your-thing kind of club. Food, casual partner-swapping, all lubricated by good bottles of wine, she noticed. Where was the other exit? They had to have one for deliveries: the fire code demanded it.

Xedo's glistening bare chest was too close for comfort. Rolls of fat hung over his bicycle shorts.

"I'm meeting someone," she told him, handing back the mask.

He winked. "We all meet someone here."

She never thought she'd be nostalgic for a bordello. Compared to this event, a commercial establishment seemed *passé*. She hoped she wouldn't run into anyone's father or cousin from the Sorbonne. It was that kind of place.

She edged toward the entrance to see if the *flics* had left yet. Then her gaze fell on Léo Frot.

Léo had moved to the Finance Ministry last year. He'd avoided her calls after she'd done him a favor. A big-time favor on his credit authorization, in return for giving her entry into the police database. Not that she felt like catching up. Especially since he was wearing a cloak and, she imagined, nothing underneath. But he owed her. And she'd kick herself if she didn't grab this opportunity to dig for a connection to Tracfin.

"You swing, Léo?"

His eyes glittered. "Call me a gangster of love, Aimée," Frot said.

Self-important, as usual.

"But you're dressed, Aimée. Get into the swing."

Léo pronounced it "sweeeng."

"How's life at Bercy, Léo?" People in the know referred to

the Ministry of Finance by its location, even though it had moved there ten years ago.

"Forget it, Aimée. I come here for pleasure, enjoyment; not work."

"Don't you remember, you owe me?"

"Not officially."

He knew everyone. "Connected" was Léo's middle name. "So, unofficially, can I reach you. . . ."

"Near the whipping post." Léo smiled and swept away, his cloak trailing on the floor.

Dangle something and reel him in, she thought. But at the whipping post, a fur-covered contraption, she hesitated. Flagellation wasn't her thing, especially with a bald man, sweat dripping down his back, moaning in ecstasy "I'm so bad, bad, bad. . . ."

Léo asked her, "Why don't you cool off?"

"Like this?" She unbuttoned the top button of her blouse. Thank God she'd worn her Agent Provocateur black bra edged with fuchsia lace. Tease and retreat, that was her plan.

Her last button undone, she shook her hair back, then forked her fingers through her hair. "You will serve me." She directed Léo to the cubicle behind him. "Now."

"Yes, mistress."

Léo, abject and wanting domination. She'd guessed right. She'd use this opportunity to worm a name out of him. And, with luck, avoid that cape and what was under it.

She sensed a presence, edging closer in the shadows of a figure wearing a harlequin mask. She saw the glint of studs on a motorcycle jacket. A hand cupped her shoulder, pulling her. Léo had disappeared into the cubicle.

The hair rose on her neck. "Get your hands off me."

"I think you and I belong together"

The grip tightened, like a vise digging into her skin, tugging her behind the billowing red silk panels. She leaned down, biting his knuckles hard. The hand let go; a yelp of pain was muffled by the mask he wore.

The exit; where was the exit?

She ran behind the silk panels, reached the door, and slipped outside. In the courtyard, the static of a walkie-talkie echoed above in the chill air. Light shone on the cobblestones from the lit apartments above. The *flic* was still questioning Dita; she'd have to wait until he left. Her mind went back to Clémence's pale face, her lifeless body, the small swelling in her belly.

Then the club's door opened. Disco music drifted out, accompanied by the clomp of boots. She had a brief glimpse of a leather jacket.

She had to leave. Now.

She kept to the shadows, hugging the building, pulled the entry door open, and ran out to the street. The orange, blue, and white light bar on the roof of the empty *flic* car bathed the buildings. Her heart beat to the clicking of her heels on dark rue Thérese. Footsteps sounded behind her, at first keeping pace. Then gaining.

Shivering in the chill air, she turned her head. A dark figure. A man or a woman, she couldn't tell; but the sheen of a black leather jacket that caught the streetlight.

She ran now. Her legs pumping, perspiration trickling between her shoulder blades. Another block and she'd reach Avenue de l'Opéra and the Métro.

At the corner, she spied the sign and ran down the Métro steps into the station. At the turnstile for the Number 7 line, she pulled out her Métro pass. Expired. Her chest heaving, she rooted in her bag for change. None.

She set her hands on the turnstile, heaved herself up, and

swung her legs over. A train rumbled on the platform below. Sprinting, and knowing she'd feel it tomorrow, she ran like hell down the steps. She regretted that last cigarette. Three weeks, two days, and four hours ago.

She caught the train's doors as they started to close, pulled them apart with all her might, and ducked inside.

A man peered at her from behind a newspaper, then sniffed in disapproval. Panting and clutching her sides, she leaned her head against the glass door. A figure ran onto the platform as the train pulled out of the station. The *mec* who'd chased her from the club? But the train picked up speed; the smell of burning rubber and the screech of metal took over as the train entered the tunnel. She collapsed onto a seat and buttoned her blouse.

Thursday Morning

STANDING AT THE kitchen window, Aimée pulled her father's old wool robe around her. Outside, dawn spread a hazy peach glow over the blue-tiled rooftops. Coffee in hand, she studied the Seine's dark green eddies and lace-like foam from a passing barge. Brown leaves swirled in the current, sucked into the depths of a whirlpool, mirroring her feelings after last night: Clémence murdered, Nicolas's notebook gone, René, wounded, in a clinic. She sighed. The list went on. Melac suspected her, and the financial *flics* expected answers concerning the hundred thousand francs plus, the source of which she had no idea about.

And, instead of finding her brother in New York, she still had only two ten-year-old letters lying next to the coffee press.

She picked up the last one, struggling with the simple English, rereading the faded childish script:

> We move all the time. Mom calls it traveling. She keeps your photo and says you're my big sister. Sometimes she talks on the phone late at night in the booths near the public restrooms. But I don't understand. She said "merci" once and that's the only French word I know. Mom doesn't know I found this address, so maybe this reaches you, maybe not. I don't know who my Daddy is—but I don't think we have the same one. You can't write me back, she'd find out and who knows where we'll be. I think we're in trouble.
>
> Julien

She stared at the name: Julien. He'd written so long ago, and here in Paris what could she do?

A wet tongue licked her ankle. "Hungry, furball?" Miles Davis wagged his tail.

At least she'd stocked up on horsemeat from the butcher. From her suitcase-sized fridge she pulled out a waxed paper parcel and spooned the horsemeat into Miles Davis's chipped Limoges bowl.

Her bedroom phone rang. No one ever called her this early except René. She felt a flash of hope. "Let's talk with uncle René, Miles." But Miles kept his head in the bowl.

She ran to her room, caught her bare foot on the clothes she'd left in a heap on the floor last night, and stubbed her toe hard on the bed frame. She yelped in pain. Hopping up and down, she reached for the phone. And she noticed an overseas number displayed.

Jack Waller, of course. With the time difference, it was late afternoon in New York. The answering machine clicked on. Stupid, stubbing her toe, and not reaching the phone in time!

"Mademoiselle, an old address turned up a new lead. I recommend that you consider coming over." His New York accent filled her bedroom, along with car horns blaring in the background. "My contact's meeting me soon. But I'll call you later. . . ."

She hit the callback number. A strange voice in incomprehensible English repeated itself several times. The gist of it, she figured, meant no calls accepted at a public phone booth.

He'd found something about her brother important enough to make him call her. That meant he hadn't given up.

Her cell phone containing his own number sat charging in her office. But he'd said he would call her back. Her message light was flashing. She'd been too tired to check the answering machine last night.

She hit PLAY and heard Melac's voice demand that she call him at his office, asking why she hadn't answered his repeated calls to her cell phone.

Her excitement over Jack Waller's message evaporated. A bad feeling came over her. Melac couldn't have seen her last night. Or could he?

Prioritize. She had to prioritize. Nicolas's notebook came first. If the killer hadn't found it yet—a slim chance existed—she had to search Clémence's apartment and question Dita. And print out last year's tax statement before her appointment.

While the statement was printing, she grabbed the closest jewelry, oversize earrings. From her armoire, she took a geometric-print vintage dress, and found the only shoes she could wear with an aching, stubbed toe, peep-toe blue wedge heels.

Grabbing her secondhand Vuitton bag, she checked among

her lipsticks, glad she'd taken care of that yesterday, and threw in mascara. She took the slim black coat from the rack. Downstairs, she let Miles Davis water the pear tree in the courtyard of her seventeenth-century building.

"Changing your mind again, Mademoiselle Leduc?" Her concierge, Madame Cachou, in the doorframe of the concierge loge, peered at her over reading glasses. "You staying or going?"

Aimée had hired Madame Cachou to mind Miles Davis during her trip. "My trip's cancelled, Madame."

"So the *flic* said. But one keeps asking for you."

"Tall, black hair?"

"More like short, motorcycle outfit. Undercover, he said."

The last thing an undercover *flic* would tell a concierge.

"With a scar here?" Aimée pointed to the corner of her eye.

Madame Cachou nodded.

Manu. He knew where she lived. Had he chased her to her home from Club Eros after all?

"He's not a *flic*, Madame."

"Your boyfriend? I can't keep up with all of them."

"If you see him again," she interrupted, giving her Melac's card, "call Inspector Melac."

"At the Brigade Criminelle?"

"Careful, he's armed and dangerous." Aimée handed her Miles Davis's leash.

Madame Cachou swallowed. Her gruff tone evaporated. "Ready for the park, Miles Davis?"

* * *

AIMÉE CAUGHT THE Number 29 bus at Bastille and fifteen minutes later entered the open courtyard door on rue de Richelieu leading to Club Eros. Fronted by green garbage bins, the club looked gray and anonymous this morning. She mounted the apartment-building stairway, the wood banister smelled of lemon oil. On the next floor, she found the name-plate Dita Louvois. The door stood ajar.

A break-in? She reached for her Swiss Army knife.

But a woman stepped out, cell phone to her ear, shifting the canvas bag she carried to her other arm. Medium height, her brown hair piled back and held by a clip, pointed Louis heels, jeans, orange lipstick, and raincoat to match.

"Dita?"

The woman looked up. Aimée noted her red-rimmed eyes. "Let me call you back, Jojo." She clicked her phone off. "*Oui?*"

"I need to talk with you concerning Clémence."

"The *flics* questioned me." Dita grabbed the doorknob, ready to shut the door. "I told them all I knew."

"It's important. Clémence was supposed to meet me last night."

"You're the one Madame Fontenay called about." Sarcasm layered her voice. "Who are you?"

"Aimée Leduc." She showed her PI license. "May I come in?"

"So you're investigating her murder? But the *flics* said it's part of all the recent robberies in the quartier. A robbery gone bad."

"Lazy *flics* would say that," Aimée said.

Dita gave a little shrug. "I've got a meeting."

"Give me five minutes, that's all."

"What's the use?" Dita's voice sounded hollow.

"I found Clémence with a weak pulse and gave her CPR until the paramedics arrived." Aimée stared at Dita. "But it was too late."

"Just a few minutes." Dita gestured inside.

The apartment—high-ceilinged rooms with raised white plaster boiserie, chipped woodwork, and paneled doors—

exuded a faded charm. With a coat of paint, in view of its proximity to the Louvre, Comédie Française, the Banque de France, and government offices in former palaces, it would go for a lot on the market. Yet, even with its cachet, this arrondissement had the lowest population density in Paris.

Green metal park chairs around a wine cask doubling as a table gave the impression of an urban campsite. A half-empty bowl of café au lait stood on a trestle. Morning light, yellow as gold leaf, slanted from the skylight.

Dita asked, "Why did you lie to Madame Fontenay?"

"Lie? Clémence asked for my help after her ex was murdered in prison yesterday." She left out the part about Clémence's blackmail scheme.

Dita took a tissue from her sleeve and blew her nose. "There's little I can say. We shared an apartment, but we hardly saw each other."

Aimée set her bag on the floor, determined to get more information. A large open leather box with several swing drawers filled with makeup sat near a rectangular gold-framed mirror propped on the floor. Pots of powder and rouge were strewn about.

"But wasn't Clémence in tears yesterday? Her ex had just left La Santé in a coffin."

"Tears? She was more angry at her cook boyfriend, the *salaud*, who was harassing her." Dita stood near the window. "Look, she needed a place, and I needed a roommate. That was the extent of it."

"How long did you know her?"

Dita lit a cigarette and blew a plume of smoke. Her hand shook.

Aimée tried to ignore the smoke blowing in her direction. Dita still hadn't answered her question.

"So, you didn't know her long?"

Dita's eyes were far away.

"Clémence came from Toulouse," Aimée said, trying to draw her out. "But you sound Parisian."

"Born and bred. Like you," Dita said without missing a beat.

Aimée noticed a takeout menu on the table and took a guess.

"Did you meet her at the bistro in Palais Royal?"

Dita nodded. Took another drag. She sat down as if she'd made a decision. "Here's what I know. We had the perfect arrangement. She worked at the bistro. Didn't need Métro or bus fare." Dita crushed the cigarette out in a saucer. "She was very young, a wild child. You know, Clémence had moved around. She got the bistro job from the owner, a fellow Toulousain. Clémence couldn't serve worth a franc, but customers liked her."

"Clémence was four months pregnant."

"Wouldn't surprise me." Dita shook her head. "From that creep Carco?"

"Not according to Clémence. Didn't she talk about Nicolas, her ex in prison?"

"Maybe once. *Alors*, we had different schedules and I needed to pay the rent. Having a roommate gives me extra so I can finish the advanced makeup course and work my way up to do the principals."

"Principals?"

"The lead actors in the Comédie Française," she said. "If that's all?"

"Nothing else?"

"According to her, she'd made her butter," Dita said. "But I'd say she was going to chase the rainbow south. Back to *Maman* and a sty full of pigs."

"Making her butter" meant she had scored big-time. Aimée sat up.

"Who was financing her butter in Paris?"

"She claimed she hadn't cashed in yet, but any minute . . . ." Dita expelled air from her mouth, shrugged. "Like always."

"Dita, she planned to show me her ex's notebook last night."

"Talk to the *flics*," she said.

"Someone murdered her for Nicolas's notebook. If it's here, I need to see it."

Dita's cell phone rang.

"Take your call." Aimée stood. "May I see Clémence's room?"

"I'm not sure you should poke around."

"I'll look around, that's all."

Dita's hands paused on her phone. "Over there. Then I need to leave."

In Clémence's high-ceilinged bedroom, she found a mattress on the floor, a poster of Johnny Hallyday at the Olympia circa 1995, a canvas carryall, and a Bon Marché shopping bag. Several *Voici* magazines were strewn on the floor.

She knelt on the floor and emptied Clémence's carryall: a pair of jeans, cotton skirts, a makeup kit with Bourjous eyeliner. Nothing else.

Disappointed, she searched the Bon Marché bag. To her surprise, she found a man's black T-shirt, Levi's, loafers and a corduroy jacket, all in fashion four years ago. A thick linked ID bracelet, engraved "Nicolas" and a form stamped "La Santé" at the top that read December 13, 1993, incarcerated; October 5, 1997, deceased. Under family members, a sister, Maud Evry with an address in Lille was listed as well as Clémence, as "spouse."

Nicolas's possessions were all contained in a shopping bag. He was a wannabee, eager to join *Les Blancs Nationaux* and elevate his status by torching a synagogue. He'd boasted of it and landed in prison.

She searched the jacket pockets and found only a used caked-hard Kleenex. He'd been someone's brother. Had his sister lost track of him or disowned him? But that was not her concern. Still, she felt she was overlooking something important. Something that was staring her in the face.

Wouldn't Clémence have had a bank account or at least wage stubs, and rent receipts? In the carryall's outside pocket, she found a much-read copy of *On the Road* by Jack Kerouac, and a pamphlet entitled *Eat Right in Your Second Trimester* from the local maternity clinic.

She put everything back with care. Her hands trembled as she replaced Clémence's meager possessions. For Clémence there would be no country air for her baby; no baby. She closed the suitcase buckle.

No notebook. She sat up, her worst fears realized, with a heavy heart. Nicolas's notebook had gone with Clémence's killer. And she had gotten no further.

She pictured the deserted Palais Royal passage, the shadowed columns. The killer could have hidden behind any of them, followed Clémence, and, taking advantage of the deserted place, argued with her, demanded the notebook, and, when she refused, strangled her.

Or had it been the chef after all, using the tunnels, who'd taken her things to make it look like robbery? Unlikely.

All conjecture. What had the notebook contained to make it so important, so incriminating?

Had someone killed Clémence for it? And had Nicolas been murdered in prison? Anyone could be silenced for a price.

She thought hard, trying to put the facts she had together: Nicolas's ravings she'd attributed to paranoia; that "they" were all in on it, he had "proof" and "they think you know who paid me off." Saddened, she remembered Clémence saying "It was big." And, what might make it more important, that Nicolas always seemed to have money. And Clémence's last words haunted her: "Nicolas said you were the one to make this right."

Back in the main room, the sunlight warmed the floor beneath Aimée's feet. From the open skylight came the chirp of birds.

"Didn't Clémence ever mention Nicolas's notebook? Did you see it?"

"Beats me." Dita chewed her lip.

"What about her papers, any bank statements? Did she pay you rent by check?"

"Cash."

"Anything else?"

Dita shook her head.

Aimée didn't want to leave but didn't know what else to ask Dita. She didn't have enough to take to the *flics*.

If only she'd found the notebook.

Dita lit another cigarette. She inhaled, sending a stream of smoke in the sunlight. "She missed Toulouse. Still a provincial." Dita dabbed an eye and shrugged.

Disappointed, Aimée picked up her bag.

Again she felt she was overlooking something. Something staring her in the face. She'd make one more try.

"Clémence was pregnant, with a new life to look forward to," Aimée said. "Her murder's not a robbery gone wrong. It's over the contents of Nicolas's notebook. But I can't prove that, since it's gone. Clémence wanted me to see it. Her ex was murdered and I can't prove that either, Dita."

Dita stared back at her, saying nothing.

She'd hoped to find something here. Anything. "Any chance Clémence kept things in storage, you know, in a locker in your cellar?"

"In storage?" Dita hesitated. "There's a bunch of old things down there. I haven't checked for ages."

Aimée stopped in mid-step, noticing a ring of long, antiquated keys sitting on a shelf of books. "They look just like the ones to my cellar." She picked up the key ring. "You won't mind if I take a look?"

"I doubt you'll find anything but dust and my old ski parkas," Dita said. "But why not? If you do find something, I'll have to send it to her mother."

Dita shoved aside one of the *Voici* magazines on the floor with her foot. "I never read these." She tossed it in the trash, then gave Aimée a questioning look. "You don't suspect Carco, do you?"

Aimée shook her head.

"You want to find this notebook."

"If I'm lucky."

"You think it would lead to her murderer?" Dita's voice held interest now.

"It's a start," Aimée said.

"The door's off the foyer. Go left. Down the stairs to #34."

* * *

AIMÉE PULLED THE string of the hanging lightbulb. A dim light illuminated the beaten dirt floor of the cellar. The humid air smelled of stone and earth. The skitter of something in the corner sent chills up her arms.

Rats.

The faded number 34 showed above a padlock. She forced herself to step over rat turds and turn the key.

The water-stained wooden door creaked open, revealing a narrow storage space, like a medieval cell. Mildew! She pulled her penlight from her bag. Several cardboard boxes, a few stacked clear plastic bins.

No footprints, due to the packed earth floor. She couldn't tell if anyone had been here recently. Still, there might be something to be found within.

She stuck the penlight in her mouth and got to work. The plastic bins held sweaters, a ski jacket, last season's winter coats, and rollerblades. More Dita's style than Clémence's.

One of the cardboard boxes, its flaps folded closed, contained photograph albums. She held the penlight closer. An adolescent Dita with a mohawk, circa late eighties. The next album was of a portfolio of head shots from Dita's theatrical makeup academy.

She tried the box underneath, hoping this one was Clémence's. An old Cuisinart mixer, never used by the look of it, and old recipe books from the fifties, like the ones Aimée's grandmother used: standard French cuisine with tips on preparing the perfect Bechamel sauce.

Another dead-end—and in a foul, dim, smelly cave. Disappointed, she faced the fact Clémence's killer must have Nicolas's notebook. The "proof" was gone. With shaking hands, she closed up the boxes. Who wanted the notebook enough to kill for it? Whoever had followed her to the Métro last night knew Clémence had had an appointment with someone. And if they'd seen Aimée, how long until they found her?

She kicked the dirt. Shoved the boxes back into the corner. And heard a *ting*.

A metal pipe? The boxes were stuck and wouldn't budge. She shone her penlight against the back wall, revealing worn stone and crumbling stucco, and a mauve metal bon-

bon tin, round, lettered in gold *P'tits Quinquins—Confiserie Lilleoise*.

Her favorite bonbons from Lille. Garrel, the sergeant at her father's Commissariat, had given her a tin of *P'tits Quinquins* one Christmas. She'd been ten years old, and she remembered the excitement of twisting open the red crinkling cellophane to reveal the flat, milky sweets, each stamped with a picture of a mother leaning over an infant. The fruit essence melted in her mouth. How Garrel had teased her, insisting that she sing the refrain from the lullaby *Quinquins*.

She unscrewed the top of the tin. Instead of bonbons, she found a plastic laminated *Carte d'Etudiant*, dated 1993, with the scrawled signature of Nicolas Evry. His photo showed reddish hair shaved to a stubble, a fuller face, but the same intense deep-set eyes.

Her heart thumping, she searched through the tin's contents for Nicolas's notebook. A bookstore receipt for a textbook from Gibert on the Left Bank, the 1993 summer schedule of Cours Carnot, a *classe préparatoire* of high-level study courses preparing students for the second year *concours*, the rigorous entrance exam for the *École des Hautes Etudes Commerciales*, the elite business school. She whistled under her breath. That was one of the *Grandes Écoles* and chose only a hundred or so from the thousands who applied to take the *concours*. This *préparatoire*, unlike the usual ones, charged a hefty tuition fee. Even to get this far, Nicolas would have had to have studied day and night, supported by his family, no doubt.

She saw a list of study groups; an advanced economics group was circled. His *lycée* report card bore the high marks of 20. A smart boy, an industrious student. She fingered a junior naval scout badge from Brittany, worn and tarnished.

She wondered what had changed Nicolas from a candidate

aiming for the *École des Hautes Etudes Commerciales*, whose alumni included ministers, an IMF president, and CEO's of the top forty French companies, into a skinhead.

Underneath a paper with his scrawl "My Insurance" was a brown leather volume.

His notebook . . . at last! She peered closer and saw worn Hebrew letters on the binding. What was this?

She opened the yellowed, much-thumbed pages. On the frontispiece were written two names in dark blue ink: Elzbieta and Karlosch Ficowska, and an address in Bialystock. Inside were pages and pages of Hebrew. Was it a prayer book?

What in the world did this mean? Why had Nicolas, convicted for torching a synagogue, kept this in what looked like his childhood treasure box? A trophy from the synagogue burning, she wondered. Somehow it didn't fit.

Nicolas must have entrusted the book to Clémence for safekeeping, his "insurance."

She'd figure out what it meant later. Right now the dusty air and the scratching of the rats were getting to her. Her arms ached from shoving boxes. Last night's sprint to the Métro had taken its toll on her legs. She stood, wishing she was in better shape.

If she didn't hurry, she'd be late for the tax-office appointment.

She put the Quinquin tin in her bag. No one would ever miss it, she thought, saddened.

Back upstairs, Aimée handed Dita the key.

"Any luck?"

"No notebook."

Dita lowered her gaze. "The *flics* called."

"Oh?"

"They want me to identify Clémence's body." She put her

hand to her mouth. "Her only family's an uncle, but he's in prison. After all, she had no mother. I had no idea." Dita shook her head. "But I thought about what you said."

Dita reached for another tissue. Blew her nose.

"You remember something, Dita?"

"Nicolas—" her throat caught and she burst into tears.

"*Oui?*" She hated to push, but if she didn't . . . . "Did Clémence mention why she stopped visiting him? Anything?"

"Bitter, maybe." Dita shrugged. "It wasn't anything Clémence ever said, but just a feeling."

"Nicolas was bitter?"

"Just that one time. *Alors*, Clémence had turned a page in her life and left him behind. But she intimated that when it was new and fresh, they'd hobnobbed with aristos. She thought she had a good catch. But everyone dropped him, I guess."

Aimée thought back to the Cours Carnot preparation, the pathway to the *École des Hautes Etudes Commerciales*. Had his study mates forgotten him?

Dita's brow creased. "*Non*. That came out wrong. I don't mean Clémence liked the high and mighty types. *He* did, but wasn't he some kind of skinhead, an Aryan supremacist?" She shrugged.

Aimée turned, her gaze catching on the trash can.

And then it hit her. "Didn't you say you never read *Voici?*"

Dita nodded. "Clémence must have gotten them for the train."

Aimée took one of the issues of the weekly tabloid out of the can. The cover photo showed a Monaco princess caught topless on some beach, with strategic portions blacked out. "Do you mind?"

"Go ahead. I'm throwing them out." Dita paused. "Do me a favor?"

Aimée nodded.

"The *flics* treat Clémence's murder like nothing, just another blight on the quartier. A danger to the *haute bourgeoisie* living here. But you're different. Please nail the bastard who did this."

Aimée stuffed the *Voici* copies into her bag.

"Count on it, Dita."

* * *

NEARING THE TAX office located in a cul-de-sac off rue Saint-Hyacinthe, once a seventeenth-century convent, still recognizable by its massive arched doorway, Aimée realized that she'd left the tax statement in the printer. No way she'd ever make it to her apartment and back within fifteen minutes.

But Chloë didn't teach until noon. After a few rings, she reached Chloë on her cell phone.

"Chloë," she said. "There's a laptop tuneup in it for you if you bring me the tax form I forgot."

"My laptop's beyond redemption, Aimée." A big yawn came over the line.

"Then keep my blue leather jacket you borrowed," Aimée said.

"A Sonia Rykiel?" Chloë said. "I couldn't take that, Aimée. I wouldn't feel right."

"Please, Chloë, the financial *flics* don't like me already."

"But where are you?"

"Place de la Madeleine."

"*Alors*, you're close to Ladurée."

Aimée scouted the line coming out of Ladurée's Second Empire front door. "Then say chocolate macaroons in fifteen minutes, corner of rue Saint-Honoré?"

"Make that an assortment in one of those precious little boxes they have," said Chloë, sounding more awake.

Aimée groaned silently. "Done."

Aimée made another call and reached the rabbi's extension, only to hear his assistant reply that he was conducting a service. She left him a message, crossing her fingers that it would reach him in time. Then she took out another traveler's check.

Fifteen minutes later, Aimée handed the signature chartreuse Ladurée box of macaroons, perfectly tied with a ribbon, to Chloë.

"You should forget things more often, Aimée." Chloë smiled. She wore a purple sweater, green skirt, pink scarf, and round red-framed eyeglasses.

Almost a match for the assorted flavored macaroons inside.

"Kidding, Aimée. Girlfriends help each other out. We'll share." Chloë looked contrite. "You in trouble?"

"More if I don't hurry."

"Can I help?" Chloë shot her a worried look.

"You've already saved my life." She kissed Chloë on both cheeks, then ran down rue Saint-Honoré, her insides churning; she was late. In the building, brown particle-board desks and partitions gave the place a temporary feeling. She wandered for ten minutes before she'd located the right desk.

"I am sorry I'm late, Monsieur," she said with a wide smile. "I got confused."

"You're not the first to say that, Mademoiselle Leduc," Fressard replied. He returned her smile. "Sit down." He was in his early thirties, she guessed. He sat on an ergonomic swivel chair before a computer screen. A glare reflected on his frameless glasses from the overhanging fluorescent light.

Aimée sat across from Fressard in a space that had once been high-ceilinged. Now, perforated gypsum-board ceiling squares, at odds with last-century plaster medallions visible in the sculpted walls, shrank the room. This chop job on a seventeenth-century *hôtel particulier* had resulted in a warren of anonymous cubicles, without style or attention to the barely visible exquisite period detail and *trompe l'oeil* murals.

She'd debated how to play this.

"I'm here to cooperate, Monsieur Fressard," she said.

"We'll just go over a few things," he replied. On his desk she saw a framed family photo, wife and yellow-sun-dressed toddler; a Smurf coffee cup; a Marseille team soccer poster tacked on his partition. Most of the front-line financial examiners were family men, sympathetic, cultivating a "we can work this out" attitude. Which usually succeeded. Most people called in didn't want to ponder the other option. The examiners adhered to a rigid code of ethics precluding bribery. Every week, the rumor went, the fisc officers met with the full staff and examined their personal financial records.

"Should I have brought my other tax statements or bank reports?" She slapped her forehead; her elbow knocked one of his files over. "*Désolée*, I'm so nervous. I've only got last year's. Should I go and get them?"

He gave her a wide smile. "No need."

She stuck her bag on his desk in the space she'd inadvertently made. "This isn't like me." She pulled out her lipstick tube. "I even forgot to put on lipstick. Silly me, this color's wrong." She took out another tube, Chanel Red, and applied it.

"We're here to take the mystery out of all those numbers." Another big smile. "That's what I like to say. And I'm here to help you."

"Wonderful. I'm not good in the math department. I need

all the help I can get." She set her lipstick down on his desk. "Does this mean you're auditing me?"

"It hasn't come to that."

Yet, she thought.

"Let's look at what's going on, explore your banking history. What do you say? We'll chat a few minutes and take the mystery away."

Did he talk this way to his toddler? Maybe it worked on her. Ivas Fressard play the good guy to gain her confidence, before another bureaucrat or financial *flic* went in for the kill?

"Any chance of a coffee?" She looked around, but all she saw were cubicles and more cubicles. And he didn't offer to get her one.

"The coffee machine's down the hall," he said. "Go ahead."

"May I get you one?"

"*Non, merci.*"

She grabbed her bag, took a few steps, and then came back. "Sorry, which way?"

"Let me show you," he said.

And by the time he'd clicked a few keys on his keyboard to shut down his computer, she'd slid the other lipstick tube under a file on his desk. He walked her across the room and pointed her in the right direction.

At the coffee machine, she took one sip of the espress, winced, and threw it in the trash. In the restroom, she checked each stall. Empty.

From her bag she pulled out the wire attached to a cigarette-pack-sized CCU, a high-quality video recorder. It fit into her pocket. The professional lipstick camera, used by Deauville casinos to spot cheaters, produced broadcast-quality video from a micro video head.

Nervously, she clicked RECORD. It worked. Then she turned it off. Now all she had left to do was to connect the lipstick camera to the wire running from her sleeve, get the angle right, and appear more confused, if possible, than she felt. Not difficult.

Back at Fressard's cubicle, she sat, put her bag on his desk, and leaned forward.

"Feel better?" he asked.

Not as good as she would if she could capture the image on his screen containing her file. But she nodded.

"I've pulled up your credit and financial history."

She gulped. Would every franc and centime she'd ever fudged appear?

"We're financial examiners here, not the enforcement arm. Please relax."

No doubt it was worse than she'd imagined.

"It's this wire deposit that caused us to take a look, Mademoiselle. A significant amount."

She bit her lip. "From where?" She leaned closer, hoping he'd turn the screen so she could see.

"The funds originate in Luxembourg," he said. "We'd like an explanation."

"So would I," she said. "I'm in the dark here. We have no business or clients in Luxembourg." She paused. "Can you show me the data?"

"The information I have is what you have also," he said.

He lied. He had a lot more pulled up on that screen than what she had access to. Just as Saj had warned. She found the wire from the video recorder, inserted it into the lipstick camera concealed on his desk, and nodded. She brushed her pocket, pressing the RECORD button.

"I notice that another deposit was wired from Luxembourg last night," he said. "Can you explain that?"

Her shoulder blades dampened with perspiration.

"I have no idea. We have only Paris-based clients. Do you investigate every foreign deposit?"

"With over thirty thousand deposits a day?" He shook his head. "But this Luxembourg bank's on the watch list. Think hard. If it happens once, maybe it's a mistake. But twice, Mademoiselle?"

Merde. "I'll wire this money back. Close my account. Avoid future errors," she offered.

"'Errors'? Quite difficult to prove at this point. That's all you have to tell me?"

"Monsieur Fressard, I've got no clue as to why someone's depositing money in my account."

His smile was gone. "Then we'll find out in our investigation, won't we?"

Surprised by his abruptness, she leaned forward. "I want to speak to your supervisor."

"He's in meetings this morning."

"Convenient." Her voice hardened. "His card, *s'il vous plaît*."

"In this branch, *we* contact *you*, Mademoiselle." His eyebrows arched. "My next appointment's arrived, so if you'll excuse me?"

"But I'd like a printout so I can check my bank statement." If she didn't ask, it would look suspicious. But she knew his answer already. And it was spelled Tracfin, and he wouldn't utter it.

"As I said, you have the information. *Au revoir.*"

"That's it?" It had all happened too quickly.

"For now. I've noted your comments, Mademoiselle."

He shut down his computer, gesturing her to the hall. "My next appointment's waiting." All *bonhomie* had gone from his voice. "Meanwhile, I recommend you draw funds from other accounts. This one's frozen."

Her rent was due in a week; Miles Davis needed food. What could she do? Her only other account, for office supplies, held only a few hundred francs! Given the speed of the bureaucracy, there was no telling how long this might take.

* * *

IN LEDUC DETECTIVE, curls of smoke drifted from burning cones of sandalwood incense. Aimée peered around the partition to see Saj on the tatami mat, surrounded by several laptops. "I've got something for you, Saj." She emptied her pocket onto the mat.

"Lipstick, cigarettes." He wagged a finger at her. "I quit. So should you." Saj paused. "How did the meeting go?"

"You'll see for yourself."

"A Monsieur Fressard left a message." Saj rolled his eyes. "And his boss. Sounds like you stirred things up."

"Then this should help, Saj."

"Eh?"

She unscrewed the tip of the lipstick. "At least it will get us on the playing field. It's a micro video head." Then she pointed to the packet of Gauloises. "A CCU high-quality video recorder."

His eyes lit up. "You did it!"

"Now you hook it up to your laptop and we pray."

"CCU? Nice, no problem," Saj said. "Just let me finish running these programs."

She glanced at her Tintin watch. No time. With Saj in charge, she could wait and view it later.

"*Bon*. You should see a Luxembourg bank here if I did it right. I've got to hurry." In the office armoire, she found an ankle-length black wool coat, military style, with a double row of brass buttons.

"But where are you going?"

"To the synagogue," she said.

On her way out of the office, her gaze caught on her grandfather's sepia-tinted photo. The one taken after he'd left the Sûreté, in his greatcoat, a dusting of snow on the rue du Louvre, standing in front of Leduc Detective. And a pang hit her. She wouldn't lose Leduc Detective. Not if she could help it.

Maurice, at the kiosk, pursed his mouth in a moue of distaste.

"Looks impossible for me to take Miles Davis to the groomer later," he said. He slapped the newspaper beneath a brick that kept the papers from blowing away. The headline read: TRANSPORT STRIKE.

As usual, the Métro workers had enlisted other transport workers to strike in sympathy. Last-minute contract negotiations had failed, and a city-wide transport shutdown loomed in a few hours.

"Last month we had the teachers' strike." Maurice shrugged. "At least it put Princess Diana lower on the front page."

When wasn't someone striking, she thought.

"I'll reschedule, Maurice. Day after tomorrow?" She pulled out her cell phone to reschedule.

He nodded.

By the look of the rue de Louvre's congested traffic, the transport slowdown, precursor to tonight's total shutdown, had started early. A full bus passed; people ran after it, shouting for the driver to stop. Bicycles and motorcycles wove among the cars.

Aimée quickened her step. A few blocks later, she turned into the Marais. Here the streets narrowed. Little light penetrated the seventeenth-century lanes bordered by high, blackened stone buildings. Glimpses of blue-gray roof tiles glistening with mist appeared as she cut through the small park at Blancs Manteaux. The creak of a swing set, shouts of children playing in the sandbox, and low murmurs of Yiddish from men clustered on the street corner. They wore black fedoras, long curled earlocks hit their coat collars, and white threads hung from their waists. The rabbi, who she'd phoned en route to her appointment, stood among them. She caught his eye and he nodded. Thank God he'd gotten her message.

"*Bonjour*, Mademoiselle," he said, joining her by the park's clipped hedge. "It's been several years."

"I appreciate your making the time, Rabbi Jacob." She extended her hand.

Instead of shaking it, he gave a small bow. "Mademoiselle, it's not my practice to touch women."

Flustered, she clenched her fist. What other *faux pas* would she commit in her ignorance of proper interactions with a Hasidic rabbi?

The tang of autumn lingered in the slight chill. The dampness, the dark corners of wet pockmarked stone, made her glad that she'd worn her warm coat. And it was modest enough, she hoped, for the Hasidic rabbi.

Thick brows beetled in his long face, a pale face framed by a black beard. "You have new information concerning the synagogue incident?"

"I'm not sure, Rabbi," she said. She placed the volume she'd taken from Nicolas's Quinquin tin on the park bench. "Does this look familiar?"

"A siddur." His voice tightened.

She wondered if she'd done something wrong again. A

prayer book? It was quiet except for the laughter of children and the peal of a church bell.

"Maybe I'm not showing proper respect, Rabbi. Forgive me."

"A daily prayer book," he said. He picked it up, opening the pages. "We have another for the Sabbath." He gave her a long look.

"The publisher's address is in Bialystock. That's Poland, *non?*"

"Where did you get this?"

"A dead girl's storage locker. She wasn't Jewish, nor was her ex, Nicolas, who was imprisoned for torching your synagogue."

He pulled his beard. "What do you want to know?"

She pointed to the frontispiece. "Were they members of your congregation?"

He leaned forward, the fine mist on his hat catching the weak light. "I don't know them. This could belong to a family member, one that turned up after the war." He shook his head. "Some things do."

"I'd hoped to return it." Perhaps this promising clue led nowhere. Again. "It seemed as though he kept it as some sick sort of trophy."

"This felon? You mean like the way they desecrate the Jewish cemeteries and take pieces of headstones?"

"Something like that," she said. "But I'm guessing."

"Anti-Semitic incidents happen all the time; in the Métro, at schools," he interrupted. "But we can't hide. Life moves on. We've repaired the synagogue. Why does all this matter now?"

The rabbi's interest in Nicolas's fate faded. He gave another little bow. "Forgive me, but I have appointments."

"Nicolas Evry died in prison right before he would have been paroled, Rabbi," she said. "Last night a girl was murdered before she could give me information which might relate to the synagogue torching."

Rabbi Jacob nodded. "Your father helped my colleague, as you did. All I can suggest is that you try tonight's evening service when the old Polish people attend. But I doubt if it will do much good."

Maybe the siddur meant nothing. But why did it turn up in a convicted skinhead's treasure box? A murdered skinhead? And was there a link to the attack on René?

THURSDAY

SWEAT DOTTED RENÉ'S brow. Gritting his teeth, arm muscles straining, he pulled the blue elastic exercise band harder. Determined he could do this, he pulled a centimeter more. Then another. His arms shook as he managed to join the ends of the thick rubber band together.

"You're pushing yourself, Monsieur Friant!" The smiling therapist, blond and soignée in her masseuse outfit, touched his arm. "I've never seen a patient work so hard so soon after surgery. Of course, we don't want you to lose muscle mass or flexibility, but take it easy. Remember, your wound's still healing."

René wished he could wear regular therapy sweats instead of the children's size, printed with trucks.

"I'm so encouraged by the effects of electrical stimulation on your hip dysplasia," she said. Another smile. "We'll keep it up."

Before he could suggest discussing tomorrow's therapy session over coffee, she pressed something into his hand. "Wonderful work. You deserve a prize. Here." She smiled as she handed him a sticker.

He looked down. A blue unicorn sticker. For a preschooler.

"Must run, my husband's waiting," she smiled. "A *demain.*"

It figured.

René grabbed the walker, made his way to his room and up the aching climb of the three steps to his hospital bed, eased himself between the covers, and collapsed. A big stupid showoff, and now he'd pay. Wouldn't he ever learn? The Leukotape strapped around his waist chafed. For two centimes he'd rip it off, but he knew the nurse would wag her finger and tape him up five minutes later.

He hated lying here, his mind spinning, his wound throbbing, blowing into the spirometer ten times a day to keep his lung moving. And attending therapy with the very married blond therapist.

He stretched his hand, winced, and booted up the laptop he'd cadged from Nana, the young nurse. She was letting him use the department's spare laptop in return for setting up her boyfriend's band's Web site. An hour's job, but he'd prolonged it.

He kept it from the eyes of the *flic* guarding him. Beside his laptop, on the duvet, he saw *Le Figaro*'s headlines: TRANSPORT STRIKE PARALYZES COMMUTERS. At least he didn't have to deal with that.

Below was an article on the continuing investigation into the Fiat Uno reported speeding away from the Pont de l'Alma tunnel, and another on Princess Diana's autopsy report. How could journalists find more to write about that, he wondered. Near the bottom of the second page he noticed: LA SANTÉ SUICIDE RATE CLIMBS—Mental health professionals demand inquiry into recent suicide. His eye caught on a name in the article.

Nicolas Evry. The skinhead Aimée had sent to prison. His thoughts went back to her, the Beretta, the blaze of the muzzle flash.

Before he could read more, the pre-paid cell phone the nurse had furnished him rang. He noted Saj on the caller ID and answered.

"René, check your e-mail," Saj said, his voice excited.

"Any good reason?"

"Click on the link, René."

René found Saj's message. "Okay."

"Can you see it?"

A blurred video feed filled his computer screen. The gray metal of a bathroom cubicle, a dizzying shot over a tiled floor. Then the sharper focus of a woman checking her teeth in the bathroom mirror.

He recognized those kohl-smudged eyes, the streaked blond wisps of hair over the leather jacket collar.

Aimée.

His heart leaped. With effort, he controlled his voice. "Care to explain, Saj?"

"Hold on to your hospital gown," Saj said. "It gets better."

René saw a Smurf cup, upside-down files. Heard the continuous rustling of paper, clicks, Aimée's voice, a man's. But what riveted his attention were the rows of numbers filling the computer screen. Bank accounts. *Their* bank account.

"Aimée's at Paribas?"

"Even better, René," Saj said, his voice vibrating with excitement. "She took this at the investigating examiner's desk at BRIF."

René's jaw dropped.

"All I know is that it involved lipstick," Saj said.

"Lipstick?"

"A lipstick camera. But that's not important," Saj said with impatience. "Recognize that icon?"

René tugged his goatee, eyes riveted on his screen. "Two wire transfers from Banque Liban to our account," he said. "Banque Liban's registered in Luxembourg."

"And has topped Tracfin's blacklist several weeks running," Saj said.

Not good. He felt a tingle in his shoulder. And it wasn't from his arm exercises.

"So this wire deposit jangled the security alerts?"

"Big-time jangle, René. That's the problem. They've frozen the account."

No wonder.

"It doesn't explain why our account received the wire transfer."

"Not yet, René. We'll trace it and find out what's going on before Tracfin does."

René rubbed his aching hip. "A perfect nut for you to crack, Saj."

"Your frozen bank account? That's *your* metier, René."

Sunlight filtered over the potted violets. A gift from Aimée forwarded from Hôtel Dieu after he'd left. A hollowness filled his chest as he wondered if she'd really shot him.

"Who knows what I'd find," René said. What if Aimée had been set up? An unknowing dupe of money launderers, or terrorists? Or, more disturbing, by her mother, a woman on the world security watch list. Had Aimée's imminent New York trip triggered events? The implications spiraled: arms payments, shell companies, offshore accounts. "Too many possibilities, Saj. None good."

He shouldn't have anything to do with Aimée now, for her

sake and his. He'd avoid making contact. Once he got involved . . . *non*. He should leave this alone, ignore the worry for her in his heart. He *should* do a lot of things, he thought.

"Banque Liban spells major trouble," Saj said. "I can't see Aimée involved in laundering money or committing a crime. Can you, René?"

The muscles tightened in René's neck.

"*Zut*, René!" Exasperation sounded in Saj's voice. "I sent you the tape Aimée discovered of the woman impersonating her getting in the taxi. Aimée didn't shoot you."

His heart told him she couldn't have. But his eyes didn't lie. Or had they, in the dark?

René's gaze went to the *flic* speaking with the nurse at the intake station. "What can I do? They're watching me."

"I missed my meditation today, René," Saj said. "*Alors*, my chakras need alignment. I need your help."

He shouldn't get involved.

"Only on one condition, Saj," René said: "you keep this from Aimée. We deal with whatever I find together, *compris*?"

He heard Saj's sigh of relief. "*Bien sûr!*"

"Do me a favor, Saj. Print it out in a continuous sequence. Messenger it over inside a floral arrangement. I'm at the Clinique du Louvre."

He leaned back on the pillow, wondering what he'd agreed to. None of his hacker friends who'd played with the big boys at Tracfin had emerged unscathed. But Aimée had a lot more to lose than hackers might. A business: her livelihood. His.

Thursday

AIMÉE LOCATED THE Cours Carnot *classe préparatoire* in a building behind the Palais Royal. Prime real estate, despite the soot-stained façades. When apartments here appeared on the market, they went from the mouth to the ear, as the saying went, snapped up via a concierge's hint before the previous owner lay cold in his grave.

Cours Carnot prepared students for the tough second- and third-year entrance exams required for the École des Hautes Etudes Commerciales. She'd come up with a story to lead her to the students in the study group Nicolas had circled. And she didn't have much time.

"*Bonjour*," Aimée said. "I hope you can help me, Madame."

The middle-aged receptionist shot her a quick smile. Hennaed hair, too much makeup. Thick silver bracelets clanked on her wrist.

"Take an enrollment brochure," she said. "That answers most questions."

The small reception area, no bigger than a closet, branched off to a hallway to where, Aimée figured, lay classrooms. A pot of orchids on a stainless-steel cube, along with an uncomfortable metal tubular chair, completed the ensemble.

"*Merci*, Madame . . . ?"

"Delair. A Cours Carnot application's inside the brochure. I assume this concerns your brother or sister who wishes to prepare for the concours?"

"My brother." Aimée took a tissue from her bag. "I need to inform my brother's friends of his funeral."

"*Quoi?*"

"It's terrible. So sudden."

"*Désolée*, Mademoiselle, but. . . ."

"See." She pulled out list and pointed to the circled group. "My brother Nicolas Evry attended your course four years ago in 1993. I'm Maud Evry." She used the name of the sister from the La Santé list of relatives. "I live near Roubaix and don't know how to contact his study group friends." She paused. "He spoke of them so often. Yet I can't remember their names. Could you help me?"

"1993? Nicolas Evry? But I worked here then, and I don't remember him."

Aimée felt her lead slipping away. Maybe he'd never enrolled. Maybe she'd be back at zero. Again.

"Could you check, please? It would mean a lot to me."

The woman set down her pen. Her silver bracelet tinkled on her wrist. "As I said, I'm not familiar with his name. Of course, there's also a confidentiality issue."

Aimée sensed a slight thaw in her attitude. "Just an address, so I could send the funeral announcement? I'm sure his friends would want to know." She leaned forward. "A suicide." Aimée blotted her eyes with a tissue.

"My condolences. But I'll have to ask the director."

If the director got involved, it became more complicated. And would take more time. Aimée's gaze rested on the file cabinet drawer with A-Z listings from the year 1997. From where she stood, her view was blocked, but she figured the lower file drawers held the previous years.

"I'd appreciate that, Madame Delair. I'm sorry to take so much of your time."

Aimée counted on the woman going to the director's office. Instead, she reached for the phone. "He's teaching a course. I forgot."

Aimée dabbed her eyes again. "It's not your problem, but

since we're from the North, the funeral's so small, and my parents *alors*. . . ." She shrugged. "If none of his friends come. . . . It's hard enough for them right now."

The woman's eyes softened as they gazed at the metal Quinquin box Aimée held. "You're a real Lilleoise, eh? My father's side came from Roubaix. Whereabouts do you live?"

She'd never gone to Roubaix, didn't know the North at all.

Didn't every city have a rue Jean Jaures, named after the socialist? But she didn't want to chance it. "But now with my job, I live in Lille most of the time. On rue des Arts," she said, reading the Quinquin manufacturer's address on the tin.

"I love Lille. All the art nouveau architecture in the *vieux quartier*. A real renaissance of a former industrial town." Before the woman could wax more specific about the wonders of Lille, Aimée glanced at the wall clock.

"*Excusez moi*, but my parents arrive at Gare du Nord in twenty minutes."

"Then I'll have the director contact you."

Just what she feared. A wasted trip.

"I'm sorry, there's just so much to do." She wrung her hands. "And so little time before the funeral. I'm overwhelmed."

The woman patted her arm. "*Calmez-vous*. Hold on a moment."

The woman took off down a hallway. She had to grab this chance. Feeling guilty but not guilty enough to stop herself, she slipped behind the counter, leaned down, and found the 1993 drawer right away. She opened it and saw folders labeled EXPENSES subcategorized "EDF" and "Tax."

She pulled open another drawer. Files labeled MINISTRY OF EDUCATION GUIDELINES and EDUCATION BROCHURES.

Footsteps sounded in the hall. Voices. Only seconds until

the woman came back. Perspiring, she scanned the reception desk. Underneath it was a cabinet labeled ENROLLED STUDENTS and another marked PAST STUDENTS. She slid it open. Names and more names. Riffling through at the back, she found "Spring 1993" and kept going until she found "Fall 1993."

With a quick grab she took it, stuffed it under her coat, and edged out from behind the desk.

"Mademoiselle?"

Footsteps. Aimée sneaked past the orchid and into the tubular chair. She blew her nose.

"I thought you'd left," Madame Delair said with raised eyebrows. "Where were you?"

Aimée sniffled, then covered her face in her hands. "I'm sorry, I can't wait any longer."

"The director concurs, Mademoiselle. Nicolas never enrolled."

Aimée stood. She had to get out of here fast. "I apologize. A mistake."

There was an accusing look in Madame Delair's eyes. "The director remembers Nicolas well. Even though he offered Nicolas a tutoring position in lieu of partial payment, Nicolas still couldn't afford to live and study. Nicolas mentioned that his family discouraged him: you in particular, Mademoiselle Evry."

Is this what had changed Nicolas?

"Such a bright boy, too!" Madame Delair said.

Aimée had found what she came for and opened the door.

"So just now you're feeling guilty?" Madame Delair's mouth tightened. "I'm sorry for your loss, but what right do you have to come here now? None of his friends would appreciate your contacting them."

But Aimée disagreed. If not, she'd find out.

* * *

AIMÉE TOOK THE short cut through Passage des Deux Pavillons, which was now open. The passage, covered by a glass roof in an iron framework, contained two levels connected by a dilapidated staircase. Once gas-lit, it had changed little since the Duc d'Orleans's architect had designed it. The nineteenth-century working ladies, nicknamed *hirondelles* after the swallows that had once lived there, had spied on prospective clients, then swooped down to bring the men to their love nests in the small rooms above.

Now she noted a rare-book shop with a closed sign in the window, a pipe shop, and a store selling only ribbons, all a bit dated. She wondered how they stayed in business.

She needed to sift through this file she'd taken to find Nicolas's friends. If any. And she hadn't eaten all day. Emerging into the sunlit precincts of the Palais Royal, she could take care of two things at once.

* * *

AIMÉE SAT AT an outdoor table of the Palais Royal bistro where Clémence had worked. An early-afternoon warmth lingered. Light filtered through the canopy formed by the double row of lime trees. Shadows dappled the metal park chairs. A cool spray from the fountain misted her cheek. She set the Cours Carnot file on the table.

"You're lucky," the waiter said, handing her a menu. "We usually stop outside service in October, but with this weather!" He smiled. "Something to drink? Or would you like to order?"

"A Salade Niçoise, *s'il vous plaît*," she said, without looking at the menu. "Does Carco work today?"

The dark-haired waiter stepped back. He looked about twenty and, from the perspiration on his brow, nervous. Or inexperienced. Or both. "He's late."

Or detained. No doubt the *flics*, after conversations with Dita and Madame Fontenay of the medal shop, had detained him in the *garde à vue*. That could stretch for twenty-four hours.

She sensed the young waiter's hesitation.

"Did you know Clémence?"

"Clémence? I think she quit."

"She was strangled." Aimée pointed to the blackened stone arcade. "Last night, right there, after work."

His Adam's apple moved as he gulped.

"My uncle called me in to work this morning, that's all I know."

"Carco's got a temper," Aimée said. "Did her quitting last night send him over the edge?"

He adjusted his rolled-up shirtsleeves and brushed off his black vest. "Carco's from Marseille. A hothead. Like all of them from the south."

"See, you do know things," she said. "Your name?"

He shrugged. "Paul. You some kind of *flic*?"

"A detective. I knew Clémence," Aimée said. "We'd arranged to meet last night."

"Carco blew up, *oui*," Paul said. "The gas line to the range snapped. The kitchen ground to a standstill. On top of that, Clémence quit. Like that. The way my uncle tells it, Carco threatened to walk out, too, if we didn't fix the stove."

"I heard Carco talking on his cell phone, Paul," she said. "He didn't seem too happy with Clémence about ending their relationship."

Paul's cheeks expanded, then he expelled a gust of air. "Ask him. Ask my uncle. They worked on the range until the *flics* took him to the Commissariat."

She fixed her gaze on him. "Did you know that Clémence was four months pregnant?"

His eyes bulged. He made a sign of the cross.

"Anything else you want to tell me, Paul?"

"Terrible. *Alors*, Carco's all bluster. He'd never hurt her. Talk to him."

"I plan to. And I'd like something to drink," she said. *"L'eau de Chirac."* Tap water, as everyone referred to it these days, after the presidential election.

His mouth turned down. Big spender. *"Bien sûr."*

She crossed her black-stockinged legs, rubbed her sore toe. And in her bag found the crumpled pack of filtered Gauloises.

Just one drag. That's all, she promised herself. She struck a match and lit the tip; but instead of letting smoke fill her lungs, enjoying that rush, she flicked the cigarette onto the gravel and ground it out.

The slow swirl of blue smoke rose from the gravel beneath her feet. Aimée peered over her oversize sunglasses at the dragonfly buzzing in the rose bushes bordering the garden. The warm rustling air enveloped her, accompanied by the muted click of clippers at work on the hedge. A nanny pushed a stroller under the lane of manicured trees. Birds chirped from nests in the arcades. An office worker sat with her feet up on the lip of the fountain.

Peaceful and quiet. Hard to believe that Clémence had been murdered here last night. She opened the thick Cours Carnot file and found stapled dossiers. About fifty. Each contained a front page with the student's name, address, field of study, enrollment, attendance, sessions, and dates. The following two pages contained matriculation exams studied for and study-group attendance.

Now to winnow it down. But how? She didn't know the exact exam Nicolas had aimed at. Most of these students by now had passed the exam and were attending a *Grande École* or had even graduated.

She remembered he'd circled the summer/fall study group in the papers she'd found in the cellar. All she had to do was search through each dossier, find those who had attended that summer's study group, and come up with a list.

After an hour spent over a Niçoise salad and fifty dossiers, she'd culled it to ten names and phone numbers: the ten who might have known Nicolas. With luck, some had been his friends. And with more luck, they'd talk to her and reveal what had turned Nicolas toward the neo-Nazi *Les Blancs Nationaux*, the significance of the Jewish prayer book, and what the connection was to René.

Her mind flickered back to her little brother's letters. What happened to *him* in the past ten years? How had he turned out? Was he in touch with her mother?

With a sigh, she pushed this thought away. She inhaled the fragrance emitted by the rose bushes, felt the sun warming her back, and ordered an espress. Near the small cannon converted to a sundial, an old woman in a tattered overcoat tossed bread crumbs to pigeons flocking at her feet. A pigeon ate from her hand. A look of rapture crossed the old woman's face.

Paul set down the demitasse of espress she had ordered, with a small square of chocolate beside the sugar cube on the saucer.

"Paul, may I talk to your uncle?"

"He's arranging with the priest at Saint Roch to offer a mass for Clémence and her baby." His throat caught.

"Do you know anyone who'd want to hurt Clémence?"

He shook his head. A man raised his hand at a nearby table for his bill.

"*Excusez-moi*," Paul said. "I've got to work."

So did she.

The Cours Carnot files presented tedious, time-consuming work, the reasons she'd hated criminal investigation. But her father always said if you didn't fire the shot, you couldn't hit the target.

Aimée pulled out her cell phone and got to work. She reached the voicemail of the first three students. She left a message saying she was conducting a Ministry of Education survey concerning their educational path and attainments after taking the Cours Carnot. Two phone numbers didn't answer; the next had been disconnected. She tried the next few; answers ranged from "My parents made me sign up" to "I didn't attend much." After thirty minutes, she had yet to speak to a single student who remembered Nicolas.

Aimée rubbed the grid marks left on her thighs from the cross-hatching of the rattan chair. Scraps of conversation floated from the benches obscured by trees . . . "Velvet cuf-flinks, body jewelry."

Not much raised eyebrows in this quartier; one kept one's private life behind the salon doors. Curious, she leaned over the marble-topped table, straining to hear more. Under the windows of Colette's former apartment two well-preserved matrons were sharing a bunch of purple grapes, lace handker-chiefs on their laps.

". . . murdered in that sex club?"

"*Non!* Can you imagine, they found the girl right here!" one said. "We're not safe in our beds!"

So word had spread in this village-like enclosure, this exclusive slice of the first arrondissement, whose inhabitants ranged from senior Banque de France and Ministry officials to concierges, shop owners, and bourgeoise matrons like these women.

She downed her espress. No time to get lulled into relaxation by the gushing fountain. She left a thirty-franc tip with her bill, crossed the gravel, and stepped under the arcade into the bistro.

From the look of the place, they needed wait staff and the sooner the better. Instead of waiters and waitresses preparing for the evening service with fresh place settings and floral arrangements, dirty dishes, soiled wine glasses, and empty wine bottles littered the tables.

On narrow rue de Valois at the bistro's back entrance, she recognized Carco right away in his white side-buttoned chef's shirt and black-and-white checkered trousers. He smoked, leaning against the crumbling wall. A pile of cigarette butts clogged the gutter at his feet.

To Carco's right stood an open semicircular window flush with the pavement, through which a chute led to the basement. Wooden produce boxes were piled next to it.

At last. She rooted in her bag, found her pack of Gauloises, and pulled one out.

"Got a light?"

He produced a lighter from his pocket. Flicked it. He had such big meaty hands. Strangler's hands?

"I saw you last night." Carco's forehead creased. "You're the detective."

Thanks to Paul, the weasel, informing him.

"And you've got a temper," she said.

"So her arty roommate hired you? The bitch."

No one had hired her. She could use a paying job. But her neck was in a noose and Melac burned to tighten it.

"Not at all," she replied. "Right now she's down at the morgue identifying Clémence's body."

The smoke filled her lungs and gave her a jolt.

"You're angry, a hothead," Aimée continued. She expelled a plume of smoke. "But the *flics* didn't question you very long, did they?"

He fixed a glare on her. "Could I wring Clémence's neck with ten *plats du jour* in preparation, appetizer garnishing, a *sous chef* at my side, the patron at my heels, and a broken stove to repair?"

He ground his cigarette under his shoe.

"Last night I never left that furnace of a kitchen for a minute. Not even for a cigarette. Even the owner backed me up." He hefted a crate of green peppers, shot it down the chute. "The *flics* believe me."

They'd let him go.

"You'd wanted to move in with her, right, Carco?" she said. "She refused. That made you livid. You followed her."

"Follow her? No point." He shrugged. "*C'est fini.*"

"Then what do you think happened, Carco?"

A mixture of defeat and sadness washed over his face.

"*Tant pis,* I should have known she had someone else," he said. "She was two-timing me."

Another man?

"With her ex in prison?" Aimée said. "I think she just felt sorry for him."

"I don't know." He shook his head.

"But you harassed her."

He leaned down to pick up some loose white asparagus that had fallen from a crate into the gutter.

"*Zut!* Try cooking for a bistro of people with no gas and one waiter," Carco said. "I didn't even know she'd quit until I saw the orders sitting there getting cold."

No chef allowed his orders to go cold. She believed him.

Despite the heat, a frisson ran down her arms. Granted that Clémence worked in a busy understaffed kitchen, still she could have told Aimée more over the phone. Clémence had held something back. Earlier, she'd refused Aimée's offer to accompany her to La Santé. Run away angry. Then her insistence that they meet. And for a brief moment she wondered again if the alleged notebook had been a ruse. A way to lure Aimée into the passage, a deserted place.

She realized Carco's eyes were tearing. "The baby wasn't mine. She hadn't let me touch in her months. Maybe she didn't know whose it was."

"Could she have gone to meet this other man?"

"I think she wanted to get the hell out," he said. "Someone called her here every night."

Thoughts spun in Aimée's head.

"A jealous man, another boyfriend?"

Was that what this was about? That *mec*, Manu?

Rather than answer her, he stomped into the bistro.

After her visit to the prison, Clémence had known too much. Had her call to Aimée complicated things, some arrangement that backfired? Aimée imagined someone—a contact—catching up with Clémence, demanding the notebook or that she keep quiet. Say Clémence refused or demanded money, attempted blackmail, desperate to leave, for some reason Aimée didn't know. An argument, and the killer took advantage of the deserted passage to stop her, choking her, then stole her bag to make it appear like a robbery.

And who was the person calling her at the bistro?

If the notebook existed, was Aimée the only other person to know about it? Did it contain the proof that Nicolas had been bribed? Say the killer knew, too. And had trailed her to the sex club, then to the Métro.

Was she next?

Goose bumps shivered her arms.

She made her way to Passage des Deux Pavillons. A caged white-plumed cockatiel warbled from an upper window; a woman shook a dust rag in a doorway. The shops lay shuttered and closed.

Nothing here.

Aimée walked back the few steps to the Palais Royal and paused amidst the alternating slants of light and shadow in the columned arcade.

"Papa, I'm a statue." A small boy stood on one of the black-and-white-striped Buren columns that were ranked in assorted heights.

"Get down, Alain," his father said. Khaki pants, guidebook in hand. A tourist from the provinces. Beside him a woman droned, reading aloud from her guidebook.

OTHER THAN STRIPS of yellow crime-scene tape on the barricade fronting Madame Fontenay's medal shop, no evidence remained of Clémence's murder. A closed sign hung behind the shop's metal shutters.

Across from her, a man wearing a blue work coat embroidered with *Monuments et Travaux* beckoned to a hardhat. "Over here. Major water leak. You know what that means!" he said to the worker.

"Means my spanner turns off the water valve if you're lucky." He grinned. "Depends on the bolt size. And how much water's in the tunnel." A moment later, he made his way toward Madame Fontenay's building, took out a ring of keys, inserted one, and opened the door she'd entered last night. Aimée followed. She stood again on the black-and-white-tiled floor at the foot of the staircase's metal rosette-ornamented banister.

A side door in the foyer leading downstairs stood open. Cranking noises and the smell of mildew came from the stairway. She made her way down the dark stone stairs into a subterranean tunnel. Could Clémence's killer have escaped this way?

Her cell phone vibrated in her pocket.

"*Oui?*"

"Mademoiselle, concerning the Cours Carnot survey. Would participation be paid for? Is remuneration involved?"

After all those calls, her first bite. "Hold on a moment. Let me go to a place with better reception." She ran back up the stairs, into the foyer.

"*Allô*, Monsieur. Can you hear me?"

"Loud and clear."

"That depends on which study group you attended," she said. "Your name, please?"

"Audric Loubel," he said. "Our study group met for a year between 1993 and 1994."

Promising, she thought. "*Un moment*, please. I'll consult my notes." She took out the first thing in her bag, the *Voici* magazine, and rustled some pages.

"Bear with me, please. They've made the survey guidelines so specific," she said. "We provide honorariums yes, to specific groups and students we track."

"Like who?"

"Of course, I've left the files at my office. Let's see, I wrote down a name. Nicolas Evry. Were you in his group?"

Silence.

"There's a mistake," he said.

"In what way?"

"Nicolas didn't attend any courses," he said, disappointment in his voice, "although his friends did."

She had to draw him out.

"That could explain a few things." She gave a little sigh. "Can you help me correct this information then? I'll need to verify that fact with you and his friends."

"But Cours Carnot knows. . . ."

"Well, they're the ones who furnished this information. I'd like to take your word, but that involves reconfiguring the survey."

"It's as I told you: Nicolas hung around us." Audric sounded young. "That's all."

A door slammed. The sound of scraping reached her ears.

"Actually, Audric, you haven't settled this to my satisfaction. Let's talk in person. Then I can get some answers and pay you today."

"How much?"

Greedy, too.

"Let's talk. Meanwhile, I'll check," she said. "Say in half an hour?"

"I'm late for class," he said. "I'll call you back later."

The line went dead.

She stared at the sheet with his address on rue des Bons Enfants, not five minutes away. And he'd known Nicolas.

The hardhat emerged from the stairs. "I need more tools to stop that leak. Meanwhile, close tunnel 3 in the south wing in case," he said into his cell phone.

The tunnel network under the Palais Royal. For now it would wait. She had to catch Audric.

Thursday

"Complaining again, Sicard?"

The La Santé prison guard handed Sicard his release papers at the last checkout booth before the gate. "Where's your happy face?"

"Right here," he said with an obscene gesture. I'll be happy never to see a sadist like you again, he thought. His shoes pinched, his old jacket hung from his shoulders. He'd lost weight inside, yet his feet had swelled. Go figure.

How many years had he waited for this moment, walking out La Santé's gate a free man? In his dreams, his girlfriend was waiting with open arms. They'd drive away in her car, her red hair trailing in the wind, to a restaurant. Good food, real food, then they'd spend the night and the next day in bed. He'd rediscover and explore every curve in her body, surfacing only to eat. And he'd go to the bank, find money waiting from his last job that his "friends" who put him in here had promised.

But, of course, the redhead had moved on two years ago, and the *mecs* he'd done the job with had served time at Clairvaux, the maximum-security prison up north, and never made good on their promise to put his share in the bank.

What he found was dust swirling in the warm wind, grit in his eyes, and no one waiting.

Still, the air tasted sweet. And he was free. Free with the twenty francs he'd had in his pocket years ago when he entered and the five hundred earned from working in the prison kitchen.

Not the worst, he thought. He could live two, three days? At the dock loading job he was qualified for (and that was several years ago), he'd earned less than a living wage. That's what had gotten him into La Santé in the first place.

Instead of the bus, he walked. He felt light, walking alone on the wide dusty boulevard, the leaves crackling under his feet, the air warm and enveloping. No walls, no alarms, no damp cell or guards banging on the bars, no fetid breath down his neck. Just a woman and a little girl hand in hand waiting at the bus stop. Real people.

So what if the woman looked at him curiously, eyeing his outdated jacket, his mincing walk in his too-tight shoes, his prison haircut, and pulled her daughter closer.

He'd paid his debt to society. Now it owed him. At least one segment of society would pay. He'd worked it all out. In his shirt pocket lay Nicolas Evry's gold mine that he'd found sewn into his cot's mattress in their cell.

Too late for Nicolas to use it now. But he could, with a little help. Sicard smiled as he walked down the boulevard, inhaling the free fresh air.

Thursday

AIMÉE WATCHED FOR Audric to emerge from his building, a limestone *belle époque* affair framed by a sculpted roofline frieze depicting nymphs holding bunches of grapes over long pillars supported by busty caryatids.

Her skirt stuck to her legs. The variable October weather ran chill one day, then blazing hot like today. But it would not be much longer until autumn arrived, with a cold wind under pewter skies.

She kept an eye out for Audric, now twenty-three years old, to match him with the blurred Xeroxed photo on his four-year-old *Carte d'étudiant*. Across the street, whiffs of chlorine came from Gymnastic, a health club, and she longed to get in the pool. Her thighs could use fifty laps.

Not two feet away from her, an old man sucked on a hand-rolled cigarette, picking a flake of tobacco from his mouth. He gave a hacking cough, hawked, and wiped his mouth on his corduroy jacket sleeve, the whole time giving her the eye.

"Old pots make the best soup, Mademoiselle," he said, leering.

"But I don't cook, Monsieur," she said.

"You go the other way?" He licked his cracked lips, fumbled with his fly.

A dirty old man, and in this heat. She sighed.

"Not the time to take out the 'bishop'." She pointed to the Commissariat on the corner. "I complain, and the *flics* will curl your nose hair."

He took off down the pavement.

She fanned herself with the copy of *Voici*. No Princess Diana photo on the cover, unlike all the others. Instead, a photo collage of former celebrities *du jour*, now replaced by new ones. The paparazzi ate them up and spit them out faster than the old man now hawking up phlegm down the street. Not a pretty sight.

She glanced at the pages of the magazine issue which was, she now saw, dated December 1993. Holidays in Val d'Isere, skiing on the slopes. Stick-like models and starlets in attire involving beaded miniskirts and fur vests at aprés-ski parties, snowmobiles parked in front of exclusive chalets with the aristos and their young throwing snowballs, a Baron and Baronne something in front of roaring walk-in fireplaces.

But it made some sense, since Nicolas had been awaiting trial in La Santé in 1993. Still, she wondered why he had kept these old magazines. Before she could ponder further, a small door in the large dark green entry opened and a figure pushing a bicycle emerged from Audric's building.

She spotted his short brown hair, pockmarked face, and thick black glasses. Audric hadn't changed much from his photo in four years. He paused on the cracked pavement, then headed up the street, walking his bicycle. He limped, despite a thick-soled shoe; one leg seemed shorter than the other.

A wide tour bus turned into the narrow street and blocked her way. The taxi behind it hooted its horn; the driver got out shaking his fist. Skirting the fracas and the bus, she saw Audric at the end of the block.

She broke into a run; but before she could catch up with him, cars blocked her way on rue Croix des Petits Champs. Now in full force, the transport strike had made all traffic grind to a halt.

She looked up and down the street. No Audric. And then she caught a glimpse of his bike disappearing into Passage Vero-Dodat.

Desperate, she zigzagged between the cars. The whole street was like a parking lot. Below the two statues in niches over the entrance to the covered Passage Vero-Dodat were dark wood-framed old-fashioned storefronts with gilt sconces and small black diamond tiles under a glass-and-iron vaulted roof.

Her grandfather had pointed out the commercial origins of the now-elegant passage; Vero had been Montesquieu's pork butcher, and Dodat a shopkeeper who'd gone bankrupt.

A bicycle leaned against a storefront in the passage. Audric stood bent over a glass display window of an antique toy store. Didn't he have school?

"Excuse me. Audric?"

He looked up from a collection of tiny Napoleonic lead soldiers. Light reflected off his thick lenses as he looked her over.

"I get it." His mouth tightened. "He put you up to this, as usual."

"I don't understand." She pulled out a card from one of the many she carried.

"Since when does a looker follow me? Get lost."

She imagined him the butt of cruel jokes. The child found in every schoolyard, the beaten-up outcast with scars both outside and inside.

"But we spoke on the phone." Her hand paused, holding out the card.

"Aimée Leduc," he read. His voice wavered. "Olivier didn't put you up to this?"

"Who?" She shook her head. "You don't seem interested in the Cours Carnot survey. I've wasted my time."

He bit his lip. "I've made a mistake."

"I doubt if you can help me," she said. "From your phone comments, you had little communication with our target student, Nicolas Evry."

"Why him?"

She pointed to the old Napoleonic metal soldiers. "Expensive, eh?"

"Not for a collector."

He seemed the type who still played with toy soldiers in his room.

He shrugged. "To be honest, Nicolas Evry can't figure in your study. He never took the *prépa* course for the École des Hautes Etudes Commerciales *concours*."

She hated doing it, but she pulled out the travelers' checks she'd intended to use on her trip to New York. It was all the money she had left to live on, with her account frozen.

"As I mentioned, there's remuneration, but I need to verify your information. Why don't you tell me about it?" She pointed toward the Café de l'Epoque.

Longing shone in his eyes, but he stepped back. "I can't . . . he won't understand."

"Understand what?"

"I'm late."

She'd lost him. "Who? Olivier?"

From the way his mouth opened in surprise, she'd hit home.

"What's his connection to Nicolas?"

Without a word, Audric backed up. But she remembered seeing Olivier's name in the files.

She caught his sleeve as he reached for the bike handlebars. "You're afraid. Why, Audric?"

"Nicolas committed suicide, didn't he? That's what all this is about." A muscle twitched in his cheek. "I've got nothing to say to you."

From the street, car horns blared.

She let go of his sleeve. "I think it was murder, Audric. Can you tell me what changed Nicolas in November 1993?"

"Changed? You related to him or something?"

Before she could answer, the alarm on Audric's watch beeped. In his wire bike basket she saw an École des Hautes Etudes Commerciales calendar. "I'm late for a lecture."

"You said he hung around you," she said. "Why did Nicolas join the skinheads?"

Audric's eyes almost popped out from behind his glasses.

"He wasn't the only one, was he?"

Audric grabbed the handlebars, swung his shorter leg over the seat. She stepped in front of the wheel.

"Maybe your parents should know their son dabbled in the neo-Nazi movement."

"It's not like that. Not that way."

She stared at him. "Or maybe you did more than dabble. Maybe you torched a synagogue." She pulled out the Cours Carnot file. "Your father's a playwright and your mother . . . they're divorced, I see; but anxious, I'm sure, to know. . . ."

He took off his glasses, wiping the perspiration from his brow. "*Non*, please, you don't understand."

"Then help me understand, Audric," she said. "Or I talk with your father."

"Nine P.M." He swung his leg over the bike. "Here in the café." And he pedaled off.

* * *

ON QUAI D'ANJOU in front of her apartment, she caught sight of a man sitting on the stone wall, legs swinging as he spooned something from a cup. Twilight hovered, and the quayside lights cast mercury-silver pools on the Seine's surface.

She heard a cough. And recognized Melac. She'd never returned his call. Did his appearance mean he'd found a link between her and Clémence?

He held an ice cream cup from Bertillon's around the corner.

"This vanilla bean's a winner," he said. "Fantastic."

She shook her head, clutching her keys. "Then you haven't tried their white peach sorbet."

"Next time," Melac said, wiping his mouth with a napkin.

Nonplussed, she shifted her heels on the gravel. "Don't tell me this is a social call."

He set the empty cup on the stone wall.

"The GSR test came back negative for gunshot residue on your hands," Melac said.

"You sound surprised. But maybe you're here to inform me of the line of investigation you're following in René's shooting."

"Sounds like you're telling me how to do my job."

That had gained her no points. She should try tact, as René often suggested. But her stubbed toe throbbed and Melac annoyed her. Especially the way he'd waited in front of her apartment.

"Liken it to an onion," he said, pausing as if in thought.

Handsome in a rough way in his black shirt and jeans. His jacket lay on the stone wall. Was he off duty?

"Every time you peel a layer, there's another one."

Something about the way his eyes flickered raised the hair on her neck.

"Who peels onions? I don't get your point."

"The financial police faxed a request for your criminal record, if any," he said. "That tells me they're mounting an investigation; it's kind of what they do."

His condescending attitude more than rankled. He knew something. Something she didn't.

"So I comply and notice the Interpol flag on your family member. I keep peeling the onion, finding cross-references, cross-searches, and my chief tells me to comply with the financial police request because they have reasonable suspicion, et cetera." He nodded. "But, of course, I'm waiting to hear what you have to say."

His false conversational tone, the ominous tone of calm in his voice, panicked her. She couldn't speak.

"You wouldn't want me to get the wrong idea, would you, Mademoiselle Leduc?"

"Instead of an onion, you could liken it to a second-rate dry cleaners," she said, pointing to the pink dry-cleaning tag peeking from his jacket pocket.

He blinked.

"All the chemicals, but still those stains don't rub out. Impossible to remove. So you're stuck with a Sauce Bernaise grease spot for the life of your jacket."

Melac lifted his jacket sleeve. "How did you know that's Bernaise sauce?"

"Just like I know you mastered simple addition but nothing more complicated."

His eyes narrowed.

"Let's see, a ticket to New York, an American mother who's a wanted terrorist, and now a financial probe by the big guys," Melac said. "Add them up and you hit a jackpot."

"What?"

"Money laundering, arms and drug deals. Big-ticket items," he said. "And a partner who's shot after discovering discrepancies in your office bank balance. Even with my 'limited' math skills, it adds up."

Startled, she stepped back into her neighbor walking his dog on the quai. A doddering white-haired man, a former member of the Academie Française, with his Pekinese. "*Pardonnez-moi*, Monsieur," she said, trying to recover.

He snorted and moved away, crunching fallen leaves.

Now she was ready for him. "But it doesn't add up, Melac. I'd never hurt René. And my mother left us a long time ago. A very long time ago. She may be dead, for all I know." Her throat caught, and she turned away. Why did her eyes well up after all this time?

"Sidonie (aka Sydney) Leduc's file's open. Active."

"You mean she's alive?" She turned and looked at him.

Melac studied her. His demeanor was removed, professional. He folded his arms across his chest. The plane tree branches rustled.

"You want me to beg, Melac? I will."

"It means no one's reported her dead," Melac said. "But in that business, they don't always identify the bodies."

She froze.

"What business?"

Melac edged off the wall. Tossed the empty Bertillon cup in the trash. "I thought you'd know."

"I'd give anything to know."

"You would?" Melac said. "I'll remember that."

He dusted off his jeans, took a step, paused. "What I do know is that your father cut a deal for her. He was a good *flic*, and it ruined his career. A shame."

He'd gotten that all wrong, too. She took a breath. To give vent to the anger rising inside her would get her nowhere.

"In point of fact," she said, "one of his partners caught in a bribery scandal shifted the blame to him. *That* ruined his career."

She controlled her voice with effort. "But you're right about one thing. Papa was a good *flic*."

"I'm not the only one interested in you, Mademoiselle."

"You're playing with me," she said, "thinking I'm a pawn that will let you take the queen."

"I heard you'd cooperate," he said. "You're the one being used."

Melac's footsteps crunched on the gravel as he walked toward Pont Marie.

Aimée stood rooted to the spot. The branches of the plane tree nodded in the wind.

Alone.

If her mother was alive, would she use her to launder money? The woman she remembered doodled on napkins, burned the milk she was heating on the stove for *café au lait*, and worried if Aimée forgot her jacket.

All the old hurts surfaced. And this brother she hadn't known existed, what had become of him? But this would get her nowhere.

She had a hunch that whatever had happened to Nicolas in 1993 would explain a lot. The siddur weighed heavy in her bag.

The streetlights' gleam pocked the pavement's surface with light. She felt someone watching her. Fear invaded her, from her head to the soles of her feet.

She scanned the quai. Deserted.

If she hurried, she could cross town to reach the synagogue, then make her meeting with Audric. Resolute, she pushed the digicode numbers, entered the courtyard, and found her faded pink scooter. With a quick turn, she keyed the ignition, hit the pedal, and the engine rumbled to life. Out on the quai, she took off her tight shoes, put them in the basket, rubbed her toe, then roared off. Using the narrow streets to avoid traffic, she hoped to make the synagogue before the service ended.

The strike and traffic dictated otherwise. Streets clogged with bicycles, buses, and cars slowed her way. By the time she reached the synagogue, the people were filing out, joining friends talking in groups, everyone discussing how to get home.

One of these people might know something about the siddur. At least there was more chance among older Polish Jews.

She parked the scooter, pulled it up on the kickstand, and slipped on her heels. Holding the prayer book, she threaded her way through the crowd and spied an older couple, the man leaning on a cane, the woman squeezing the cheek of a toddler.

"Forgive me for disturbing you, but I want to return this siddur to its owner."

The old man shrugged. "Ask the rabbi."

"Of course," she said. Hoping to gain more, she opened the

much-thumbed pages. "Before I bother him, I thought it better to check with someone in the congregation."

The yellowed pages crinkled. No one paid attention. "Do you recognize these names?"

She pointed to the two names written in dark blue ink. The crowd had dwindled and the old couple's gaze was locked on the red-cheeked toddler. She gave it one last shot.

"Elzbieta and Karlosch Ficowska from Bialystock?" Aimée said.

"Pronounced *Beeyelischtok*," the old woman corrected. "That's where I come from."

Excited, Aimée leaned close to her. "This wouldn't be you, would it?"

The old woman pulled up the reading glasses hanging from a chain around her neck. Scrutinized the names. Then pressed the siddur to her chest for a moment.

"But that's Effie and Carl!" She nudged her husband, the old man. "Effie and Carl Ficou! Look!"

"Eh, they're dead, Myra, you forget things."

"I don't understand," Aimée said. Disappointed, she realized the old woman had made a mistake.

"I only saw this siddur every day," Myra said. "Where did you get this?"

"The names differ, Madame."

"We didn't keep our old names. What for? To remain the target of those hunters?" She took off her reading glasses. "After the camp, I can't remember my old name half the time, not that I want to. It's from another life. But look at that fascist Le Pen, nothing's changed here since Dreyfus and the Stavisky affair." She shrugged. "We're Jews, we wander, that's what we do. Ready to leave at a moment's notice. My bag stays packed at the door. My daughter calls me '*fer-*

ukt'—crazy—and my granddaughter gets excited and asks when I'm going on a trip."

Aimée wanted to focus this talkative Myra on the names.

"You're sure it's Effie and. . . ."

"Carl. *Bien sûr.*"

The old man leaned forward. "Murder, I call it."

Aimée leaned closer.

"What do you mean?"

Myra took a handkerchief from her bag. Blew her nose. "A hit-and-run, left to die. What has the world come to, leaving old people to die in the street? So few escaped the Warsaw ghetto, and then they died in a Parisian gutter."

Stunned, Aimée tried to think. Why was this siddur Nicolas's insurance? How did this involve René?

"When did this happen?"

"Like yesterday, I can see Effie in my kitchen peeling potatoes for latkes."

Aimée plumbed her brain. Latkes?

"You mean December, at Chanukah? Last year?"

"It's some years ago, Mademoiselle." The old man pulled her sleeve. His eyes were kind. "Myra remembers not so good. Forgets."

"Do you remember?"

He sucked in his breath. Hard to do with his false teeth. "Open-heart surgery . . . I don't remember time so good myself."

What could she do?

"How can I give this to the family?"

"Too late. They moved," the old man said. "It was in the papers, our Yiddish paper," he said, "and a small mention in the French ones. They don't write about all the incidents. At least this one, people heard."

"What happened?"

"Effie's little grandson saw them run over."

Aimée took out a kohl eye pencil, the first thing she felt in her bag.

"Can you tell me where the family lives now?"

"Their daughter, Rachel, works for the SNCF." The old man leaned on his cane. "She transferred to Lyon . . . Strasbourg? I'm not sure. Got married."

"They were your friends; can you try remembering anything else? Could this have happened in 1993?"

His face crinkled in thought. A look of pain crossed his face.

"You're doing a good job, so helpful," she said, concerned that she'd upset the old man.

"I had my operation when?" He scratched his chin. "That's right. In 1993."

The same year the synagogue in the Marais was torched. Hadn't Nicolas said this was bigger than people thought? She'd discovered this couple's prayer book in his belongings. Had he run over the old couple and left them for dead?

Or was she looking at this the wrong way? Nicolas could have acted with students from the Cours Carnot. Had he taken the fall for all of them for the synagogue burning?

But what kind of insurance was it to keep the prayer book of a couple who'd been killed? That only made sense if someone else had done it. If having the siddur pointed to them.

But she hadn't found anything inside.

And why hadn't the *flics* connected the hit-and-run to the burned synagogue?

"Monsieur, where were Effie and Carl run over?"

He lifted his cane. Pointed to the sky. A pale glow silhouetted the jagged rooftops.

"Over there," he said. "Now I remember."

The light came from near the Opera. Place Vendôme, or. . . .

"The wax museum. Effie and Carl took him for his birthday."

"You mean the Musée Grévin? But that's in Passage Jouffroy."

"They lived two streets away." He shook his head. "Killed on their doorstep on rue Bergère. A crime."

Someone there might remember. After all, it had made the papers. She could check this out.

"*Merci*, Monsieur."

He stared at her. "You know who ran them down?"

His age-spotted hand gripped hers with a slight tremble.

"I think so. But proving it's the hard part."

* * *

HER SCOOTER WOVE through the cars on rue du Conservatoire. Her left hand gripped the handlebar; her right held her cell phone to her ear. Paco, her contact at *Le Monde*'s newspaper archives, had put her on hold.

She fumed at the stalled traffic and wanted to jump the scooter onto the pavement. But due to the strike, the sidewalks were full of commuters walking home.

"How do you spell their name again?" Paco's voice sounded tinny and the reception wavered. Everyone in the world was talking on their cell phones right now.

"F-I-C-O-U, Effie and Carl."

"Nothing so far in November 1993."

Her heart sank. Had the old man remembered wrong? Was her theory shot to pieces?

"There's an article concerning a big demonstration by Le Pen supporters, and a list of the injured, but not those names."

Even if Nicolas had their prayer book, she couldn't link him to the hit-and-run. He could have found it and kept it. A coincidence? But she didn't believe in coincidences. And it made no sense for a rabid neo-Nazi to keep it as his "insurance."

How did this connect to René's injury? What bigger picture didn't she see? Another scooter cut in front of her. She saw the red tail light and braked just in time.

"They don't print victims' names," Paco said. "At least until notification of the family."

That helped her not one bit.

Her nerves shot, she wiped the perspiration from her brow. The smell of roasting meat, smoke; she turned to see a bistro.

Smoke and fire . . . of course. The date the synagogue was burned. She should have told Paco that first.

"Try November third."

Paco sighed. "The microfiche machine jammed. I'm re-threading. Wait a minute," he said. "Could this be it? 'On rue Bergère, a fatal hit-and-run of an old couple while their young great-grandson looked on. Police in the quartier are asking anyone who saw a vehicle on rue Bergère at 10 P.M. to help with their inquiries. Neighbors were alerted when the cries of the three-year-old boy reached them and the couple were found'."

"That's it?"

"*C'est ça.*"

She swerved into rue Bergère. A street of white limestone Haussmann-style buildings with iron balconies, a few shops open. "Does it give an address?"

"No clue here."

"*Merci*, Paco. Do me a favor, fax it to my office."

She'd try the section of rue Bergère nearest the Musée Grévin. At least shops were open. At the second store she entered, the young Arab man, stacking cartons of yogurt, nodded. The small corner shop was clean and compact, and every inch of space was filled with canned goods and grocery items.

A sprig of ivy trailed from plants in the window. The radio perched near the security camera softly played Arab music.

"1993? I signed the lease and opened my shop on November first."

He'd been open only three days. Excitement ran through her. She hoped he'd remember.

"Do you remember the old Jewish couple who lived near here killed by a hit-and-run driver?"

The corners of his mouth turned down. "Horrific. I remember that child crying."

"What happened?"

He shrugged. "I didn't see the accident."

"Did the *flics* question you?"

"For a few minutes."

"But you heard the child crying. Maybe you heard something else?"

He stacked another carton of yogurt.

"Made me sick," he said. "I thought maybe I'd made a mistake to open here. But I tell you, I still see that three-year-old boy with blood on his little teddy bear."

Her stomach lurched. "You mean the child was hurt, too?"

"Praise to Allah, *non*. I looked out the door and saw him."

"Can you show me where?" she interrupted.

"You a *flic?*" His eyebrows rose.

She handed him her card. "Aimée Leduc, private investigator."

"I'm Mahmoud." He wiped his hands on his blue work coat, shook her hand. He called out to a woman in the back to help a customer, then led her to the street.

A pool of yellow light from the street lamp shone on the cracked pavement. Rain puddles streaked with motor oil glistened purple.

"Try to picture that cold November evening," Aimée said,

prompting him. "It's late, the street's dark except for that street lamp."

She waited.

"I heard the child crying."

"And it sounded wrong," she said. "You felt it was unusual for a parent to let a child cry like that."

"The child pointed that way." Mahmoud indicated the gutter. "But when I asked him what's the matter, he just said '*Grand-mère*'."

"Can you remember if you heard brakes, a car driving away?"

"I just saw the couple." He pointed to the gutter. "I thought they'd fallen down. But all that blood . . . and the old woman's eyes were open."

"Did you see anything else, like her handbag or things that might have fallen out?"

"Now that you mention it, *non*."

A distracted look filled his eye. "It felt like time slowed. Like, how do you say . . . slow motion?"

Tragedies did that. Time slowed, and each moment passed in freeze-frame.

"I can't forget. The little boy cried and I held him. The neighbor from upstairs," he pointed to a dark window, "she leaned out, then called the police. But she's moved now."

"Do you remember anything else?"

He shook his head. "Everyone thinks Arabs and Jews hate each other. But in Palestine, my neighbors and the corner butcher were Jews. We lived together. I don't understand what their people and my people do to each other. We're cousins." He shook his head again. "It wasn't right, what happened to those people, and that little boy. He'd picked up a dirty candy wrapper from the gutter."

And then it hit her. "Did you have customers that evening before the accident?"

"I'm open until midnight. People come in all the time."

"But you'd just opened, were still building your business. You said you couldn't forget that night."

He nodded. "It was tough at the beginning. I didn't have many customers."

"So you'd have a few customers, maybe people not from the quartier but en route somewhere else?"

She pulled the Cours Carnot file from her bag, pointed to Audric's photo. "Think back. He limps." Then she showed him Olivier's photo. "Did you see either of these boys?"

Mahmoud studied the blurred *carte d'étudiant* photos. "Why?"

She tried a hunch. "Could they have been with another boy, a skinhead type?" She remembered Nicolas in the video that convicted him. "I'm asking because that night, the skinhead burned a Jewish synagogue in the Marais."

"Religious persecution? Against Jews, you mean."

"The couple were Jewish."

"But the *flics* called it a hit-and-run."

She opened the *Voici* and pointed to the page. "Do you recognize him?" It was Olivier's photo, with a twig-thin model draped over his shoulder.

"I don't understand," Mahmoud said.

She thrust the file photo toward him for comparison. "He's the same person."

"So?" Mahmoud fingered the prayer beads circling his wrist. He wanted to get back to work. Or was he hiding something?

"Did either of these boys come into your shop?" she asked again.

She didn't hold out much hope.

"Four years ago? You're asking me to remember customers who might have come into my shop?"

The light blurred on the cobblestones. Her toe throbbed, and she'd reached another dead end.

"It's a stretch, I know, but I thought since that night's remained so vivid in your mind. . . ."

"I wish I could help you," Mahmoud said.

"Such a crime, to leave old people lying in the gutter, their little grandchild looking on," Aimée said, trying one last time. "If that happened to my grandparents, I'd. . . ."

"Let me see that again," Mahmoud said. He stared at the photos. He stabbed Olivier's picture with his finger.

Shivers of excitement ran up her spine. "You remember now, don't you?"

He nodded. "This one was drunk. He broke a display case and made a scene when I refused to sell him wine. But it happened before the old couple's accident. With all that happened that night, it paled in comparison. I remember now. My wife was terrified and wanted me to move."

Mahmoud saw them drunk the night of the synagogue burning; Nicolas had the old couple's prayer book, not his trophy but what he planned to use as his insurance. Insurance for or against what?

"There's a customer," Mahmoud said.

"One more thing, please," she said. "Do you remember anything they said?"

"Apart from calling me a dirty Arab?" He gave a small shrug. "That's part and parcel of doing business."

* * *

ON HER SCOOTER, Aimée headed toward the café to meet Audric. She'd confront him, insist that he take her to Olivier, who hadn't answered her calls.

Ahead of her, theatregoers spilled from the Thèâtre du Palais Royal, blocking traffic. Impatient, she squeezed the handlebar brakes, overhearing the well-dressed theatre crowd discussing the adaptation of Feydau's seventeenth-century farce. Others moaned about the already-full taxis.

A couple crossed in front of her. The man—salt and pepper hair, bags beneath his eyes—looked familiar. But everything else about him looked different. He wore a new suit, his hair was brushed back, and his arm embraced a woman's shoulder. And he was laughing. Then he looked up.

She locked eyes with a surprised Morbier.

She'd never seen him nonplussed before. Or with a woman. In this case, an attractive older woman with full red lips who adjusted her gold speckled shawl as her bubbling laugh floated above the conversations and car horns.

Morbier on a hot date? Had the earth shifted on its axis and the planets spun out of orbit?

"What a surprise, Mademoiselle Leduc."

Mademoiselle Leduc? He'd never called her that either.

But then she remembered him in a tuxedo at his office at the Brigade Criminelle.

"Aren't you going to introduce us?" The woman's words lingered in the air.

It seemed like she and Morbier stared at each other for a lifetime. Why had Morbier kept her secret? And why did a pang of irrational jealousy shoot through her?

"I'm his goddaughter, Aimée Leduc, Madame."

"Aaah, of course," she said. Warmth and the scent of gardenias emanated from her. "Those big eyes, I should have known from the way he talks about you."

He does?

"Please call me Xavierre," she said. "*Enchantée*, Aimée."

Horns beeped behind her. "The pleasure's mine, Xavierre."

Aimée leaned forward to kiss Morbier on the cheek. "Get Melac off my back like you promised," she whispered in his ear, "or I give Xavierre an earful."

Then she winked at Morbier. "Enjoy the rest of your evening."

She popped the gear into first and took off.

* * *

AIMÉE PRESSED THE buzzer of Audric's apartment. He hadn't shown up at the café. No answer, but she hadn't expected one. She tried the phone number listed on Olivier's file once more. Again, no answer.

She rounded the corner past the Commissariat and watched the buildings that backed on to Audric's rear courtyard. A cat slinked by in the shadows.

She wanted a cigarette so much, she could taste it. Too bad she'd run out of stop-smoking patches.

A side door opened, shooting a ray of light over the cobbles. Then a limping figure crossed the street. Audric.

He was speaking into his cell phone.

She could learn more by following him than confronting him.

She slipped off her heels and darted among the parked cars. Barefoot, she kept to the shadows, trailing him past the looming hulk of the Banque de France, pausing every so often to wait in a doorway.

Audric kept up a fast pace despite his hobbling gait. He paused mid-block, bent, and tied his shoe. Afraid he'd see her, she ducked behind a pillar and waited. And then on the busy rue des Petits Champs, she lost him. Frantic, she looked both ways. Only a couple, arm in arm, laughing.

She broke into a run. Half a block later, she saw him on the steps of the small church fronting the oval-shaped Place des Petits Pères.

She huddled in the bakery doorway.

She recognized the person next to him right away from the *Voici* photographs. Olivier. Tall, slender, blond, and with a sneer.

Their words carried over the square. "You worry too much, little boy." And then they entered the church.

Aimée ran, shoes in hand, up the wide steps, through the quilted leather church door and into dim, candlelit Notre-Dame des Victoires. Thousands of book-cover-sized plaques commemorating answered prayers covered the vaulted stone walls.

A lone man kneeled at the main altar. She saw a few old women at the side altars. Organ music soared, filling the church. Nicolas and Olivier stood in back, near the stand of flickering votive candles.

Audric gazed up at Olivier with a kind of hero worship. Beauty and the beast, she thought.

She edged closer to hear them, pausing behind the confessional.

"It's serious. I'm warning you, Olivier, be careful, she's going to—"

At that moment, a black-frocked priest emerged and beckoned to her. "Mademoiselle, you're next."

Nervous, she stepped back. "Not tonight, Father."

The priest swept away, but not before Audric spotted her.

Alarm crossed his face. "You followed me again!"

"Who the hell are you?" Olivier demanded.

Nothing for it now but to confront Olivier and get answers.

"Sounds like you're afraid I'm going to rake up your involvement with Nicolas," Aimée said, stepping between them. "Count on it. Remember November third, 1993? The Marais synagogue was burned, an old couple was run over?"

Audric's mouth dropped open.

"I don't know what you're talking about," said Olivier. But he didn't meet her eyes.

She shifted her bare feet on the cold uneven stone, feeling vulnerable and at risk even in this church.

"But a witness remembers you, Olivier. Drunk, making a scene at a shop outside of which an old Jewish couple was found run over, in the gutter, their great-grandson crying, with blood on his teddy bear. You drove off drunk, right? To escape. But not before Nicolas took this."

She held up the siddur. "His insurance policy."

"And that proves what?"

"He went to prison for torching the synagogue. You made an arrangement with him, no doubt. I assume you paid him. But if news of the couple's killing ever hit the fan, he wouldn't go down for you. Not for vehicular manslaughter, hit and run, fleeing the scene. That's three counts."

Olivier looked her up and down. "You look normal, even chic, but you sound like you escaped from the mental hospital."

A few voices raised in song joined the organ music near the altar. No one paid the three of them any attention.

"Nicolas couldn't afford Cours Carnot," she said. "A shame, considering the promise he showed. Audric, you told me how he hung around your group. How he thought of you as his friends."

Audric backed away.

Olivier caught his arm. "Little boy with a big mouth."

"H—how was I to know what she was after?" Audric stumbled against the confessional.

"Enamored of neo-Nazis or seeking thrills, I don't know which, you joined *Les Blancs Nationaux*. For Nicolas's initiation, he boasted on video about torching the synagogue."

"I knew him: a loser," Olivier said. "So what? What's all this to you?"

His insolence marked him as dangerous. She became wary. But she'd gone this far. Now she had to get him to open up.

"It was my testimony that put Nicolas behind bars," she said.

"Eh?" Shock painted their faces.

"And I'll do the same for you. Before Nicolas was murdered in prison, he told me things. It's time the blame shifts to where it belongs."

She'd kept talking, all theory, but neither of them denied any of it.

"He was in prison; what else would he say? Where's your proof?" Olivier demanded.

"The *flics* are going to re-open the investigation." She was lying, but they didn't know that. "Clémence, his ex, was murdered last night, and that triggered renewed interest." She watched their faces for a reaction.

"I didn't go with them." Audric's lips trembled. "My father wouldn't let me."

"Shut up," said Olivier.

"Don't get me in trouble, please. Nicolas couldn't drive. He didn't have a car. There's been a mistake."

"I said shut up, Audric."

"But you drive, Olivier," Aimée said.

"So do millions of other people."

"You had Nicolas murdered in prison. Then you had to shut Clémence up, to get Nicolas's notebook from her and destroy it."

"You're crazy." Olivier's voice wavered.

"I'm sure you didn't plan to strangle her in the Palais Royal. But if she taunted you, demanding money to keep quiet . . . ? She wasn't easy to manipulate, like Nicolas. She'd blackmail you forever."

Olivier's eyes widened. She'd gotten to him.

"That's right." Aimée pulled out the *Voici*. "You go for models. Nicolas kept these in his cell, and it burned him. Ate at him that while you partied, he got a crowded cell, rats, cockroaches." She paused. "He was covered with bites. Lice crawled over his clothes."

The votive candles guttered in their red glass holders. The smell of burning wax hovered. Barefoot, Aimée shivered in the chill emanating from the cold stone.

"Why are you hounding me and making such crazy accusations?"

"Prison will make an interesting change for you, Olivier. Those inmates like blonds."

Olivier's mouth hardened. His gaze was defiant. "Big talk. But you're spinning fantasies. Lies. Nicolas committed suicide, and you can't prove a thing." He snorted. "I hate bleeding hearts who think they're out for justice."

She'd struck a nerve.

But he backed away. Covered his chest with his arms as if protecting himself. Then a look of bewilderment crossed his face.

Shadows danced on the walls. Fabric shushed on the stone. The smell from the holy water font, incense drifted from the altar.

"Don't you want to get out in front of this, Olivier?" she said. "Tell the truth. Youth's on your side. You were eighteen years old, drunk, mixed up with neo-Nazis. It can be explained."

Audric's lips trembled. He took Olivier's arm. Audric said, "Nicolas agreed and got paid off. None of the rest happened. Tell her."

Olivier pushed Audric away so hard that he hit the wooden prayer kneeler in the darkness. "Not me. I didn't do it." His voice came out in a strangled cry.

But he knew who *had* done it.

Aimée leaned down to help Audric up. The church door swung shut. Olivier had bolted.

She ran outside to hear a roar and see gray puffs of exhaust as Olivier took off on his motorcycle. No way she could catch him barefoot. She'd parked her scooter at Audric's.

But she'd rattled Olivier's cage. Big-time. Now she had to find out what he was hiding. She counted on Audric.

She slipped on her peep-toe heels. And noticed a ladderwork of runs in her black stockings. "I'm walking you home, Audric. And you're going to tell me what happened."

"I can't. Olivier will. . . ." He chewed his thumb.

"Hurt you?"

"It's not that way. He's like my friend."

"But not really your friend."

Too cool to let Audric call him a friend.

"You scared him away. He didn't go home." Audric pointed to dark windows in the Place des Petit Péres. "We're in the same economics class, and if I . . . no way."

Audric had changed his tune. Afraid. Now she'd have to convince him.

"Up to you. I'm sure your father will be pleased to hear about this."

"Please, don't get me in trouble," Audric interrupted.

"I want to show you something."

Aimée led Audric across the Place des Petits Péres, a small oval, its corners lopped off by some royal architect. Past the building of Louis XIV's wigmaker, now a wineshop to the Palais Royal residents.

Into the Palais Royal, quiet except for the gushing of the fountain and the echo of her heels clicking over the flowerlike mosaic patterns. No other sound met them. Eerie in the moonlight, deserted, it seemed as though she could hear a slight gasp, almost a collective tremor, as ghosts retreated.

Sixty pavilions in three colonnades surrounded the garden, which was soot-stained and shadowed by globed lights. The air felt warmer tonight, due to the vagaries of the October weather; yet she shivered, thinking of Clémence.

She stopped in front of the medal shop and checked her watch. "I timed it. It took us less than five minutes to walk here from Olivier's."

Audric stared at the one remnant of crime-scene tape on the barricade. "What do you mean?"

"Clémence worked at that café. Easy for Olivier to follow her."

Audric swallowed. "He was at my place last night."

"Why lie for him?"

"Lie? But he brought his entourage. I didn't invite those models. Or their mess. Or the way he pissed off my cousin's dealer."

Audric clapped his hand over his mouth.

So Olivier hung with a fast crowd and did drugs.

"Drugs don't interest me," she said. "Tell me what happened."

"His model girlfriend drank all my father's champagne. Olivier partied. We were supposed to be working on our class project."

She understood. Audric was bookish, a brain, thus useful to Olivier.

"My father returned from the theatre excited." Audric pointed to the Theatre du Palais Royal. "His new play, a Feydeau adaptation, just opened. He and Olivier talked for hours. Ask my father. I fell asleep."

Aimée leaned against the wrought-iron fence tipped by gold spikes. Damp ivy trailed in the distance, glistening in the moonlight, a scent of night-flowering jasmine from the garden mingled with the smell of old stone. But she couldn't put the image of Clémence out of her mind.

"Did you know Clémence was pregnant with Nicolas's baby?" she asked. "Instead of her giving me his notebook, the 'proof,' I found her strangled behind the barricade. The police will question Olivier. And you. Better for you to tell it all now, show you want to cooperate."

Audric turned away, but not before she saw his stricken look.

"I told you." He took a breath. Exhaled. "Most of it. The rest I don't know; it's just a feeling. About Nicolas at Cours Carnot."

"Go on."

"Olivier dared Nicolas to join *Les Blancs Nationaux*, to undergo the initiation. I think Olivier wanted to himself, but his father's in the ministry—and his mother, too."

"So instead of joining, he torched the synagogue with Nicolas?"

He shrugged. "I wanted to go. But my father made me stay home that night. Then, when Nicolas had money all of a sudden, *alors*, I thought Olivier had helped him."

"From a feeling of noblesse oblige? I don't think so, Audric."

"And then we never saw Nicolas again." Audric's mouth twisted. His teeth chomped nervously, then he regained control. "Gone, like smoke. Turns out he was in prison." Audric wrung his hands now. "And you put him there!"

Did all spoiled rich aristo kids expect to get away with murder?

"Arson's a crime, Audric. How would you like your apartment set on fire?"

His mouth twitched again and he covered it with his fist.

"Olivier bragged to you about the synagogue, the couple he'd hit, didn't he, Audric?"

Audric shook his head. "That's the funny thing. He didn't. He wouldn't talk about it."

* * *

LOW-LYING FOG MISTED the Seine, blurred the streetlights. A clammy wetness clung in the air. Aimée gunned her scooter over Pont Neuf onto Ile Saint-Louis. All the way, Audric's words haunted her. If Olivier had burned the synagogue, she needed proof. With Clémence and Nicolas dead, unless Olivier admitted it, his guilt was almost impossible to prove. Mahmoud, the shopkeeper, had recognized him and put him at the location where the old couple were run over. But an Arab shopkeeper's testimony, years later, wouldn't hold up. It would only put him in danger of retaliation by Olivier's high-powered parents.

The more she thought about it, the more it didn't feel right. She recalled Olivier's shock at the mention of the hit-and-run. The only honest reaction she'd noticed from him. Had she assumed too much?

But she had a nagging feeling that René's shooting was a result of the threat she posed. To whom, and about what, remained the questions.

She parked her scooter. Tired, she mounted the worn marble stairs and opened her door.

Miles Davis scooted into her waiting arms. Licked her face. Rubbed his wet nose in her ear. She had a man, albeit with four legs and a spiky tail, who snored on the duvet. But all hers and eager to see her.

"*Alors*, Miles Davis," she said. "You need spoiling after Madame Cachou fed and walked you."

She threw him a shank bone from the fridge, ignoring the pile of mail Madame Cachou had left on the secretaire. She heard the insistent ring of her cell phone from her bag. She reached it on the fifth ring.

"*Oui?*"

"Lady, don't you answer your phone?" The New York accent boomed over the crackling line.

"Please, Monsieur, go ahead." She kicked off her heels and

grabbed a pencil. Hopefully, she leaned forward. "I'm ready. You found an address for my brother?"

"When we meet. When's your flight?"

But she'd forfeited her ticket. With her account frozen and her travelers' checks needed to pay the rent, she was stuck. Not to mention that Melac wouldn't let her leave the country.

"But, Monsieur, my plans changed. I told you that earlier. Tell me on the phone."

More static.

"Look, lady, this costs money. And you owe me."

"*Bien sûr*. E-mail me the information, that's easier."

She stood up and reached for her laptop bag.

"I don't do e-mail." A snort. "And I don't report on the phone. You understand?"

Understand? Did he think other people were listening? Or hacking into her e-mail? Horns and what sounded like a street cleaner roared in the background.

She didn't get this. Or him. "But you called mentioning a contact in your message. That you found out about my brother."

"Right. On condition she speaks with you in person."

"In person? Impossible right now, Monsieur."

"No deal then, lady. Forget it." The phone buzzed. He'd hung up.

Her heart sank. Why couldn't he understand and give her the information over the phone? Why did every lead vanish in smoke? Or was there an agenda behind Waller's insistence that she leave Paris for New York?

She noticed the blinking light on her answering machine. Two messages. With her pencil she pushed PLAY.

"Aimée, I'm following the wire transfers," Saj said, excitement in his voice.

Saj had risen to the task. Did she smell René's hand in this? But that couldn't be.

"The wire transfers jumped two accounts in twelve hours," Saj said. "One to a bank in Malta, the other to Guernsey."

Well-known money-laundering locations for offshore accounts and shell companies. Seemed even more like a setup to her.

"More later." He clicked off.

She hit the next message. A woman's voice.

"Remember you gave me your card? It's Dita."

Clémence's roommate. Surprised, Aimée gripped the pencil.

"This *mec* asked for Clémence this afternoon. Maybe it's not important, but. . . ." Her voice paused, hesitant. "He told me he'd been Nicolas's cellmate and had something for her. He mentioned a book, that's all. But I thought of the notebook you were looking for. A strange *mec*, he sent chills up my spine. Hard to explain. When I told him Clémence was dead, he seemed more angry than sad."

Nicolas's cellmate Sicard, out on parole. She tried to remember what Clémence had said about him. If Sicard had Nicolas's notebook, she had to see him. Her hopes rose.

She called Dita back. No answer.

How could she find him? Think. What options existed for a new parolee: family, friends, a hotel or a halfway house set up for transition? Every prisoner's condition of parole involved reporting to a case officer weekly. And the case officer would have his address.

She called her contact in the parole office. By the time she collapsed into bed beside a warm Miles Davis, she had an address.

Friday

AIMÉE PUT A franc in the *tronc*, the metal donation box under the round domed basilica of Notre-Dame-de-l'Assomption, and lit a candle for René. From the baptismal font she heard a crying infant held by a priest in a cassock intoning prayers. A well-dressed family completed the scene.

Outside the church, she headed to the side door, down the stairs to the basement stone crypt, and was met by the warm and inviting aroma of paprika and garlic. Polska, the resto in the crypt below the church, served Polish dishes to a mix of the quartier. Wild mushroom ravioli headlined the chalkboard special. Reasonable and filling in a quartier noted for couture boutiques and the nearby Ritz.

Morbier sat at a table covered by a red-checked tablecloth, among Polish workers and executive types who worked nearby.

"Borscht?" Aimée said, noticing his soup bowl with surprise. "You're a *bifteck* and *frites* man."

"*Pas mal*. Try it." Morbier raised his napkin, tucked it into his shirt collar. This was the Morbier she knew, clad in a worn tweed jacket with leather patched elbows. The tired look in his eyes, nicotine-stained fingers, and mismatched socks, one blue, one black, were familiar.

"For Xavierre." She set a bouquet of apricot-colored roses on the table and sat expectantly. "So, how long have you two . . . ?"

"We're not here to discuss that."

A hurt look flashed in his eyes and then vanished.

"I just thought you should know. . . ." She hesitated. That irrational pang of jealousy stirred again. She'd never seen him with a woman or looking so happy before. "That she's beautiful. I enjoyed meeting her."

"I don't want to talk about it, Leduc." His tone was curt and all business.

So his hot date had gone wrong? Concerned, she leaned forward.

"Having a bad day, Morbier?"

"I've had better." Morbier nodded to the waitress, pointed to the chalkboard *prix fixe* menu. "She'll have the same."

Aimée noticed the moustached man with big biceps who ladled the borscht. Hard not to, since the man's eyes flicked Morbier's way every few minutes.

"You're making the moustache nervous," she said.

"Jerzy? That's not all I want to make him."

"Eh? Jerzy's planning a heist?"

"*Indicateurs* need to cooperate. I'm reminding him." Morbier kept a web of informers who furnished him with the pulse of the community. Like all good *flics*. He nodded to Jerzy. "My visit's a little reminder of our deal." Then he turned a penetrating gaze on her.

"You rub people's hide the wrong way, Leduc." He shook his head, reaching for his spoon. The crevice of his right jowl sported a whisker tuft he'd missed shaving. "Countless times. It's like you enjoy it."

"And you call this helping me with Melac?"

"Consider this more than a warning. Melac's interested in you. And not in a good way."

Her knuckles tightened on the napkin. The waitress, a barrel keg of a woman, set down a plate of steaming borscht and tossed a basket of bread in the middle.

"So he doesn't like me." She ripped a piece of bread off. "I'm not competing for Miss France."

But she groaned inside.

"I noticed." He glanced at her black leather pants, worn cashmere sweater, and denim jean coat. "*C'est grunge, c'est-ça?*"

He pronounced it *greunch.*

"Then you know I've cooperated, even furnished him with a video. What's Melac doing to catch the woman who shot René? Instead of investigating, he suspects *me.*"

"The financial *flics* find you interesting too."

"Someone's framing me, Morbier."

He held up his thick age-spotted hand. "Not my turf. You asked for my help with Melac. I tried. But he's got this bee in his bonnet that you're laundering money."

"Why not say I'm milking the moon? That makes as much sense."

"Wake up, Leduc." He wiped his soup bowl clean with a chunk of bread. "Haven't you ever wondered if she'd use you one day?"

Fear crawled up her spine.

Her mother. He meant her mother.

She pushed the bowl of borscht away. A wave of soup splashed over the rim, leaving a deep pink stain on the cloth. "Melac's theory makes no sense. Who knows if she's even alive?"

But the wheels were spinning in her mind.

"Unless you're not telling me something, Morbier?"

He shrugged. She couldn't read the look in his eyes.

"Wait a minute," she said. "That's what it's all about, your helpfulness connecting me to Jack Waller in New York. It's just to track my mother, isn't it?"

Morbier set down his spoon. "Paranoid as usual, Leduc. That woman—"

"'Woman'? You can't even say her name, can you? You've always refused to talk about her."

The waitress took the soup bowl and shoved a plate of *tarama*—fish eggs with a side order of sauerkraut—in front of her.

"There's nothing to say." His mouth tightened. "Eat your sauerkraut, Leduc; they do it well here."

She tasted the sweet-and-sour cabbage. And let her fork fall on the plate. "How well do you know Jack Waller, Morbier?"

"Jack Waller?" A lift of his eyebrows. And then Morbier's face changed, his gaze faraway. "I knew him as Jacques Weill. Our fathers were *cheminots*, railway workers, at Gare de Lyon during the Occupation."

Morbier rarely spoke of his childhood. Or the war. She remembered a tale fueled by a late-night bottle of red. The empty shops and his family's hunger drove him to trap pigeons in the park for dinner.

"Resistance comrades. That creates a bond, Leduc."

"To hear people today, everyone served in the Resistance, *non*? Funny, considering only three percent of the population participated."

"Resisting took different forms," Morbier said. "Small acts of courage. Especially if you needed to put food on the table. My father and Jacques's loaded the wrong freight on rail cars, they did what they could."

His voice was wistful. "Jacques's family moved to New York in the fifties."

"Jack Waller will only talk to me in person. He says I have to come to New York or forget his help."

Morbier paused. "And that's suspicious?"

"It smells."

"Ingrained habits die hard, Leduc."

"Meaning?"

"Jacques made captain in the NYPD, no small feat. Freelanced, did some work for the Company and Interpol."

"You mean the CIA?" She clutched her napkin.

"They all do that," he said. "Reciprocal arrangements, man on the ground the best thing, you know."

His matter-of-fact tone grated on her. What she had

thought suspicious now stank to high heaven. "You connected me to a man who works with Interpol and the CIA?"

"Who else, Leduc? He knows the terrain. A retired New York City police captain. Who better?"

Surprised, she took his hand. "You're naïve, Morbier."

He snorted. "I've been called a lot of things. But naïve? Never."

"My mother's. . . ." The words stuck in her throat. She kept her hand on his. "Good God, don't you see?"

"That she's on the World Watch List? *Bon*, you're looking for this brother, *non?*"

And then an awful thought hit her. What if the letters were a plant? A ruse to get her to New York?

But why would anyone think that would draw her mother there too? And after all these years, why now?

"*Et alors*, Leduc." Morbier cupped her hand with his for a moment, then let go. He removed his napkin, took out a packet of tobacco and Zigzag papers, and with a deft movement rolled a cigarette. He tamped the loose blond tobacco into the tip, lit it, inhaled, and sent out a plume of smoke.

She wanted to grab the cigarette from him.

Instead, she waved the smoke away to join the cloud hovering over the smokers in the basement crypt.

"Leduc, I try to help you, and you see phantoms, monsters."

She shook her head. He didn't get it.

"This obsession with the past—your mother—it goes nowhere." He knocked off his ash into the Ricard ashtray, took a toothpick packet from his pocket. Aimée recognized the goose-feather toothpicks he used. Le Coq. Her father had used them too.

"You're a big girl. Face it. If Jacques found a link to this 'brother,' you're lucky. Otherwise, take it the way it's meant." He put an open hand over his mouth as he picked his teeth.

"What do you mean?"

"What if she buried her past and doesn't want to be found, Leduc?"

But I'm her daughter, Aimée wanted to shout. And she was again eight years old on that rainy March afternoon after school in an empty apartment.

The voice she repressed that never went away murmured doubts. Had her mother left to protect her? The phrase from her little brother's letter—"I think people follow us"—came to her mind. Years later had her mother been with another child on the run? The horrible thought that her mother might not have succeeded in hiding her little brother came to her. Lies or the truth? Her thoughts swirled. She didn't know what to believe. Already Waller, whom Morbier trusted, turned out not to be who he purported to be.

In the course of a few days René had been shot; Nicolas had died before his parole, a suicide or a murder victim; Clémence had been strangled; and Tracfin had been set on her tail. It all linked somehow. Only she didn't know how.

"Remember, after the Berlin Wall collapsed and the Stasi files were opened? The radicals, the terrorists with new identities, who'd made new lives, had jobs, families. All shot to hell. Think about that."

What made him mention that? "You referred me to Waller. Now are you saying to leave it alone?"

Morbier stubbed out his cigarette and slid an envelope under his plate. "This consumed you. Night and day you hounded me for a contact in New York. Remember? Sometimes it's better to let sleeping dogs lie, but you wouldn't let go. I thought, *bon*," he shrugged, "you'd try, get tired, give up. Then you'd finally move on. But your partner's been shot, your business is in trouble, and now you're blaming Jacques. Is that the thanks I get, Leduc?"

She started. Was she paranoid? Yet the more she told Morbier, the more she stood to lose.

"I'm late." Morbier stood, wrapping his scarf around his neck. "But think about this, Leduc. The business your grandfather founded, the place your father put his heart and soul into running to provide for you . . . think about what he'd say."

"Papa?" Her heart sank. "Say to what?"

"Risking it all for a mother who abandoned you. That's a slap in his face. To his memory."

Stunned, she grabbed his hand. "How can you think . . . you knew her."

"A long time ago."

"People buckle under pressure, Leduc." He spoke slowly. And he almost sounded sympathetic. "Nets tighten; and to survive, people do things they're not proud of later."

"But it's not that at all."

Morbier's eyes narrowed. "Eh, then what?"

"I don't know."

He invoked her father's memory to get her to turn her mother in. Morbier assumed a money-laundering network ran through her; they all did. The only reason they let her walk free on the street was as bait.

"Let's hope it's not too late when you decide to come clean."

"Too late?"

"That you're not in a cell at La Santé."

Her blood ran cold. "You're threatening me, Morbier."

"Right now, it's cooperate or face prison."

With that, he shuffled ahead.

"Monsieur, you forgot something." The waitress pointed to the envelope Morbier had left.

"An incentive for my friend." Morbier shot a glance over at Jerzy, now red-faced and perspiring.

A payment for his informer. "And keep the roses."

In life, one always paid. And even when you paid, she thought, you were on your own.

Whoever had wired that money was linked to Nicolas, not her mother. She was almost certain. But she couldn't prove that or anything else.

All the way to Leduc Detective, she wondered if her father would want her to turn in her mother to save herself. She doubted she could.

Friday

"OLIVIER'S HIDING THINGS, Roland." Gabrielle paced back and forth in Roland's book-lined study.

After Olivier's enigmatic message about a ghost, he hadn't answered his phone. Or come home last night.

"What twenty-three-year-old doesn't keep things from his parents?"

"And there's a prison inquiry into Nicolas's suicide."

"Another inquiry like all the others?" He sighed. "But I'll talk to him." Roland caught her around the waist. "Slim and elegant, Gabrielle, you still have the body of the young woman I took against the armoire in your father's house."

In 1968, after a protest at the Sorbonne; she remembered her bell bottoms on the library floor. That scorching September, the geraniums wilting in the heat on the balcony. The way he made her feel. The way he still made her feel. She felt a stirring in her chest. She pushed it aside.

"Roland . . . it's serious."

"Very serious." He pulled her back, licked behind her ear. "I agree."

Gabrielle heard the long buzz of the apartment door. Olivier had forgotten his key again. She kissed Roland, then grabbed her briefcase. "Must be Olivier. Don't forget."

He returned her kiss and breathed in her ear. "Later, *ma chére*." She ran, briefcase in hand, to the apartment front door.

No Olivier. Disappointment washed over her. Instead, she saw a lithe woman in heels, black leather pants, and denim coat, wearing oversized earrings. There was an inquiring look in her large kohl-rimmed eyes. The new neighbor, she wondered. They'd heard that a model had moved into the building.

"May I help you?"

"Madame de la Pecheray? I'd like to speak with Olivier, please."

One of Olivier's conquests?

As the woman handed her a card, Gabrielle noticed the copper puzzle ring on one of her fingers.

"Aimée Leduc," she read, "*Detective Privée*. What's this concerning?"

"May I come in, Madame?"

"But why, Mademoiselle Leduc?"

Gabrielle glanced around the hallway. The concierge was dusting the stained-glass windows, no doubt listening.

"It's a private matter."

Gabrielle's gut wrenched. The blackmailer?

"This concerns a police investigation," Aimée explained.

The concierge continued dusting the same spot on the window.

"I'm busy, Mademoiselle." This Leduc woman bothered her. The tousled unstudied chic, the raw energy vibrating from her, and the determination in her eyes.

"Maybe you'd prefer to hear via official channels first?" Aimée shrugged.

Gabrielle stood aside and let her in.

"*Entrez*. I'm listening, Mademoiselle." Should she disturb Roland in his study? Better to keep this short, stay on the defensive, and deny whatever popped up.

"On November third, 1993, a synagogue in the Marais was torched."

Gabrielle willed down her fear and managed to keep her face expressionless. "I fail to see how this involves me."

"A witness says your son participated with Nicolas Evry, who took full responsibility for the incident and was arrested, convicted, and imprisoned."

Gabrielle's spine stiffened. The woman had some pieces but nothing to link them together.

"There's a mistake," she said.

"Olivier denied it too," Aimée said.

Gabrielle tried to remember to keep breathing.

"If you've already spoken with Olivier, then what's the point of this?"

The Leduc woman shook her head. "My client believes Olivier's covering up," she said. "If he doesn't come forward, he's in trouble. He may be charged as an accomplice in a vehicular manslaughter and fleeing the scene of an accident."

Shaken, Gabrielle grabbed the foyer's fluted pillar to restore her balance.

"You're still here, Gabrielle?" Roland strode into the foyer. "The Minister's dropping by in ten minutes to finalize last minute arrangements for my investiture."

Even though the Leduc woman was still right there, she felt him draw her close. She leaned into him. Trying to draw strength. What was that look in his eyes?

Friday

AIMÉE RECOGNIZED HIM. His graying temples, clear blue eyes, and Lobb shoes. The man in the Palais Royal who'd held her penlight as she tried to resuscitate Clémence.

Olivier's father.

"But I know you, don't I?" he said, smiling. "I'm Roland de la Pecheray." He extended his hand and shook hers. His grip was warm and firm. "We met at the ministry reception, *non?* Or after?" His smile faded. "Oh, now I remember. That poor young woman in the Palais Royal was your friend."

"Olivier's friend, too, Monsieur," Aimée said. Feeling awkward, nevertheless she made herself go on. "And Nicolas Evry's ex."

"Olivier knew her? I don't understand." An expression of concern appeared on his handsome face. He was dressed in a navy blue blazer over an open-necked striped shirt. He ran a hand through his hair, his brow furrowed. "That's why you're here?"

Miniature topiary trees were aligned across the marble claw-footed table in the hall. A tarnished silver bowl filled with deep orange-red persimmons stood in the middle. Several eighteenth-century oil landscapes hung in gilt frames. The place breathed old money.

They might be aristos, with *de la* before their name, but they were worried parents, and here she was, lying to them.

"Olivier refuses to understand the implications," Aimée said. "I tried to explain. He needs to tell the truth and quit shielding whoever burned the synagogue."

"Who says this?" Gabrielle interrupted.

"My client's requesting that the police re-open the investigation," she said. "New evidence has come to light."

A stretch.

"What client?"

"I'm not at liberty to say," she said. "But the evidence suggests that your son's implicated in an old Jewish couple's death later that same night."

"Impossible," Gabrielle said, leaning against her husband's shoulder for support. "How can you accuse Olivier?"

"A hit-and-run driver left the old couple dead in the street, their three-year-old grandson looking on."

"Terrible," Gabrielle said, shaking her head.

"My son didn't have a license; he didn't even drive in 1993," Roland said. "We bought him a motorcycle just last year."

Aimée shifted her feet on parquet floor.

"My client discovered evidence suggesting that Nicolas Evry received payment to take the blame," Aimée said, "and go to prison."

She paused to let that sink in. How would Olivier, a nineteen-year-old, obtain that kind of money unless from his parents?

"You're making this up," Gabrielle said.

"On November third, 1993, a witness described your inebriated son Olivier making a scene in the corner shop on rue Bergère just meters away from the subsequent hit-and-run incident."

Shock painted Gabrielle's face. "But that's not proof."

Roland stared at Aimée.

"You're asking us to turn our son in? For something he didn't do?" he said.

Aimée pulled out the newspaper clippings faxed from Paco. The black-and-white photo of the charred synagogue, the bouquets of flowers as if at a shrine in the gutter where the old couple had died.

"I'm asking your son to tell the truth," she said. "And I'm seeking your help in persuading him to speak with the authorities. Much better—"

"'Better'? You're making unsupported allegations—"

"My client's allegations," she interrupted. "Did Olivier prevent Clémence from furnishing proof of his complicity? She was strangled not five minutes away from here."

Roland's mouth dropped open. "Five minutes away? *Mon Dieu,* a whole quartier lives five minutes from that spot. Why, we both work in the Palais Royal, I cross it every day, but that doesn't mean I strangled that young woman."

"Don't say any more, Roland." Gabrielle disengaged herself and opened the front door. "Allegations, rumors, will be dealt with by our attorney, Mademoiselle."

The door shut in Aimée's face. At the stained-glass window, the concierge straightened, rubbing her rag with vigor. Intelligent people summoned their attorney, Aimée thought, especially ones with something to hide.

Friday

"*QUELLE HORREUR!*" NANA, the young uniformed nurse, halted behind the clinic's meal-tray cart. "Monsieur Friant, what's all this?"

Caught, René's fingers froze, poised on his laptop. The hum of working printers filled his clinic room.

"You're in therapy, not supposed to be doing anything but your exercises," Nana said. "That's doctor's orders."

Tell that to the furtive instigator of the bank wire deposits to Leduc Detective, whom he was tracking.

René smiled. "I'm exercising my mind, Nana. Part of mind–body wholeness. Crucial to recovery; my therapist insists."

He'd trailed hackers, good ones, geniuses who redesigned software games while they played them. But this one displayed more savvy, more flair, almost arrogance. Mocking him.

"Got these for you, Nana." René pointed to the blue cornflowers next to his bed. "The blue matches your eyes. We'll keep this between us, eh?"

Nana wagged her finger. "Naughty boy."

She left with the cornflowers and a grin.

René knew that Tracfin's legal jurisdiction extended only so far. It had been granted limited access by several EU member countries, but only relating to banks with reciprocal relationships in other EU countries. Even if Tracfin suspected money-laundering, its investigation could only proceed to a certain point if the bank was located inside a non-reciprocal country. However, he and Saj, in hacking mode, observed no such restrictions. He wasn't going to stop to count the number of laws they'd broken already.

René operated on the principle that no system was safe. He'd seen it proven time and again. It took a few clicks to wire money; a fax with a forged signature as in Aimée's case was easy to obtain from a bank file; and the transfers zipped just beyond Tracfin's reach.

René hit Saj's number.

"You seeing what I'm thinking, Saj?" René said.

"I'll need to get back to you." Saj's voice sounded strained. Stiff. "In the meantime please note, of course, we'll honor the account, but at present we've suspended our operations."

René's skin crawled. "What's happened? Who's there, Saj?"

"Rest assured we've erased unnecessary data, Monsieur, and backed up your profile, but you'll need to proceed with other inquiries."

"The *flics*, Saj? Just tell me."

"Think on a larger scale, Monsieur. Remember to consult the Bercy office."

BRIF was there. The financial *flics*. The phone went dead.

Sweat broke out on René's brow. Things were worse than he'd imagined.

He took a breath, realizing he had to keep calm. At least try to. And think.

He surmised that BRIF had closed Leduc Detective and taken the computers, but that Saj had managed to delete Aimée's video and the bank data. René trembled. He looked at the pages spitting from the printer. This was the only proof now, here in his clinic room. The rest, in Leduc Detective's computers, had been deleted.

How long before BRIF—Tracfin—traced certain links to his hard drive?

Some of that he could fix with a phone call. He could transfer the office files to one of his hacker students. But he had to work fast.

And proceed by himself, before they found him. Before they locked Saj and Aimée up.

Friday

AIMÉE PARKED HER scooter in the small tree-lined Place Dauphine, enclosed on three sides by seventeenth-century townhouses. Her goal, the two-star hotel with a sagging stone façade in need of steam cleaning, held a few rooms set aside for paroled prisoners in transition. They were never far from the eyes of the law, since the Tribunal was across the square.

"Sicard?" The young man behind the small reception counter shook his head. A smug look crossed his face under brown hair combed back in a short pompadour. "Haven't seen him. Don't believe he's in."

"Believe this," she said. "I'm with the parole board, making the routine parolee room check."

The smug look disappeared. "Room check? Since when?"

"Do I make the rules?" she said. "Just routine, checking for arms, drugs, the usual. What room, please?"

"Better come back later."

"I'd like to." She shrugged. "But I'm behind, two other sites to check." She reached into her bag. Pulled out her bank-account printout, pretended to consult it.

"His parole officer asked me to drop off some papers."

"What kind of papers?"

Use your imagination, she wanted to say.

She smiled. "A job came up."

Most parolees needed jobs. And soon, considering the price of accommodations. She figured this *mec*, himself a parolee by the look of him, worked in lieu of rent.

"But Sicard. . . ." He stopped.

"Go on," she said. "Sounds like you know more that I do." She kept the smile on her face. "What's your name?"

"Joêl," he said. "Look, I'm busy."

"So Sicard roped you in too, eh, Joêl?" She shook her head. "Offered you a slice, in return for some help."

Joêl watched her, expressionless now. "I don't know what you're talking about." But now she was sure Joêl was involved. She wondered why Sicard had cut in another person for a share of the money.

"I don't blame you, Joêl," she said. "Sicard told you about

his foolproof plan. But you're not the only one. He botched the first blackmail attempt; now he needs a patsy."

He sputtered. "I didn't do anything."

"Not yet, you haven't."

"Listen, I'm clean. I can't get in trouble now."

"That's why you're going to talk to me about Sicard's plan."

"But you're. . . ."

"I'm magic," she said. "I can make this go away. Phhfft, like it never happened. But Joêl, I need your cooperation."

"Plan? Sicard never talked about a plan."

"Shall I chat with your parole officer?"

He shook his head. Not a hair of his pompadour moved.

A moment passed. "I read things."

She nodded. "Like what?"

"I read him things, that's all. He likes to get 'current' after all his time locked up. Newspapers, like that."

"Magazines, too?" She held up the *Voici*.

"That's right.

She put our her hand. "His key, please."

* * *

A FEW MINUTES later, she unlocked the door of *chambre* 17 on the creaking fourth floor. Thick wood beams supported a slanted ceiling over a dark narrow room with peeling walls. She saw the outline of a single bed and a chair. Medieval, almost monastic. She hit the light switch, and a single hanging bulb illuminated the sloping wood floor and the papers on the bed.

Finally!

But they were only La Santé release forms, indicating that Sicard had been set free the day after Clémence's murder in the Palais Royal.

That didn't help.

Where was the notebook? Dita's message said Sicard had tried to contact Clémence, he'd unnerved her, and he'd mentioned a "book." That had to be the notebook, either here or with Sicard. It began to seem like Clémence, desperate for money, had lied. But she didn't know for sure.

If Clémence's killer had taken it, she was back to square one.

She had to search the room before Sicard returned. She got on her hands and knees and checked the floorboards, then the mattress, the sheets and pillow. Nothing. She eyed the cracks in the walls, above the door frame. Her fingers came back covered in dust. She turned back, and her eye fell on the cracked porcelain bidet with a high tank above it.

Nothing behind the bidet. She stood on the rim, used her Swiss Army knife to pry up the lid. She felt something. Her hand came back with a wet plastic Monoprix bag. Water dripped down her arms.

She dried the bag off, washed her hands. From the hallway came creaking noises. She grabbed her knife, listening. The creaking continued, as footsteps moved down the hall.

She had to get the hell out.

A laundry cart blocked the stairs on the narrow landing.

Merde!

A door on the right was labeled EXIT. Good. She'd leave by the back stairs and go through the bag's contents at her office.

But inside the small foyer she found that the door to the rear stairs had been nailed shut. A definite fire code violation. She faced a leaded-glass window overlooking the Seine. The plastic bag ripped open. Onto the worn tiled floor tumbled a child's first reader, an Asterix comic book, lined paper with a penciled word '*bonjour*' misspelled with a *d* instead of *b*.

She crouched down.

Underneath the rest of the torn bag's contents, she discovered the brown leather notebook Nicolas had tried to give her in La Santé.

At last! But pages had been ripped out. Sicard must have taken the important ones. Dejected, she scanned the few pages of Nicolas's clear handwriting that remained.

She recognized the page Nicolas had showed her in prison, filled with numbers. Looking closer, she realized it contained a list of payments to a post office bank account. Three thousand francs each month, like clockwork. Until this month.

She turned the page to find a passage referring to his sister Maud, a Le Pen supporter, his distaste at Maud's high-minded rightwing tone, how he'd joined *Les Blancs Nationaux* to "show Maud" and take Olivier's dare. And how the video had "cooked his goose." That was all.

She could trace this bank account; she knew it would lead to the de la Pecherays. She'd hoped for more; a link to Olivier, to the old couple, the synagogue; but it wasn't there.

Disappointed, she stood up. Then she felt a thickness under the cover. She wedged out a much-folded paper. A letter from Maud, dated January 1994. Maud wrote that she would find whoever put him inside, find out who was to blame, punish them. It was not her little brother's fault. Maud demanded that he leave Clémence, saying she couldn't support him and that *putain*. Aimée shuddered at the vindictive tone. There were a few rambling lines about Maud's "little episode," how she "didn't mean to hurt people but it was all his fault."

Then she opened a folded telegram. Stamped "received and cleared La Santé," the telegram header read "Clinique Pyschiatrique de Lille": "Informing you Maud Evry committed yesterday for mental breakdown. Stop. A danger to herself and others."

Aimée's mind reeled. She felt a fleeting sympathy for Nicolas Evry.

The hallway door creaked open. A rush of damp air passed her. She looked up to see a man filling the doorway.

"That's personal," he said. "Mine."

She rose, backing up against the wall, her right hand gripping her Swiss Army knife behind her back. In two strides Sicard was close enough to grab the notebook.

"I'm with the parole office, Sicard," she said. "Joêl gave me your key."

"I know. The fool." Sicard, muscular, in his early thirties, dark blond prison-cut short hair, wore shapeless pants hitting above his ankles.

She moved the knife a centimeter at a time along the wall, eyeing the door, ready to sprint past him.

Sicard caught her left wrist in a steel grip.

"The parole office never heard of you," he said. "Who are you?"

Useless to lie now. "The truth?" she said. "Aimée Leduc, a private detective. My testimony put Nicolas in La Santé."

He stared at her.

"But I made a mistake," she said. "Nicolas tried to give me his notebook the day I visited him. The day he was killed."

"That's what *you* say."

"He didn't tell you?" She had to keep him talking, find a way to get past him and escape from this narrow, stifling place.

"How do you know Nicolas didn't commit suicide?" Sicard said.

"Nicolas wanted to expose them; he thought he had evidence," she said, her words coming fast. "That he'd get justice for the murder of that old couple."

Sicard stuck the notebook in his trouser pocket. Her moist hand held the knife, but she couldn't move. Sicard pinned her left arm against the wall.

"But you know all that, Sicard," she said. "He told you. You two shared a cell."

"Sharing a cell doesn't mean sharing secrets," Sicard said. "We were scheduled for the same parole date, but his lawyer screwed him. I found him hanging in the kitchen."

Sicard wouldn't need a job if he could get blackmail money. But she'd noticed his awkward gait, as if his shoes were too small. A small sag of defeat in his shoulders. Whatever he'd found, he hadn't figured out how to use it.

Perplexed, she wondered why.

"Weren't you supposed to give this notebook to Clémence?"

"Too late."

"Then why tear out some of the pages, Sicard?"

"They're at the copy shop. They weren't any good to Nicolas any more. Someone should make money with them." Sicard gave a short laugh. "You think they're beating down the door to hire me? The dock where I worked doesn't want to know me. I can't even pay for this place after tomorrow."

"And blackmail's easier."

His eyes glittered. "You're going to help me."

"You want to go down, implicated in Nicolas's murder?"

"Eh? Not me. In prison, you pay a guard ten thousand francs and it's done. But you'll never prove it."

Sweat trickled between her shoulder blades.

"I don't have to," she said. "Why did you get Nicolas work in the kitchen?"

"Quit changing the subject."

"It's a plum job, Sicard."

"Why not? He liked serving the VIP wing." Sicard let out a snort. "Better leftovers. Magazines."

She nodded, putting it together. "Those *Voici* magazines. He saw photos of Olivier with models, and it made him burn."

Sicard gave a quick nod.

"It's more than that, Sicard," she said. "What did he do for you in return?"

"Promised to help me when we got out."

"That's a lie. Come on, Sicard. What did he do for you?"

"Like I told you."

"Do you have children, Sicard?"

He shrugged. "Never had the time."

She nodded to the comic book and primer lying on the worn tile floor. It fit together now.

"I think you can't read, Sicard," she said. "That's why you needed Nicolas, and now Joêl."

Sicard kicked the wall. Plaster dust fanned over the tile. "Shut up."

"You don't understand the words in the notebook," she said. "It drives you crazy, so close and yet so far."

"Nicolas was stupid. Those aristos screw you."

"In return, Nicolas was teaching you to read, wasn't he?"

Shame and surprise showed on Sicard's face.

"Nicolas could have gone to a Grande École," she said. "He was bright, sharp, not like the other *mecs* in prison."

Sicard averted his eyes. But he hadn't let go of her arm. His grip was so tight, it was cutting off her circulation.

"That was the deal: you got him the job in the kitchen and he would teach you to read," she said, trying to think how she could use this to get away. "Why not scratch each other's back; nothing wrong with that."

"At night, Nicolas showed me letters." Sicard's words came slowly. His brow furrowed. "How to turn them the right way."

A dyslexic. He'd confused *b* and *d*.

"Then someone hanged him by his own socks from the meat hook," he said.

From the open leaded-glass window came the toot of a barge, the sound of lapping waves. She thought of making a break for the window, but it looked too small to climb out of and there would be a long drop below to the riverbank.

"And they'll get away with it, Sicard." Her breath came fast. "If you let them."

He wrenched her arm with the knife, grabbed the knife, and put it to her throat.

"You're my ticket out," he said. "I'll make them pay in my own way."

She had to reason with him. Perspiration dampened her brow.

Her eyes went to the hallway door, but he twisted her arms behind her, pushed her forward. Now he held her own knife pointed at the back of her neck. The sharp tip felt cold at the base of her skull.

"You think a little notebook will threaten the spoiled son of a ministry type, Sicard?" she said, gasping. "They have more people in their pockets than you'll ever know."

"Not if you help me." He tightened his grip. "With your help, I'll play them like a piano."

"Better you find work. I'll give you a job, Sicard."

According to her father, Vidocq, the first head of the Sûréte and a former thief, had said often that it took a crook to catch a crook.

"My firm needs part-time surveillance staff," she said. "We'll arrange it with your parole officer."

"Just like that, you're offering me a job?" He gave another short laugh. "Desperate, eh?"

"My neighbor, Chloë, teaches a literacy class. You can learn to read."

"Shut your mouth till we get to the car."

The hair rose on her neck.

"What car? Where are you taking me?"

"My money's gone and your promises don't put food in my stomach."

"But it could," she said. "You don't have to do this, Sicard. For kidnapping, you'll go right back to La Santé."

He opened the hallway door, looked both ways. No laundry cart, no maid. Deserted.

Sicard steered her across the landing, down the narrow winding stairs.

Too late.

Her arms were wrenched behind her painfully. Voices came from below. In that brief moment, Sicard tensed, holding her back. The voices receded. A door shut.

He shoved her forward, the knife point digging into her skin. His other hand squeezed her like a vise.

They reached the next landing. The last flight of steep, winding stairs was her last chance. She took two steps down; Sicard towered behind her. A master at this once, she prayed she remembered the technique René had taught her from the Dojo. A karate-type move he'd adapted to offset a mismatch with a *mec* twice his size, it was dependent on speed and surprise.

Now or never.

In a quick movement she snapped her head down as far as she could, gritting her teeth in pain at the wrenching of her arms. She squatted and butted her rear against his knees. Hard. Taken by surprise, Sicard's grip loosened. He let her go with a shout as he lost his balance.

He tottered, his arms reaching out, trying to catch the railing to break his fall. She heard a crack as his back slapped wood and he crumpled down the stairs.

He was still breathing. She straddled his body, reached into his pants pocket for the notebook. In his shirt pocket she found the copy shop receipt. He stirred, moaning.

She found her Swiss Army knife on the floor beneath the Versailles brochure rack in the lobby and nodded to a surprised old woman behind the desk.

"Treacherous, those stairs," she said. "Terrible. An accident just waiting to happen."

She reached for the phone on the woman's desk. Punched in 17 and handed the woman the receiver. "I'd ask them to hurry. The poor man's in pain."

* * *

Aimée wiped perspiration from her brow as she crossed the Conseil d'Etat forecourt in the Palais Royal. She willed down the trembling in her shoulders and legs. There was no one to witness but the yawning high windows framed by pillars and topped by bas-reliefs and statues forever sightless and frozen in stone.

She took tortoiseshell glasses from her bag, found her black wool cloche, and pulled the brim low on her brow.

She mounted the Ministry of Culture's wide staircase. Only vestiges of its former glory as Cardinal Richelieu's palace remained. The doorknob she turned was mounted on a gold plate adorned with embossed griffons.

"Madame de la Pecheray's in conference," said her secretary, a man with a pointed Van Dyke beard and a dismissive air.

"May I leave this with you?" She smiled, handing him her card. "She asked me to contact her today."

He scanned an appointment book. "I don't see your name," he said, eyeing the lit-up phone console on his pristine desk. "No guarantees that she'll receive this before tomorrow. She's in meetings all afternoon."

Aimée doubted that. But there were other ways to find out.

At the outer reception door, her arms still smarting from

Sicard's grip, she paused to put on her coat. A messenger walked in, clutching several Frexpresse envelopes under his arm.

"By four? Impossible," said the secretary. "I can't disturb Madame de la Pecheray." He paused. Aimée heard mumbling. "That important? I'll try Tania. See if she can bring it in to her. No promises, though."

Aimée slipped her arm in her coat. Down the hallway, white-plastered, gold-curlicued, Louis IV–sconced, she heard laughter. Inside of what looked like a series of high-ceilinged staff rooms, two women stood around a small espress machine. Secretaries.

Perfect. But she said a little prayer, just in case.

Aimée rushed in. "*Excusez-moi,* it's an emergency. My cousin Tania . . ." she stifled a sob . . . "her father's had a car accident."

Startled looks greeted her.

"Tania Assouline?"

She had to mobilize them fast before they questioned her.

"He might not make it," she said. "I can't remember which office Tania works in. Please help me find her."

"Tania, the councilor's secretary?" asked one woman, stubbing out her cigarette in a coffee cup.

Aimée nodded, gave another sob. "Is that upstairs?"

"First door on the right."

"*Mais non,*" said a blonde setting down her coffee. "Tania's organizing de la Pecheray's investiture in the Grand Salon."

The woman took her arm. "Take the back stairs, it's quicker."

Before she could reach the Grand Salon, she saw Gabrielle at the end of the hall conversing with several men in pinstriped suits. Aimée speeded up, but before she could reach her, Gabrielle had turned the corner.

By the time Aimée made it to the corner, Gabrielle had disappeared. She could have gone into any of the offices lining the hall. From the stairs on her right she heard the clattering of heels. A voice. She took a chance and ran down the modern stairs.

On the lower level, the hallway fanned into a wide underground corridor. Gabrielle's blond head bobbed in the distance. Thank God. A sign with CANTINE and an arrow pointing left appeared on the stucco wall.

But Gabrielle passed the canteen turnoff and went into a tunnel, which narrowed. Gabrielle lowered her head, speaking into a cell phone. To get reception down here, she must have a phone with special transmission for national security, Aimée thought.

Aimée tried to keep pace with her. Where was she going? And in such a hurry?

Now the tunnel branched in several directions. From somewhere came a moldering smell of damp, the drip of water. Tools and what looked like plumbing equipment lined this section. She figured they were under the fountain in the Palais Royal now.

Gabrielle turned left. The tunnel snaked and darkened. Ahead, lights illumined a rusted metal electrical control panel. She remembered the plumbers descending into the tunnel under Madame Fontenay's building. The old woman had mentioned tunnels underneath Palais Royal, implying that the chef, Carco, could have gone underground and surfaced at the medal shop.

But Gabrielle knew her way through the tunnels too. Shivers went up Aimée's neck, still sore from the knife scratch.

Gabrielle's heels clattered up the chipped stone stairs.

Moments later, Aimée found herself facing an immense blackened boiler, cold and unused for a century by the look of it. A whiff of perfume lingered among the musty smells. Gabrielle had come through here.

She found a door, opened it, and stood in a hallway among spotlights on black metal stands sheeted by red, blue, and orange gel filters. A forest of mobile spotlights.

"*Excusez-moi.*" She smiled at a lighting technician wearing a workcoat. Cables and extension cords webbed the red-carpeted floor.

"Did you see a blond woman just come out, Monsieur?"

He shook his head, chewing a pencil, and split wires off a power cord with pliers.

"Better watch your step," he said.

Opposite, she saw the double glass doors leading to the Palais Royal hemmed in by crates of sound equipment. The tunnel Gabrielle traveled could have branched to another tunnel on the other side of Palais Royal where Clémence had been strangled.

So easy.

"How can I get out, Monsieur?"

He pointed behind him. "Use the temporary exit."

"*Merci.*"

Aimée pushed through the heavy swinging doors and found herself in the darkened Comédie Française theatre. A set was being erected by a stage crew. But no Gabrielle. How could she just disappear?

And then Aimée saw a flash of blond hair in a second-floor balcony box. She retraced her steps, hopped over the cables, and took the steps up to the balcony floor. A red velvet rope with gold tassels blocked the way. She slipped under the red rope and tried each door. She found Gabrielle in the third balcony box, huddled on a red velvet theatre seat, speaking into her cell phone.

Gabrielle looked up in alarm. She wore a dark blue Chanel jacket, a twisted rope of pearls around her neck.

"Who are you?"

Aimée removed her glasses and the hat and stuck them in her bag. Her fingers found the button on the micro recorder by her wallet. She pushed RECORD.

"Remember me now? I've got proof now that you paid Nicolas to cover up your son's role in the synagogue burning, Madame," Aimée said, catching her breath. "And I don't think you'll want your lawyer present."

"Aah, so it's you. But I attempted to leave the money." This well-coiffed woman looked frantic, a different person from this morning. Lines creased her well-made-up face. Her mouth, with perfectly applied dark red lipstick, trembled. "Money, that's what you want," Gabrielle said. She scrabbled in her pocket. Her hand came back with an envelope thick with francs. "Why didn't you tell me at the apartment? Count it."

Aimée figured Clémence had tried to blackmail her.

"Not my style, Madame."

"'Style'? *Alors*, you'll buy style with this," Gabrielle interrupted. "Give me this notebook. Tell your client there will be more when I see all the proof. But deal only with me, leave Olivier and my husband out of it."

"I don't think so."

Gabrielle scanned the theatre. Nervous and in a hurry, Aimée thought. Itching to have her gone. Gabrielle had made a rendezvous to meet someone.

Aimée wondered who.

On the blue spotlit stage, technicians moved scenery with the façade of a chateau painted on it back and forth, to directions shouted from the director. A sound track of baroque chamber music played low. No one heard or paid them any attention up here in the balcony.

Gabrielle thrust the envelope at her again.

"Take it," she said. "Consider this over. Finished."

"But it's just the beginning," Aimée said.

"What's wrong? I came as fast as I could. *Maman?*" Olivier stood in the red-velvet-lined balcony box. Anger suffused his face as he recognized Aimée. "You!"

"It's all here." Aimée held up Nicolas's notebook. "Records of the money sent to Nicolas to keep quiet. The old couple's prayer book. One count of vehicular manslaughter, if you're lucky."

"But my son didn't kill anyone," Gabrielle said. "He knows nothing about that old couple."

Aimée stepped close to Olivier. "Explain it to her, Olivier."

His face went white. "You're obsessed." He backed up, shaking his head.

"Then I will. You torched the synagogue," Aimée said. "Then ran down the old couple. You were drunk, you didn't care. You left their little grandson crying in the gutter, covered with blood."

"What are you talking about?" Olivier said. But the pretense of outrage didn't reach his eyes.

"No one connected the accident to the synagogue fire until now," Aimée said. "At first I thought you were covering up for someone else."

She still did. If she pushed him enough, maybe he'd crack.

"Nicolas kept their prayer book for insurance," Aimée continued. "He refused to cover up any longer. You paid a guard to silence him for ten thousand francs, the going prison rate. Clémence was pregnant and broke. She attempted to blackmail your mother. You couldn't risk her opening her mouth."

"But Olivier had no idea," Gabrielle said, twisting her pearls. "You can't believe my son—"

"Audric told me everything, Olivier," Aimée interrupted. "Nicolas had given me proof, or so you assumed," Aimée said. "So to discredit me, you had René, my partner, shot Monday night."

"Who?" Genuine surprise filled his eyes.

Olivier wouldn't get away with it this time.

"Count on the Brigade Criminelle launching an investigation," Aimée said. "It's just a matter of hours until you and your parents sit in a cell."

"Wait." Olivier shook his head. "Don't involve them. It's all my fault."

A quiver of unease shot through Aimée. This was too quick.

"What do you admit?"

His lanky frame crumpled on the seat. "Nicolas, Clémence, the old people."

"And René?"

"René? I don't know who you're talking about," Olivier said.

Gabrielle's eyes widened. "Impossible. You never went to the synagogue." She shook her head. "Papa found you, he told me he picked you up that night."

"Shut up, *Maman*."

"He said he'd smashed the car bumper. . . ." Her voice trailed off.

"Keep quiet, *Maman*." Olivier stood and stepped in front of her. "I did the rest, but I didn't touch your partner. I couldn't have."

Olivier's words stopped Aimée in her tracks.

"What do you mean?"

"Monday night I was partying at the rave in Neuilly," he said.

"I didn't get back till dawn. How would I know your partner anyway? I saw you last night for the first time at the church."

She wished she didn't believe him.

"My boy's innocent." Gabrielle's voice trembled.

"*Non*, I did it," Olivier said. "I confess. Even so, you won't convict me. That's not proof."

And now Aimée knew. The pieces fell into place. Why hadn't she seen it before?

"Forget the heroics, Olivier; quit covering up," Aimée said.

"Look, all this started as a schoolboy prank," Gabrielle said. "Things got out of hand. We wanted to protect him."

Burning a synagogue, a "prank"?

"'Protect him'? You were protecting your job and your husband's position."

"Can't we keep this quiet? We can come to an arrangement." Gabrielle's voice rose. "What does it matter now? The poor boy's dead. We paid him, I admit. That's all," Gabrielle said. "It's terrible that he committed suicide. I feel responsible."

"It wasn't suicide. He was murdered." Aimée stared at Gabrielle. "Don't you see? Nicolas was out of control. Your husband had to stop him."

"My husband?" Taken aback, Gabrielle's hand flew to her mouth.

"Stop it!" Olivier shouted, his eyes flashing.

She'd touched the right nerve.

"Your husband picked up a drunk Olivier after the synagogue burning and ran over the old couple. Instead of owning up, he fled."

Gabrielle was speechless. Her face sagged. She looked a decade older.

"I saw your husband minutes after Clémence's murder Wednesday night," Aimée said. "He escaped to the ministry via the same tunnel under the Palais Royal you just used. He'd returned to make sure the job was done right."

"Wednesday? Impossible." Gabrielle shook her head. "Roland was negotiating with delegates about the proposal to disclose the National Archives documents. No one can leave negotiations."

Her instinct said Gabrielle was telling the truth. Then who had murdered Clémence? But two things seemed certain.

"Face it, your husband covered up his crime. And he's still covering up."

"Or maybe it was you, Madame?" Out of the corner of her eye she watched Olivier for a reaction. "Did you engineer the coverup?"

"Liar!" Olivier's fist shot out.

Aimée caught his arm, twisted it, and shoved him down onto a red velvet seat. "Make another move and I break your fingers. One by one."

"I won't let you hurt my parents," said Olivier in the voice of a scared child. "Not you or anyone." His lips trembled, tears brimmed in his eyes. He looked desperate. "Let me go."

"What's the matter, Olivier?" Gabrielle said. "What haven't you told me?"

"How can you of all people ask me that?" He stared at his mother, lip quivering, an accusing look in his eyes. "All through my childhood, there were whispers, people stopped talking when I entered a room. Did you think I didn't know why *grand-père* hanged himself? They wanted to imprison him for deporting Jews."

A dawning recognition formed on Gabrielle's face. She gestured to Aimée, who let go. Gabrielle caressed Olivier's hair, then took him in her arms. "*Mon petit, grand-père* couldn't live with his mistakes."

"But Papa didn't mean to." A sob escaped Olivier. "He didn't mean to hurt the old couple. I don't want Papa to hang himself too."

"Oh, my God," Gabrielle's voice quavered.

She held her son tight. Her eyes were pools of pain.

Aimée felt for this woman who had to decide between her son and her husband.

"My son can't go to prison for what Roland did." Her voice was firm as she spoke her decision. "I've done things I'm not proud of. But no more. It's time to tell the truth, break this curse."

Curse? Aimée recalled an incident years earlier: a government official had hanged himself in his garden to avoid revelations concerning his notorious Vichy past.

Aimée stared at her. "Robert Bressac was your father?"

Gabrielle gave a small nod.

"No wonder you're working to keep the National Archives sealed," Aimée said.

"You think revelations of my father's past still matter? Will they bring him back to life? Or the people he sent to their deaths? They're gone. Smoke." A tired bitterness crept into her voice. "I just bleach the government's dirty linen." A small shrug. "My boss, *le ministre*, has more to hide than anyone. But he can keep the lid on for only so long."

Aimée glanced at her watch. "We need to have a little talk with your husband."

Gabrielle averted her eyes, but not before Aimée saw her fear. "*Non*."

"Didn't you say you wanted to break this 'curse' and tell the truth? Now's your chance." Aimée pulled out the micro recorder. "It's all on tape anyway."

"You can't use that," Olivier said. "It's illegal."

"Try me."

Aimée pointed to the red-velvet-quilted door of the box. "But we don't want to be late for your husband's investiture ceremony at the ministry, do we?"

Gabrielle blinked back tears. "Please, can't this wait?"

Until Roland de la Pecheray became entrenched in the ministry, making the case against him harder to mount? She flicked open her cell phone and hit *La Proc's* number.

"I'm sorry, Madame. Nicolas waited four years, and look what your husband did to him."

* * *

IN THE MINISTRY of Culture's high-ceilinged anteroom to the Grand Salon, Aimée picked out Roland de la Pecheray hovering near two ministry assistants. He wore a black morning suit and striped silk tie. Pride suffused his face as he saw his wife and son approach. He rushed forward.

"The ministry staff organized a champagne reception following the investiture, Gabrielle." He took her arm and Olivier's. "May I escort my family, whose love and support has brought me here?"

Through the salon's open doors, Aimée saw a crowd of well-dressed dignitaries gathered within cream-and-gilt-edged walls. They exuded an almost palpable power. Chandeliers glittered with Bohemian crystal. A scent of honeysuckle wafted through the open balcony doors overlooking the Cour d'Honneur below.

"Monsieur de la Pecheray," she said, stepping forward, "I suggest you first view Nicolas Evry's notebook. In your office."

He paused in mid-step, the smile frozen on his face.

"Roland, let me offer you advance congratulations. *Formidable*!" said a smiling white-haired man in a blue suit.

Roland nodded, smiling. "*Merci*, Conseiller."

The *conseiller* patted him on the back and entered the salon.

"Admission is by invitation only, Mademoiselle," Roland said to her in an undertone. "Please leave before you're escorted out."

"I wouldn't like to make a scene, Monsieur," she said, "but I will."

Roland let go of Gabrielle and Olivier. "What's going on?"

Gabrielle's lip quivered. "Roland, talk to her."

"Now? You're crazy, Gabrielle."

Roland caught the eye of a security guard, motioned to him.

"Not a good idea, Monsieur." Aimée raised her voice. "Your son's on tape admitting that you ran over an old Jewish couple and drove off, leaving them for dead."

"She tricked me, Papa. I didn't mean to tell. But you know people. Explain about the accident, and I'm sure they will understand."

Roland's lips pursed. "Putting words in my son's mouth, Mademoiselle? Hounding and coercing him? I'm pressing charges."

Aimée thrust the notebook pages in his face. "Not a good idea. Nicolas Evry recorded payments received from your bank account to shut him up and serve a prison sentence in place of Olivier. And then you engineered his hanging in prison. You were afraid of what he might say once he was released on parole, afraid it would injure your career."

The security guard approached, speaking into a small microphone clipped to his collar. A few heads turned.

"But losing this post is nothing compared to conviction of double murder," Aimée said. "Clémence was pregnant."

"What the hell . . . I don't understand."

Aimée stepped forward and flashed her father's old police ID with her photo glued to it at the guard. She had to keep de la Pecheray off keel until the *flics* arrived.

"My unit's cooperating with Groupe R and the Brigade Criminelle," she said to the guard. She hoped Morbier wouldn't find out and shoot her before she could explain. "It's imperative that Monsieur de la Pecheray and all of you cooperate."

The young guard, in a ceremonial blue, red, and white military uniform with a red sash, looked from her to Roland de la Pecheray.

"Let me see that." The guard took her ID. "Ministry security doesn't take orders from the *flics*."

"You do now."

Voices and the buzz of a loudspeaker came from the grand salon. "*Mesdames et Messieurs, Monsieur le Ministre,* it's with great pleasure that we welcome a distinguished ministry official to the position. . . ," a man's voice droned.

"Gabrielle, tell them I'm coming," Roland said, shooting her a look. But Gabrielle stood, in shock, staring at her husband.

"There's some mistake." De la Pecheray was smiling now. A thin smile. "The minister's waiting. We'll clear up this misunderstanding afterward."

Turning to the guard, Aimée said, "National Security's involved. Within three minutes you could be called on to evacuate the ministry. Tell the minister that there's a delay."

The guard blinked.

"Do I need to remind you of the lives that are at stake in this building?" she said, mustering as much authority in her voice as she could. "All branches work together regarding National Security. Put emergency protocol in place. Now."

"*Alors*, you mean there's a bomb threat?"

"Smart boy. Move."

He hurried inside as he spoke into his collar microphone.

Aimée kicked the doors shut after him. They shuddered on

their intricate gold hinges. Now only Gabrielle and Olivier stood beside Roland in the long hallway.

The honeysuckle scent was stronger now. Pigeons cooed from the balcony.

"Weak, spoiled idiot." Roland glared at Olivier. "And after all I've done for you." He hissed at Gabrielle. "The years it took to climb the ladder because of your father. Now you pay me back like this, Gabrielle? Some pangs of conscience? A little late for that."

Gabrielle stepped back.

"Fix this, Gabrielle. Make a call," he demanded.

Her eyes wavered. Aimée couldn't lose her now.

"I'm afraid not, Monsieur," Aimée said. "*La Proc's* en route to question you."

"You'd be surprised at Gabrielle's connections, Mademoiselle," Roland said with a little smile. "The ministry takes care of its own. No one here likes surprises. You and that notebook will disappear."

"Threatening me like you threatened Olivier? Tell your wife the truth."

He shook his head. "Make the call, Gabrielle."

"You think your wife will get you off the hook and put her son in prison?"

Roland shoved Aimée against the half-open glass balcony doors. The long blue drapery caught around her ankles. She stumbled onto the balcony, into the sunlight. Roland's hands circled her neck, squeezing tight. She couldn't breathe.

Screams came from the anteroom. Her arms flailed against the carved stone edge of the balcony. Her body pressed against the ledge, and she was pushed further and further until her shoulders hung in midair. With all her might, she kneed him in the crotch.

She heard a "*Wheuff*," footsteps, voices.

"Monsieur de la Pecheray, we're waiting for you!"

Roland grimaced in pain. She struggled loose and saw the startled exchange of looks between the minister in his morning coat and his staff members.

"What's the meaning of this?" the minister demanded.

"He tried to kill me," Aimée said, panting. "He was pushing me off the balcony."

Blue-uniformed *flics* edged through the crowd led by *La Proc*, Edith Mésard, in a tailored black suit.

"*Et alors*, never far from the action, Mademoiselle Leduc," *La Proc* said.

Aimée straightened, catching her breath.

"Nice to see you, too, Madame *la Procureur*."

Friday Afternoon

"AND WHY HAVEN'T you furnished this information to the Brigade Criminelle, Mademoiselle Leduc?" Edith Mésard, the investigating magistrate, tapped her red-lacquered nails on her briefcase.

"Considering the sensitive nature of the information involved," Aimée said, twisting the ring on her middle finger, "I thought it wiser to contact you."

"What else, Mademoiselle Leduc?"

Edith Mésard, *La Proc*, dealt with crime on a daily basis. Bank robberies and bribery cases before lunch; murder and crimes of violence she saved for the afternoon.

"Four years ago, I testified in the case you helped prosecute against one Nicolas Evry." Aimée handed her the notebook, Sicard's copy-shop receipt, and the microcassette. "But this is evidence that Olivier de la Pecheray was the guilty party in the synagogue arson and, further, that his father killed an old Jewish couple in a hit-and-run vehicular homicide."

"Are you saying that there is sufficient reason for me to recommend reopening the investigation and to prosecute a newly posted ministry official?"

Aimée faced Edith Mésard in the closet-size glassed-in *guardien's* loge adjoining the Comedie Française. "Technically speaking, de la Pecheray's post hadn't become official; but, put that way, *oui*."

"That depends." Edith Mésard gave a little shrug in her tailored black jacket. "Roland de la Pecheray's confession would help."

"Help?" Frustrated, she shot a glance at Gabrielle and Olivier getting into one police car, Roland into another. "De la Pecheray's wife admitted paying off Evry to take the blame for their son. You have the bank-account information in Evry's notebook. His son admitted on tape that his father ran the old people down and fled the scene. He attacked and almost killed me. What else do you need?"

"It's a start, Mademoiselle Leduc." Edith Mésard put the notes from her conversation with Gabrielle de la Pecheray under her arm. "However, Madame de la Pecheray confirmed that on Monday, the night of the attack on Monsieur Friant, her husband attended a ministry party with a hundred and thirty officials and employees who'll testify that he never left."

"He hired a lookalike," Aimée suggested.

"You give de la Pecheray too much credit," *La Proc* said. "De la Pecheray not only 'appeared' at the party, he worked the room. He couldn't have been impersonated. I find it difficult to believe he found you a threat, Mademoiselle Leduc."

"So he tried to throw me off the balcony because he liked me? He was afraid Evry had told me the truth. He was afraid I'd found out too much: about the old couple he'd run down, and about the strangling of Evry's woman."

But Mésard had sowed doubt in her mind. Why would he hire a an impersonator to shoot René? Yet if he hadn't had René shot, who had?

Edith Mésard signaled to her driver. "Melac informed me that Tracfin has assembled evidence of your firm laundering illicit funds. You've got big problems of your own, Mademoiselle."

Hadn't Saj found the wire deposits' origin? A link, something?

"What evidence?"

"I shouldn't even have revealed that," Edith Mésard said. "But considering what you've brought to my attention, which of course I will say came from an anonymous source, maybe I owe it to you. Forewarned is forearmed, Mademoiselle Leduc."

And with that, Mésard's heels clicked over the stone pavers to her waiting Renault. If de la Pecheray hadn't had René shot, or murdered Clémence, she was back at zero. All this for . . . what?

But right now she had a "big problem" to deal with. Saj hadn't answered her call to Leduc Detective, nor could she reach him on his cell phone.

Ten minutes later, she unlocked Leduc Detective's door. Her desk, René's, and the shelves were bare. Only outlines in the dust showed where their computers had sat. BRIF must have impounded their computers and, no doubt, taken Saj in for questioning.

Fear licked up her spine.

How could they do that?

Never mind how. They had.

She sat at her bare desk, cradling her head in her arms. Discovering Nicolas's notebook, confronting Gabrielle de la Pecheray, obtaining the truth from Olivier, and furnishing the proof to Edith Mésard had gotten her nowhere. Meant nothing. She was still a suspect, no closer to finding the woman who'd attacked René.

Failure. Her best friend had been shot, her business had ground to a halt. She felt her grandfather gazing down from the framed photo on the shelf. Could hear him saying once again, "A nice mess you've gotten yourself into, Aimée."

She racked her brain trying to think what she could have done to have endangered René. Revenge, love, or money were the three motives for crime, he'd always say. He'd based his career in the Sûreté and later in Leduc Detective on that.

What was she missing?

She sat up and checked the answering machine. No messages. But in the dust on her desk she saw finger marks. Words. And then she made out, in Saj's hand, LUX-SWISS-CAYMAN.

Luxembourg banks to Swiss banks, on to Cayman Islands accounts, the usual route traffickers used to launder money.

She didn't know how it fit, but she knew who could find out. She punched in Léo Frot's old number at the Finance Ministry. Three departments later, she found him.

"Léo? Too bad we didn't hook up at Club Eros."

"I lost you at the whipping post," he said, his voice low.

She suppressed a shudder thinking of the whip, the cubicles, and the figure in leather who'd chased her to the Métro.

"I'm going there tonight," she said, letting out a big sigh, "if I get my work done. Tracing funds to a Cayman bank is really holding me up."

"Forget it, Aimée. No more favors."

"Pretend you don't owe me, Léo." He never liked being reminded. "Call it a simple favor so I can finish up soon." She honeyed her voice and paused to let that sink in.

"How soon?" A hopeful tone crept into his voice.

"Depends if you can help me or not," she said. "Tracfin's tracing an account I need."

"Tracfin's a different branch under the Ministry of Economy," he said. "Not my stomping grounds."

"But you know people, Léo."

He knew everyone and massaged egos to get favors.

"And if I do it?"

"*Alors*, if not I'll be here all night."

"Before ten?"

Like hell she would.

"Count on it."

* * *

TEN MINUTES LATER, a knock sounded on Leduc Detective's door. Taking her bag, she opened it, keeping her hand on her Swiss Army knife inside.

Luigi stood outside on the landing with a sheepish expression. He shifted his feet and put a finger to his lips, pointing to Viaggi Travel's open door.

She started to speak, but he shook his head. Warily, she followed him. He closed his office door and turned off the light.

"Not so fast, Luigi." What had she walked into?

Luigi clicked on a small desk lamp. "But it's for you."

A telephone receiver lay on the green blotter of his desk.

"A call for me here? Why?"

His eyes flickered over the knife. Then he pointed to his ears, then to her office.

Before she could say anything, he took his jacket from the chair, turned, and left. She picked up the receiver.

"*Allô?*"

"Aimée, they bugged the office, your phone, your apartment," René said. "There's a *flic* outside my door."

Her heart thumped.

"René, are you all right? Where are you?" Her words raced. "Melac refuses to tell me anything."

"Just listen."

"But your surgery. How are you feeling?"

"Aimée, I've got one minute. Can you listen for once?"

She swallowed. "Of course."

"Write this down."

She scrabbled for a pen on Luigi's desk. Found one with green ink. "Go ahead."

"2-0122-7389. The wire deposit originated in Luxembourg, then was routed to Switzerland—"

"Then to the Caymans," she interrupted.

"How do you know?"

"Saj wrote that in the dust."

"Keeping the office clean, as usual." René snorted. "Tracfin's investigation stopped at the Caymans. Follow the money. Write this down: a Lichtenstein account, number 7894-8334."

"Meaning?"

"Guess who?"

"I thought you were in a hurry, René?"

"You can blame it on our friend Nadillac," René said.

Amazed, she fell back in the chair. "You mean he put up a hundred and fifty thousand francs just to discredit me?"

"By linking you to money-launderers, he'd invalidate your testimony and save millions for his firm," René said. "After receiving our report of his sabotage, the last thing his firm wanted was to let it be known. It would have shown the leaks in their system. So they 'encouraged' him to route company money via a wire transfer to you from hot spots on Tracfin's blacklist. Then, big surprise. The money's all back in his firm now, like it never left. He covered his tracks. Who'd check a brief discrepancy in his firm's accounts, he figured. Who was to know, eh? The firm never lost the money, but now we're involved in a money-laundering investigation."

A master of his metier, René astounded her sometimes.

"Expose Nadillac, Aimée."

"With my teeth? How can I? They took our computers, René. My money says Tracfin's analyzing them now."

"And it's impossible for me to break into their internal system unless I'm on site."

But, courtesy of Léo, she could.

"No problem, partner. I can."

"How?" It was René's turn to be surprised. "Never mind. Get to it. Now, Aimée!"

Then the peal of a church bell rang in the background.

"Watch out, Aimée. Be careful."

She heard laughter, ". . . fresh forest mushrooms folded in the omelet. Next time dinner's my treat. . . ." Was René standing outside? A door shut, she heard footsteps; the church bell was muffled now. She heard more footsteps.

"Monsieur René! You're late again for pool exercise therapy."

"I miss you, partner," she said, but René had clicked off.

She ran to the window, opening it to the sound of the pealing church bells of Saint-Germain-l'Auxerrois, the former parish church of kings, at the nearby Louvre. A Romanesque, Renaissance, and Gothic mixture, painted by Monet. She heard those bells every evening, the same infamous ringing that had signaled the sixteenth-century Saint Bartholomew's Day Massacre of the Huguenots.

And not three blocks away.

René had given her a clue to his location. Close to the church, a clinic or hospital big enough to have a pool, near a café or resto. She pulled open the drawers in Luigi's desk, pulled out the Yellow Pages. She found only one clinic in the first arrondissement, Clinique du Louvre on rue des Prêtres Saint-Germain l'Auxerrois. Samaritaine, the art deco department store, stood at the end of the block. An advertisement listed the clinic's special services as orthopedic therapy and hydrotherapy.

He'd been almost a cobblestone's throw away the whole time.

On Luigi's phone, a high-end digital console affair, she dialed the contact number she had obtained from Léo Frot.

The phone was picked up on the first ring.

"Monsieur Ritoux, please," she said.

"Who's calling?"

"It concerns a confidential matter," she said. "I need to speak with him right away."

"Please identify yourself and the matter this concerns."

And have him file it away?

The phone's digital display flashed the number she'd called.

She trusted no one. She would only speak with Ritoux.

"It's vital, Monsieur," she said. "He's unaware of important documentation. I want to deliver it."

"This office isn't open to the public. We have no contact with individuals."

We'll see about that, she thought, reading an address which had popped up in the digital display. Tracfin showed up as being in the ninth arrondissement. Nice feature! She'd have to get one of these phones.

"Funny. I thought in the government you *served* the public."

She hung up and ran back to her office. There was no time to search it for bugs. With her penlight, she grabbed an outfit from her disguises in the back armoire, stuffed it in her bag, away from any prying camera. Five minutes later, in the hall bathroom, she'd changed into an express delivery uniform. She checked her Tintin watch. She had to hurry.

* * *

THE TAXI LET her off in the mist on narrow rue de la Tour des Dames.

She buzzed the intercom near the gate. "Express for a Monsieur Ritoux, from Bercy."

"Eh? This time of night?" She heard the clearing of a throat. Maybe she'd woken the guard up.

"I just do what I'm told," she said, "and it's cold out here."

Getting inside depended on speed, on not giving the guard time to think about following procedures.

The gate buzzed open. The guard, in his forties, a bear-like man, stretched his arms over his head. "Bercy always informs me if they're sending a delivery."

Before he called and checked, she had to get inside Ritoux's office.

"It's urgent," she said, walking fast. "Which floor?"

"*Alors, Mademoiselle*, since when do they use female messengers?" He blocked her way.

Merde! Now she'd have to distract his attention

She stopped. "Do you have a problem with that?"

"Show me ID and the envoy slip," he said, alert now, a grin spreading over his face.

Envoy slip?

"So you think we should still be barefoot, in the kitchen with babies, eh?"

"Hold on." He extended his pawlike hands in mock surprise. "Just following procedure. Where's Philippe?"

The usual messenger, or a trick question?

"Like I know?" For the second time today, she flashed her retouched father's police ID with her photo pasted on it. "A last-minute directive from the minister's office, requiring Monsieur Ritoux's response."

"Still, I need the envoy slip to sign you in."

She shrugged, glanced at her watch, then his name tag. "It's your neck, Boulet, not mine. Don't you get it? Classified documents, covert operation, that's why they use us, not the regular messenger. Safer."

"What?" Boulet looked uneasy now.

She said, "You'd better hurry, since the minister's waiting for Ritoux's response."

"Second floor," he said. "Third office door."

She ran, perspiration dampening her collar. Her bluff would last only so long.

In a doorway on the second floor, she shimmied out of the jumpsuit she'd worn, putting it in her bag. Then she smoothed down her pencil skirt, buttoned her blouse up to the collar, smoothed back her hair, and put on tortoise-shell-framed glasses again.

She knocked, opened the door, and strode through an office reception area. Deserted.

"Monsieur Ritoux?"

A man poked his head out of an office. "Didn't we request those files half an hour ago? What's with you people?"

She shrugged.

"Junior clerks! Glad I don't work downstairs any more." He glared. "What are you waiting for? Ritoux's steaming."

She backed up. "I'm new."

"That's the problem downstairs, you're all green and know nothing. End of the hall," he said. "The *big* door. Even you can't miss it. Tell him I'm coming too."

A big door, all right. Massive and wood-paneled. She paused to take stock of the building. Tracfin was housed in an old mansion, and Ritoux, by the look of it, had the master suite.

She squared her shoulders. Knocked and stepped inside.

Another reception area with a desk. Empty, but an open office door loomed on the right. She opened a drawer, took out some Tracfin correspondence, and put the letters on top of the notes she'd made of René's information.

Gritting her teeth, she walked inside the inner office.

"Sorry to take so long," she said, smiling. "We had issues with filing procedures."

A few heads looked up.

"Monsieur Ritoux, *excusez-moi*, but we think you should see this."

A man with oversized seventies-style frame glasses, wearing suspenders, cocked his head.

"But who are you?"

"I'm new, from downstairs, a junior clerk. Our team found this data. It came from a confidential informant relating to a case . . . well, it doesn't give the case number."

He hit SAVE on his desktop computer. "Where's Despaille?"

"En route, Monsieur." She hoped Despaille was the impatient man who'd directed her this way. "Here, Monsieur Ritoux."

She set the file down, opened it, and pulled her numerical notations out.

"What does this mean?"

He had garlic breath.

"A wire transfer from this account was moved five times. We found it significant that the transferred funds landed right back where they had originated."

Ritoux shoved his glasses onto his forehead and squinted, scrutinizing the paper. "Who's working on the . . ." he paused, reading the numbers . . . "the flagged wire transfer from Luxembourg and the SAR report we discussed tonight?"

"Over here, Monsieur Ritoux," said a man working on a laptop. "We questioned the employee, that long-haired hippie."

"Him . . . that one? Then get him in here to explain this!"

Saj? Aimée tried to melt into the woodwork.

"Distribute the updates, Mademoiselle," he said. "That's your job, remember? Besides sniffing around with your team."

"Of course, Monsieur."

She consulted the file in her hands and tried to look efficient, but she knew she had to get out of here fast and somehow warn Saj.

"Where's the 2134 Bursar's Report?" said a man at her elbow.

What could she do? Flustered, she riffled through the papers. "2134? But they put in the 2130. Can you believe it? Let me get the right one."

She backed out of the room and into the reception area, turned, and bumped into a man, his tie loosened, his shirt sleeves rolled up. Saj stood behind him.

She froze. Saj stared at her. "What in the . . . ?"

"Monsieur Ritoux," she interrupted, her adrenalin kicking in, "needs this man to explain the information he's just received about a wire transfer routed five times from a Luxembourg bank account and then *back again* according to information provided by a confidential informant."

The man shook his head. "What's that to me?"

She dropped the file, spilling papers all over the floor, and kneeled to pick them up. Saj kneeled, too. They only had a second.

"It's Nadillac's scam," she said in an undertone. "The money's all back home."

"Understood," said Saj.

Saj handed Aimée the papers he'd picked up, with a wink.

* * *

A COUPLE WERE getting out of a taxi at the end of the street. She couldn't believe her luck. "Clinique du Louvre, *s'il vous plaît*," she said to the taxi driver.

She knew Saj could handle himself. With the account numbers René had furnished, he'd get out of Tracfin in an hour. Or less, knowing Saj. Maybe they'd even hire Saj to do the backdoor work they couldn't.

She'd known deep in her bones that her mother had no part of this. Just Morbier, and his suspicions. She felt vindicated.

In the rearview mirror, she noticed a taxi following them, turning left when they did. A few blocks later, it stayed a car length behind as her driver weaved into rue Montmartre, then past Les Halles.

Not good, with the Clinique du Louvre only a few blocks away. She couldn't lead whoever was tailing her to René's location. It would be smarter to get her old backup laptop from the armoire at home, feed Miles Davis, then figure out where to go next.

She reached over the seat and handed the taxi driver fifty francs. "Make a right up there. See?" She pointed to a clump of trees and parked cars.

He nodded.

"Then speed up and finish the ride without me. But don't go near the original destination. *Compris?*"

He nodded again. "Like in that old Lino Ventura movie?"

"That's right."

She crouched on the floor. As the taxi veered right, she hit the left back door handle and heaved herself out, covering her chest with her arms. She rolled over the sharp cobbles, feeling each one, and ended up on fallen branches. She waited until the car following her receded down the street.

Nothing broken, but there were oil stains on her skirt and dirt under her fingernails and an ache in her ribs. She walked toward the red Métro sign, rubbing her side. But the Métro gate was shut. The strike!

She punched in Morbier's number. Only a message. She swallowed her pride.

"Morbier? Pick up if you're home. Can Miles Davis and I borrow your couch tonight?"

A beep and the message ended. She waited. Then the phone buzzed.

* * *

SHE BREATHED IN the musty air of her dark apartment. A faint rose fragrance came from the dining room, the only remnant of her dinner with Mathieu four nights ago.

"Miles Davis?"

There was no answering scamper of paws across the wood floor.

Usually, Madame Cachou walked him at night and brought him back. But considering Madame's bursitis, she figured Chloë might have helped her out tonight. She didn't want to switch on the light, which would activate the cameras the *flics* had mounted in her apartment.

In her bedroom, she rooted in her armoire and found the old backup laptop and grabbed her stovepipe jeans and a vintage YSL black-and-white polka-dot silk spaghetti strap top. It was the first thing to come to hand, but better than her oil-stained blouse.

She was still on the run, from whom she didn't know. Gabrielle, Olivier, and Roland de la Pecheray had been carted off for questioning at the Brigade Criminelle. She'd discovered that Nadillac had moved the money to discredit her. But none of them had had anything to do with René's shooting. Perplexed, she realized that she was no further than before in finding out who had tried to kill him.

Think. She had to think and put together the facts she had. Someone had set this all up with painstaking thoroughness. A woman her height, in clothes like hers, who could get into this building. Chloë? But Chloë was her friend. That was silly.

The only woman unaccounted for was Nicolas's sister, Maud. But she'd been committed to a mental institution in Lille.

She wiggled into her tight jeans, stuck the phone in her back pocket, and stepped into black stilettos. On her way out, she took Miles Davis's horsemeat from the fridge, stuck that, too, in her bag, and grabbed her black military-style wool coat for warmth.

Chloë must have returned from walking Miles Davis and, noticing the dark apartment, taken him upstairs. Thoughtful as usual. She envisioned a cup of tea from Chloë's ever-full teapot, a place to sit down and think.

She had to go upstairs to check, if only to put her mind at rest and to pick up Miles Davis. She felt guilty even suspecting Chloë.

The stairs creaked, narrowing as she reached the fifth floor where the *chambres de bonnes*, the maids' rooms, were located. She heard the droning of a radio, a speech broken by intermittent applause. She recognized Jean-Marie Le Pen's voice, the distinctive haranguing tone of his call to "Keep France for the French."

As she was about to knock, she saw the chinks of light around the edges of the doorframe and smelled gas. Her smile faded.

"Chloë?"

Miles Davis's yelp answered her.

The door wasn't locked. Aimée stepped inside.

Miles Davis was chained to the open skylight of the attic room. As he jumped on his hind legs, his yelp turned into a keening whine.

Each time he jumped, the chain attached to his collar choked him.

"What in the world?" She dropped her bag, rushed over and lifted Miles Davis up. She loosened the chain digging into his furry neck and held him close. His tongue licked her face all over; his leash trailed on the floor.

Then the door slammed shut behind her. The deadbolt clicked into place.

Chloë faced her, wearing a demure navy blue suit and perfect navy pumps, like an Air France hostess. Tortoiseshell glasses rested on her nose. A different person confronted Aimée.

"I'm disappointed, Aimée," Chloë said. "I warned you about Mathieu, as your friend. But did you listen? *Non.*"

Aimée scanned the room, and her gaze fell on the beige crocodile loafers peeking out from under the bed. The ones worn by the woman in the security video. Shoes she'd never be caught dead in.

"You shot René and framed me," she accused Chloë.

She'd believed that Chloë was a friend, confided in her, entrusted her with Miles Davis.

"Who are you?" she asked.

Suitcases sat by the door; a pile of clothes was heaped on the bed. Chloë was moving out.

"I studied you. Every detail. Now it's your turn," Chloë said. "You have to suffer."

Aimée backed away. Something crackled under her feet. A cellophane candy wrapper. She recognized those red candy wrappers. *P'tits Quinquins* from Lille.

And finally it made sense.

"You're Nicolas's sister, Maud Evry," Aimée said. With Miles Davis in her arms, she took a step back. Her head knocked against the slanting roof and her back met the wall. There was nowhere to go in this closet-sized garret under the eaves. "But you were in Lille, in a mental institution."

"Let's say I left on my own terms." Maud smiled again. "But I was not in time to save Nicolas."

Aimée tried to control her rising panic. Somehow she had to get to the door, slip the bolt, and summon help.

"Save him?" The pieces fell into place. "*You* killed Clémence."

"That *putain*, nothing but a cheap slut. She never listened either."

"Clémence was pregnant with his baby. You killed your own blood."

Maud's mouth twisted sideways. "You're lying."

"You vowed to make whoever put Nicolas in prison pay. Revenge. That's what this is about."

"High marks," Maud said. "I wanted you to know. I almost told you myself."

"Chloë . . . Maud, you need help. We'll call your doctor."

Aimée stepped toward the door.

"For more shock treatments?" She shook her head, her eyes glazed.

"*Non*, of course not," Aimée said, trying to think fast, "but let's sort this out."

A short laugh. "You call isolation in a straitjacket 'help'? They chained me, like your dog."

A copper pot boiled on the cooktop; heat filled the room. The smell of gas mingled with the odor of rot from the roof timbers.

Maud gave a little sigh. "The *putain* gave me no choice." She flicked on all the burners on the gas stove. Little rings of blue flame blossomed. "Ever try dog meat?"

Miles Davis emitted a low growl.

"They say it tastes like rabbit."

With a quick movement, Aimée lifted Miles Davis up through the narrow open skylight and shoved him onto the roof. She counted on him to scamper to the flat part framing the gutter.

"Silly girl!" Maud stepped closer, a small snub-nosed revolver in her hand.

Prickles ran up Aimée's spine. She was being threatened by a psychotic with a gun, whom she'd thought was her friend. She edged around the bed piled with clothes and towels, toward the stove, scanning the dirty frying pans, the knives on the counter.

Miles Davis's barks from the roof competed with Le Pen's rising rhetoric from the radio . . . "We must stop immigrants from stealing French jobs."

The blue rings of flames licked higher, close to a lace curtain.

"Turn off the gas." Aimée grabbed a wet towel from the bed and threw it on the burner, dousing the flames.

"Why did you do that?" Maud said.

The gas pilot flame in the small old-fashioned water heater unit flickered above the sink. Gas fumes laced the close air.

"Don't you see that the pilot light's too near the burners?"

“You put Nicolas in that stinking hellhole.” Maud’s voice rose. “Full of lowlifes and filthy immigrants. Now you’ll pay.”

She echoed Le Pen.

“He was brilliant, he had a bright future, but he turned to the skinheads,” Maud said.

“Blame yourself. How could he study for entry to a Grande Ecole when you refused to support him?”

“He’d get no help from me while Clémence was around.” Maud’s eyes narrowed. “I told him.”

“He needed money, so he agreed to take the blame for Olivier de la Pecheray and went to prison,” Aimée said. “After four years, he’d had enough. He wouldn’t cover up the death of the old Jewish couple any longer.”

“Jews, Arabs, *Noirs d’Afrique*, that’s right. Unless the government takes control, they’ll infest us.” Maud stood so close, Aimée could see the fine beads of perspiration on her fingers holding the gun. “They’re like rodents. *They’re* the ones to blame.”

“Wrong,” Aimée rejoined. “Olivier’s father had Nicolas murdered in prison. And he was going to get away with it. Nicolas knew too much; he presented an obstacle to Roland de la Pecheray’s climb up the ministry ladder.”

The gas smell became stronger. The place could blow up.

“So *you* say.” Maud’s smile disappeared. “It’s a crime how those Jews stick together. They still control the banks. We should have taken care of all of them in the ovens.”

Aimée whacked Maud hard against the door. The revolver blasted a white flash. Burning pain grazed Aimée’s rib. Plaster rained down as a thin white powder from the bullet’s impact. She had to shut the gas off before it exploded; she couldn’t understand why the bullet hadn’t ignited it.

She clutched her side, stretching for the burner knob, but her fingers wouldn’t reach far enough.

Maud grabbed her legs. Aimée twisted, kicking Maud sideways. Haze burned her eyes; gas reeked, fogging her brain; pain smarted along her side. She felt the gun prod in her ribs.

"Your turn, Aimée Leduc."

She gritted her teeth. "Not in your lifetime."

Aimée spun, hitting Maud with all the strength she had. Maud howled with pain. Le Pen hadn't stopped orating.

Aimée pulled a chair under the skylight, somehow hoisting herself up. Another gunshot stung her leg.

"You're not going anywhere," Maud shouted.

But Aimée kept pulling herself up. She crawled over the skylight ledge, panting for air, and slid, face first, down the blue slate tiles. She grabbed a pipe, hanging on for dear life.

Warm wetness spread over her ribs. She saw a dark red stain over her chest. The YSL blouse was now totally ruined. Her jeans leg had been ripped by a bullet. Gas fumes came from the skylight under a smatter of stars. Below, the Seine glittered, pockmarked with lights. But everything felt far away. A tongue licked her ear and she realized she'd reached the flat part of the roof.

Shots pinged, ricocheting off a drain pipe. She bundled Miles Davis close, crawling along the gutter, pulling herself forward by her fingertips. At the edge of the roof, she tied the end of his leash around the pipe, wrapped the middle part around her wrist, and took the phone from her back pocket. If she didn't hurry, her building would blow up. With trembling fingers she hit 18 for *Sapeurs Pompiers*.

"Hurry, there's gas leaking on the fifth floor." She struggled for breath. "17, quai d'Anjou."

"Your name?"

"Forget my name, there's a woman inside with a gun; the place will blow up."

"A terrorist attack? Do you see explosives?"

If she said yes, they'd activate Plan Rouge, putting all response teams on first alert.

"*Oui*, a whole room of *plastic!*"

She put the phone down. Breathed, filling her lungs with air. Miles Davis whimpered in her arms and her phone trilled.

"I'm waiting for you, Leduc," Morbier said. "Where are you?"

Her black high heel fell off her foot and slithered down the slate roof, then over the gutter. She didn't want to look down.

"On my roof." Lightheaded, she hugged Miles Davis for warmth.

"Again?"

Why wouldn't her brain clear? "Things got hot, I needed air."

"Leduc, what the hell do you mean?"

"Nicolas's sister shot René, Morbier. There's gas leaking from her stove. She's downstairs in my building with a gun."

"What? Don't tell me—"

But she never heard the rest. The shock of the explosion lifted her in the air and closer to the stars. The roof tore, splintering tile, wooden beams, and plaster. The last thing she saw were tiny shards of glass, twinkling like starlight against the rooftops.

Saturday

"Half the roof blew into the Seine," said a voice. A voice she knew. Alcohol and antiseptic smells assailed her nose.

Aimée blinked. Her eyes opened to see bright lights shining on her bandaged raised leg. Then the green walls of a hospital room. She could see and breathe. She grew aware of throbbing pain. René, wearing a back brace, spoke to someone behind the curtain.

"I was so worried. You okay, René?"

"Better than you," René said, parting the curtain. "Walking, talking, and communicating online with Ritoux at Tracfin for an hour this morning. He almost likes us." René grinned. "Saj's working at the office. We're back on track."

"And Nadillac?"

"In custody," René said. "He's insisting that his firm put him up to the wire transfer to protect their 'assets.' Complaining and whining as usual."

She pictured the short, overweight hacker in a cell and brightened.

René's brow creased. "Lucky the explosion didn't kill you, Aimée."

Or the fall.

"Where's Miles Davis?"

René paused. Her heart ripped open.

"*Mon Dieu*, he's dead, isn't he? It's my fault."

"*Non*, it was thanks to his barking that the rescue unit found you. They're awarding him a canine badge of honor."

Morbier parted the curtains. The bags under his eyes were more pronounced; there was stubble on his chin.

"A little messy, Leduc. Maud Evry's body parts rained down over the entire block."

Aimée didn't like to picture the cleanup.

"Other than that, no fatalities," Morbier said. "The firemen contained the blaze right away. Amazing."

"Thank God you held on to the leash, Aimée," René said. "They had to cut it off your arm."

No wonder her skin felt as if it was on fire.

Morbier picked up her charred cell phone. "Dead. But Jacques called me."

A shiver went up her arm. "Waller has information about my brother?"

Morbier pushed the cuticle back on his thumb. "Maybe next time round, Leduc."

What did that mean? "Care to explain?"

Morbier read her look. "Jacques is en route to the Congo right now."

For a retired NYPD officer, he sure got around. Before she could press for more information, a saccharine-smiling nurse pushed the curtain aside. "Time for your medication, Mademoiselle."

She'd think about her brother and Waller's angle later.

"Open." The nurse put a funnel device in her mouth. "Just swallow."

She gulped.

"Good. Now drink some water."

Aimée sputtered, pushing it away.

"What's the damage?" she asked the nurse.

"*Quoi?*"

"My injuries?"

"Arm lacerations, a bullet graze and bruising to the third rib, a low-grade infection in your leg wound." The nurse swabbed her arm with alcohol, raised a thick hypodermic syringe, flicked the glass with her finger, and pushed.

Aimée winced in pain. "They use this size on horses, don't they?"

"No need to be funny." The nurse gave a little shrug. Smiled. "*Pas mal*, considering how close you flew to 'heaven'."

Aimée waited until the nurse left. "Call me a taxi, Morbier."

"*Et puis*? You're injured, Leduc."

"Have your *flics* removed the cameras and bugs from my place?"

"You know about that?" He looked at his feet. "I read this wrong. I'm sorry."

Morbier apologizing?

"Just get it taken care of. Now, Morbier," she said. "I'm going home."

"Stubborn as usual," Morbier said. He rubbed the stubble on his jaw. "Take my advice, Leduc: enjoy the peace here and recover. They won't let you out without signing a waiver."

"I hate these places." She sat up. Everything swayed, then righted itself. "Can you hand me my clothes?"

"Those?" René pointed to a plastic bag with her torn, bloody clothing, which emitted a smoky scent.

A crime. Her vintage YSL silk top, a rag.

"I need a favor, Morbier."

"You want to stay at my place? Hire a nurse?"

"I want to borrow your coat, Morbier."

"No taxis, remember? There's a train strike and they're scarce as hen's teeth." He shook his head, then draped his coat around her shoulders. Sighed. "I'll drive you."

She paused. "And we'll pick Miles Davis up en route."

He shot a look down the hall, then nodded. "We better go out the back."

"Coming, René?"

René grabbed his crutch. "About time, too."

* * *

DUSK DESCENDED OUTSIDE Aimée's open balcony door. The quayside lights gleamed, diamond-like, against the gel-black Seine. Even the roof-repair scaffolding couldn't mar the view, she thought. An orange-brown leaf fluttered inside on the wood floor. Every part of her hurt, but she was home.

A bandaged Miles Davis nestled at her feet on the recamier, yellow plastic pill bottles lined up like toy soldiers on the side table, candles flickered. On the answering machine, a red light blinked. One message. She hit ANSWER and leaned back.

"I'm sorry, Aimée." A pause, and she heard Mathieu take a breath. "Inexusable, but can you forgive me? If you're there, pick up. I need to explain."

Another pause. "My wife threw me out."

Aimée leaned forward and hit ERASE.

Miles Davis looked up, his ears pricked. She heard a key turn in the front door lock. No doubt René, with her laptop and a new cell phone.

"In here, René," she said. "Hungry? I can order takeout. Feel like sushi?"

Melac, in his black leather jacket and jeans, hair combed back, set a distinctive black-and-white-lettered Fauchon bag on the dining table.

"I brought an assortment," he said. "Had no clue what you like."

She elbowed herself up and winced. Her arm burned. "Who gave you my keys?"

He pulled a screwdriver from his leather jacket pocket, smiling.

"You want the cameras removed, don't you?"

The smile reached deep into his eyes. Large gray eyes. Why hadn't she noticed them before?

She let her bandaged arm fall back on the pillow. The breeze ruffled her toes peeking from the end of the duvet.

"So you're apologizing, Melac?"

"For doing my job?"

Her body hurt too much to argue. "I accept."

A weight, like body armor, lifted from him. "I've had this place under twenty-four-hour surveillance, half the time by myself."

Married to the job. Like all of them. Like her father.

"You don't get out much, do you, Melac?"

He blinked. "The Lille *clinique* sent a report alerting us to Maud Evry's escape. Regulations, forms, it took time to obtain the proper medical protective warrant."

Look where following rules had got her.

"A little late, Melac."

"Blame the transport strike. We were stuck on Pont Neuf in traffic," he said. Paused. "Maud Evry had done this before."

Aimée cringed inside. With her good arm, she pointed to the kitchen.

"You'll find plates in the first cupboard."

"That I can handle," he said, eyeing her, a softness in his look. "But I don't know about the rest."

"The rest?" she asked.

"You."

Acknowledgments

Immeasurable, heartfelt thanks to Dot Edwards; Barbara; Jan Gurley, MD; Max; Susanna; Elaine; Terri Haddix, MD; Jean Satzer; Michael, Leonard, Marion, Don Cannon, Carla, and Sarah and Ailen.

In Paris: Sarah Tarille, *mon amie* and *flâneuse; toujours* generous Anne-Francoise Delbeque and the red-soled Louboutins; *la petite Zouzou;* Gilles Fouquet for his expertise; Pierre-Olivier—Aimée's historian; Benoit Patission, security at the Ministry of Culture and *Centre de Monuments Nationaux,* Palais Royal; Elise, Jean and Damien Lesay; Isabelle, for our long ago afternoon with *les enfants;* Elke Tsalkis; Cathy Etile—Police Judiciare; Frederic Carteron, formerly Police Judiciaire; Jean-Claude Mulés, retired Commissaire, Brigade Criminelle; Libby Hellmann; Arthur Phillips.

And nothing would happen without James N. Frey, Linda Allen, extraordinary Laura Hruska, Jun, and my son Tate.